Feeding Frenzy

Feeding Frenzy

AN ARISTOTLE 'SOC' SOCARIDES MYSTERY

Paul Kemprecos

A Perfect Crime Book
Doubleday
New York London Toronto Sydney Auckland

A PERFECT CRIME BOOK
PUBLISHED BY DOUBLEDAY
a division of Bantam Doubleday Dell Publishing Group, Inc.
1540 Broadway, New York, New York 10036

DOUBLEDAY is a trademark of Doubleday,
a division of Bantam Doubleday Dell
Publishing Group, Inc.

Library of Congress Cataloging-in-Publication Data

Kemprecos, Paul.
    Feeding frenzy : an Aristotle 'Soc' Socarides mystery / Paul Kemprecos. — 1st
ed.
        p.   cm.
    "A Perfect crime book."
    1. Socarides, Aristotle Plato (Fictitious character)—Fiction.   2. Greek
Americans—Massachusetts—Cape Cod—Fiction.   3. Detectives—Massachusetts—
Cape Cod—Fiction.   I. Title.
PS3561.E4224F44   1993
813'.54—dc20   93-3243
                                                                                      CIP

Book design by Claire N. Vaccaro

ISBN 0-385-42486-8
Copyright © 1993 by Paul Kemprecos
All Rights Reserved
Printed in the United States of America
September 1993

FIRST EDITION

10   9   8   7   6   5   4   3   2   1

TO CHRIS SOCARIDES, A GENTLEMAN
AND A SCHOLAR

ACKNOWLEDGMENTS

I'd like to express my grateful appreciation to my neighbor, Alex Carlson, who generously shared his knowledge of big ships; to Mcg Ruley, who suggested that a book about hungry creatures lurking under the sea would be scary indeed; to Kate Miciak, who beat me over the head with my manuscript until I turned it into a book; and to Christi Houghton, my best friend and cheerleader, whose patient and loyal support sustained me through the ups and downs of this project.

"The greatest griefs are those we cause ourselves."

—SOPHOCLES

Feeding Frenzy

 Chapter 1

Twenty-one minutes after midnight, seven miles east of Cape Cod, deep in the bowels of the Liberian freighter *Pandora,* demons began to stir.

The malignant forces slumbering in the ship's dark cargo hold were quickened into life by a moving wall of black water three stories high. The onrushing wave buried the *Pandora*'s bow under a foamy avalanche. The rounded stern lifted high into the spumy air. With no resistance to slow its spinning blades, the *Pandora*'s cavitating propeller chewed at nothing. The drive shaft from the engine room accelerated. A bolt-rattling shudder swept along the ship's three-hundred-fifty-foot length.

In the cavernous hold, a thin strand woven into a three-quarter-inch nylon line snapped under the strain of shifting cargo.

The *Pandora*'s bow rose sluggishly, the deck leveled, the propeller bit hungrily into the water. The ship
surged forward.

High above in the dimly lit bridge, Captain George
Zervas, commander of the *Pandora,* braced his shoulder
against a bulkhead until his ship steadied on its course.
The captain glanced at his watch: 12:25 A.M. He lit an
unfiltered Camel cigarette and took a deep drag. The
storm throbbed with a deep vibration, as if a thousand
cathedral organs were stuck on the lowest bass chord, but
an inner peace reigned in the captain's mind. Zervas had
weighed the external forces of wind and water against
steel and welds, factored in navigational skill and experience, and concluded that the *Pandora* would come
through her stormy ordeal beaten but intact.

Zervas was neither a hysteric nor an oblivious fool
when it came to dirty weather. The captain had been
punished by the fierce summer *meltemi* of his native Aegean, and sailed through storms on both oceans. For all
its blustery violence, a New England northeaster was no
more dangerous than anything in his experience. He had
done all he could. Long before clouds blotted out the
stars, the crew had battened down the watertight hatches
and pumped seawater into the freighter's ballast tanks
for more weight and stability.

Zervas believed in the old adage that any ship, even
a fifty-year-old relic like the *Pandora,* was stronger than
the men who sailed her. His instincts were right about
the *Pandora.* She had been a survivor since the day she
slid off the ways at Maine's Bath Ironworks in 1942.
With the champagne barely dry on her hull, she was

dodging torpedoes from the German U-boat wolf packs that prowled the East Coast. Only once was she damaged. In March '43, a sub's deck gun scored a direct hit amidships before rescue planes chased the attacker away.

Passage of a half century and the neglect of uncaring owners accomplished more than the German *untersee* navy ever hoped for. Cancerous rust patches scarred the hull above the waterline. Reddish tears of oil and grime runoff streaked the blistered black hull. Corrosion ate away at the jutting masts and cranes. Water from a leaky bilge had settled to one side, and the ship listed drunkenly to starboard.

In her glory days, when she was named the U.S.S. *Eagle,* her shiny decks were manned by a seasoned crew of American merchant marines. Now she was registered in Monrovia, a west African port where she had never dropped anchor. Her home was in Panama. The ship's owner was a multinational shipping company in New York whose principals were Maltese. Most of her crewmen were Panamanian. The officers were Greek.

Zervas had been on boats since he was able to walk. He was born on Santorini, the black-sand, volcanic island north of Crete. The first breath of air to fill his lungs was moist from the mists of the Aegean.

George Zervas was of shorter-than-average height, with dark hair and a pencil-thin mustache, but he carried himself with military stiffness and placed a great premium on dignity.

Had he not made a fateful decision five years before, Zervas might have commanded a supertanker or a cruise ship. Dog-tired from bridge duty on a small, undermanned tanker, he left his mate in charge, and went to his cabin for a nap. His slumber was cut short by an ear-splitting grinding. The mate had run the tanker onto a shoal that ripped into the ship's bottom. Oil storage tanks ruptured; black number-two crude poured into the ocean off the Brittany coast. The spill cost millions to clean up, infuriated fishermen and hotel owners, and brought down the wrath of the French government and international environmentalists.

Evidence on the real cause of the disaster, a mal-function in the tanker's ancient navigational instruments, disappeared before it could be introduced at a hearing. The ship's owners were insulated by layers of corporate paper and protected by political influence. In the end, George Zervas was held responsible. His captain's license was revoked. He got his papers back eventually, but his reputation as a ship killer stuck like the smell of death. The only berths available to him were on rust buckets a voyage or two away from the scrap heap.

Zervas took almost any ship handed to him. He learned not to be particular or to ask too many questions. He had a wife and two children to feed back in Santorini and he looked forward to the day he could retire. He accepted his fate stoically; what must be, must be. He was a proud man, nonetheless. The ships under his command might be derelicts. His crews could look like pirates. No matter. His uniform was always spotless and the creases ironed to razor sharpness.

Now he rarely left his command to others, and never in a storm.

Zervas walked over behind the helmsman, a wiry

young Panamanian named Jésus. The helmsman stood, legs wide apart for balance, with his slim artist's fingers curled around the sixteen-inch-diameter wheel. His flat Indian profile was plated in reddish copper by the soft ruby light from the gyrocompass dial, and his face was set in a beatific expression. He looked like a saint in a Renaissance painting. He stared at the nothingness beyond the rain-dashed wheelhouse windows. Occasionally he glanced at the compass and adjusted the wheel, really an electronic switch which relayed commands to the hydraulic system that moved the great rudder of the aging freighter.

Having the Christos guide his ship tickled the captain's Hellenic sense of irony, but Jésus was a natural helmsman. He had been at the wheel for hours and might have to remain at his post until the *Pandora* was safely out of the bad weather. Bringing in a new helmsman would have been dangerous; the Panamanian had an instinctive feel for the tempest. Better to let Jésus steer until he was exhausted. Luckily, the young man showed no sign of tiring.

The captain had ordered the helmsman to maintain a course slightly to the east of the wind direction. If the freighter tried to go directly northeast into the waves, it would take a brutal beating. At this angle, the seas should break to one side of the bow. The engine room was keeping the ship at two knots, bare steerage way, the minimum speed necessary to maintain headway.

Satisfied with the ship's course, Zervas checked on Manos, the first mate, who was hunched over the pale glimmer of the radar screen. Manos was a bright, good-natured Athenian in his midthirties. Zervas sometimes wondered what he had done to be sentenced to the purgatory of duty on the *Pandora,* but he kept his questions to himself.

Ragged whitish patches of storm clutter from waves and rain splotched the radar monitor. The captain studied the ghostly images, then recorded the digital position reading on the long-range navigation receiver. He went to the navigator's table and penciled a circled dot on the chart to show the *Pandora's* current position. He wrote the time inside the circle and on the outside, the distance from the last position.

He planned to head north and west again, around the great curling arm of Cape Cod, for a straight shot to Boston, as soon as the ship was safely clear of land. He had radioed ahead that the storm would delay him. The anonymous people who awaited *Pandora's* cargo were impatient. They promised him a bonus if he got the cargo to Boston that morning.

Zervas thought about the dozens of black steel drums in the hold. They had been quietly loaded in the dead of night just before the ship left New Orleans. The bill of lading said the ship carried chemicals. The barrels themselves were stenciled with the word FERTILIZER. He wished he had had time to supervise the loading, but it was impossible to be everywhere. Most of the crewmen came from farms and knew little of ships and sailing them. They were paid rock-low wages and gave equal effort in return. Manos was a good man, but even the first mate could be lackadaisical. Zervas hoped he wasn't carrying dope, but he didn't much care. His mind was on sunny Santorini and his family. Maybe he could retire with the unexpected windfall from this trip, buy a little boat, and take tourists on trips around his island.

The captain went over to whisper a few words of encouragement to the helmsman. He again checked the radar and the loran and went back to the chart. He penciled another circled position dot and grunted softly. The waves and wind were driving the *Pandora* southward. He ordered Jésus to adjust course a few degrees more to the east. The new tack would take them into deeper water. There the swells were farther apart.

Time passed, and Captain Zervas made further calculations. They were back on course. He let his thoughts drift home. But while he dreamed of whitewashed houses hugging the black lava cliffs, trouble was brewing less than a mile to the east. As if angered by the plodding progress of the defiant old freighter, the storm had reached deep into the ocean, packed thousands of tons of water into a giant sea, and sent it winging toward the *Pandora*.

Captain Zervas took the Camels from his breast pocket and stuck a cigarette in his mouth.

Now only a half mile away, the rogue wave rolled toward the unsuspecting ship like a snowball going downhill, growing to a terrifying size, absorbing mass and velocity from the waves in its path.

The captain offered a cigarette to his first mate.

The wave was a quarter mile away, bearing down hard. The hissing, foam-crested, white-veined monster was more than sixty feet high, taller than the ship's rigging.

Manos took the cigarette and borrowed the captain's lighter.

An eighth of a mile away.

He was savoring his second puff when the *Pandora* seemed to stop, then rise in the air. Within seconds, the towering wave dashed over the bridge and aft house as if they were pebbles in a stream. The ship veered wildly to starboard.

Zervas and the first mate were hurled to the deck.

Still clutching the wheel, the helmsman fell to his knees.

In the crew's quarters under the aft house, eight Panamanians sat on the floor in a haze of cigarette smoke playing cards while those who weren't nauseous watched from their bunks and fingered their rosary beads. When the wave caught the ship, the bunks tilted at a crazy angle. Bodies hurtled out. The poker game became a tangle of arms and legs. Chips and cards clattered across the deck. Beer bottles became lethal projectiles.

In the black hold where only the rats could bear witness, a stack of barrels, each about a yard in height and two feet in diameter, shifted weight, pressing against the line that secured them. More nylon strands parted.

The wave had flung the freighter onto its starboard side, and now it oscillated in the other direction like a great pendulum. Again, the men in the crew's quarters were tossed about like dice in a shaker. Again the barrels shifted. The ship rolled to starboard.

The weakened nylon rope snapped under the strain.

Barrels broke loose, rumbled across the hold like bowling balls, and crashed into the starboard bulkhead with a metallic thundering that sent the rats scurrying for cover.

Up in the bridge, the helmsman pulled himself erect, swearing, and fought to regain control of the ship.

The freighter rolled again. The barrels skittered across the hold and slammed into the port bulkhead.

As the rudder came under control and the propeller powered the ship forward, the wallowing began to abate and the deck leveled. Zervas and his first mate helped each other to their feet. In the crew's quarters, men picked themselves up, tested for broken bones, and started to argue over how the poker chips should be split among them.

Manos staggered to the bridge telephone. He called down to the engine room. The engines were fine, the second engineer reported breathlessly. Manos cranked the telephone again and got through to the crew's quarters. A man named Rodriques answered. Things were in a mess, he said, but nobody was seriously hurt.

Captain Zervas brushed the knees of his uniform, tucked his shirt into his belt, and found his cap. He went over to the helmsman and patted him on the back. The man's jersey was soaked with sweat. Zervas praised his helmsmanship, and said he'd be relieved as soon as they rounded the Cape. Jésus nodded. His grip on the wheel tightened.

While Manos picked up the scattered charts and navigational instruments, Zervas listened to the droning voice of the NOAA weather announcer on the radio. The forecast was encouraging. The storm was moving away.

The captain located his pack of Camels. The butts were crushed but smokable. He offered the mate another cigarette and lit up himself. He took a deep drag, blowing the smoke through his nostrils. Outside, the storm still raged, but the captain was satisfied that the ship had weathered the worst. He was carving out his own mental island of tranquility, thinking about the gifts he would bring home to his two rambunctious children and his wife.

The ship's telephone jangled. Three rings was the signal for the bridge to answer. But the phone rang at least a dozen times. The rings were jerky and spasmodic.

Manos picked up the phone. "Bridge."

He listened a few seconds without speaking. A deep furrow creased his brow.

"Well?" the captain said.

"I don't know," the first mate replied. "Listen."

He held the phone to the captain's ear. Zervas heard a frenzied cacaphony of screams and shouts. He took the phone in his hand. "Hello!" he yelled.

No answer. Only the awful racket. Like the waiting room to Hell.

"What *is* it, Captain?" Manos asked. "Is the crew fighting?"

Zervas shook his head in puzzlement.

A brawl was the first thing to enter his mind, too. The crew had been cooped up and bounced around in their stinking cabin for hours. There would have been drinking and gambling. He paused. No, these weren't voices raised in anger. They were cries of terror.

He barked into the phone again.

A man's voice came on. The words were unintelligible, more like a wet gargle than a sentence.

"Who is this?" the captain snapped.

"Mah, mah, Manuel. It's Manuel."

"This is the captain. What's going on? Is there a fight?"

"No fight, Captain. It's . . . *Dios.* Nononono. They come! Aieeeee!"

"Manuel!" the captain shouted. "What are you saying?"

There was no answer. Only the screams of men in torment. What was going on? There was no way to get from the bridge to the crew's cabin without going onto the storm-washed decks. That would have been suicide. The phone suddenly went dead. Zervas cranked the handle. No answer. He tried again. Still nothing.

As he stood there with the useless phone in his hand, he became aware of a change in the ship's motion. A good seaman becomes one with his vessel, absorbing its rhythms through his feet. The captain's legs were telling him the ship had lost power. The *Pandora* was starting to founder.

He rang up the engine room. There was no answer. Angrily, he cranked the phone. He heard a click on the other end. Someone had picked up the receiver. He could hear the sound of heavy breathing.

He shouted hello. The labored panting continued for a few seconds, then became a harsh whisper.

"I can't talk. It's watching me."

"What are you talking about?" the captain demanded. It sounded like the engineer's voice, but he couldn't be certain. *"Who* is watching?"

"It . . . Ohmigod. Nooo." There was a crashing noise. Metal on metal. Glass shattering. The phone went dead.

Zervas felt the hairs on the back of his neck rise. The storm roared around the ship, but he heard only the silence on the other end of the line. He was a worldly man who had seen everything and had only been afraid a few times in his life. This was beyond his experience. What was happening to his ship?

His thoughts were cut short by a terrified scream. Jésus had let go of the wheel. He was pointing through the window at the darkness outside the ship. Zervas rushed to the man's side and squinted into the night. He saw only sheets of torrential rain slashing against the glass.

Zervas grabbed the man's shoulder. "What do you see?"

Jésus pointed again. His eyes rolled insanely.

"Noo," the young man said. He began to gibber in Spanish. Then he turned and bolted. He ran to the doorway leading out onto the deck. The captain called after him, but he opened the door and stepped into the full fury of the storm.

Zervas ran over and stuck his head outside. Bullets of rain stung his face. He caught a glimpse of the helmsman. Then a huge sea swept the deck and the man disappeared. The captain retreated into the bridge and secured the door. Even as he wiped the saltwater from his stinging eyes he was thinking of his next move. Manos would have to take the wheel. The captain glanced around.

The first mate was gone, but Zervas was not alone.

There was *something* in the cabin with him, standing in the semidarkness near the navigator's table.

Zervas opened his mouth. Nothing came out. He almost gagged with fear.

It came closer.

It reached out toward him. Zervas screamed. It screamed back, mocking him. His legs took over, and he turned and ran to the door. He pushed it open and launched his body into the teeth of the storm. He ran down the slippery deck. The raging force of the wind ripped at his uniform.

The ship lurched. Zervas slipped and smashed his knee, but he was only dimly aware of the stabbing pain. He grabbed the rail and tried to pull himself up. A wave washed onto the deck, burying him in foam. Zervas gripped a stanchion. Another wave pounded the ship. His hand slipped. He was brushed off the ship like an insect.

The freighter was on its own now, pummeled by the full Atlantic fury. Adrift without a hand on the helm, it yawed broadside to the waves. Wind and ocean tore at the rigging. Masts and cranes snapped as if they were made of balsa wood.

A hairline crack appeared where the ship had been welded after the sub attack. Within seconds, the crack widened. Water poured into the engine room. The diesels stammered and died. More water coursed through the scuttles.

Battered, capsized, and leaking, the freighter still had enough buoyancy to float. But a crewman had forgotten to secure the lids on some deck vents. Water found the openings, coursed in, and traveled down to the bilge. The ship's natural list became more pronounced, every deck at a sharp angle. Parallel to the waves now, the *Pandora* broached, then went over on her side.

The ship took on more water, still afloat, kept alive

by air trapped in her hull compartments. Wind and waves savagely hammered at the freighter and pushed her closer to the mainland. Water continued to pour into her belly until the weight became too much for the hull to bear. Before long the weight of the water overcame the buoyancy.

The *Pandora* buckled amidships, and with an agonizing groan that was almost human in its sad desperation, the wounded ship slid beneath the angry surface of the sea.

Chapter 2

It was one of those hot leaden mornings that we sometimes get on Cape Cod in the summer. The prevailing
southwest wind off Nantucket Sound had sighed to a
butterfly's wingbeat. The air was heavy with the smell of
schooling fish and ripe with rain squalls aborning. On
days like this, the old dorymen who used to hang out at
the fish pier would feel an aching of ancient memories in
their bones. They'd squint ominously at the unclouded
sky. "Weather breeder," they'd mutter restlessly; keep
your foul weather gear close by. *Some*thing is sure to
happen, whether you want it to or not.

I guess the old salts were right. The day started
with a black Ford Ranger pickup truck roaring into my
clamshell driveway and skidding to a stop. Behind the
wheel was Albert Nickerson, called Allie Nick to differ-

entiate him from the legions of Nickersons who prolifer-
ate in these parts. He got out, strode to the boathouse,
and banged on the front door of the boathouse. He didn't
see me crawling around in the garden. I had been hunting the marauding tomato worm who was stripping the
leaves off my Early Girls.

I stood and brushed the dirt off my hands. "Hey,
Allie, I'm over here."

Arms swinging like scythes and shoulders angled
sharply forward, Allie marched over to the garden. He
looked like a snapping turtle who didn't have anyone to
bite.

"How's it going?" I said.

"Some son of a bitch stole my harpoons."

"Your *tuna* harpoons?"

"Four of them. Brand new. Fishermen's supply is
out of stock, and there's bluefin all over the place. What
the hell am I supposed to do, Soc, stick them with dinner forks?"

I calmed him down and got the story. The harpoons
were tied to his boat's pulpit, the framework that ex-
tends off the bowsprit. He discovered them missing halfway across the harbor and had to turn back. He was
sputtering with rage. A single bluefin tuna can bring up
to fifteen grand on the Japanese market. The tuna spot-
ters were reporting bluefin everywhere, and it was driving him crazy.

I told Allie I'd sniff around and meet him in an
hour at Elsie's restaurant. I got in my GMC pickup and
poked in at a couple of town landings. At one were some
cars with college parking stickers. I walked down to the

beach and saw a bunch of hung-over young guys playing Moby Dick using an old wooden barrel as the white whale.

They weren't bad kids. They apologized, and said they'd scoffed the harpoons while they were party cruising in a Boston Whaler the night before. I lectured them about hurting somebody's way of making a living and left it at that. Allie saw me with his recaptured harpoons from Elsie's coffee counter and came out smiling. He wanted to pay me. I refused, saying it was a personal favor, but he insisted on giving me a secondhand 9.5 horsepower Johnson outboard from his truck. I could keep it or sell it, he said, and dashed off, harpoons in hand, to catch some bluefin.

I didn't need an outboard, but my pickup truck sounded like a popcorn popper, and I'd been putting off repairs until I had some extra cash. Back at the boathouse I called the marine engine shop I deal with, described the motor, and said I'd give them a commission if they could find a buyer for it. The mechanic said somebody had been in the other day looking for a used motor, but he didn't know who it was. He'd ask around.

My fishing partner Sam had gone off to the Cape Cod Mall in Hyannis, fulfilling a promise to his wife Mildred that he'd made when Jimmy Carter was still president. I went back to the garden. Kojak the cat came over to see what I was doing. He sniffed a denuded plant that looked like a miniature saguaro cactus, then collapsed in a dusty black heap. Some wormhound.

The telephone rang inside the boathouse. Gary Cozzi was on the line. The marine shop had just called him and said I had an outboard for his skiff. I told him he could look at the motor any time he wanted to.

"Things are pretty busy here at the beach, so I won't be able to come by until later," he said. Gary is head lifeguard at Quanset Beach.

"I'm not busy. I'll bring it by and you check it out."

Gary said that would be fine. I scrubbed the dirt off my knees and elbows and was running cold water over my head when I remembered the Red Sox were playing the Yankees today. Quanset Beach would be a nice cool spot to sit and listen to the Yankees go down to defeat. I made a couple of tuna sandwiches on stale onion rolls after picking off the green mold spots and filled a Thermos with lemonade. I put the food in a rucksack with my Walkman and a bottle of Ban de Soleil number 15. Then I pulled on a bathing suit, a Talking Heads T-shirt, and a Red Sox ball cap, grabbed a folding plastic-and-aluminum beach chair, and headed out to the truck. Kojak was still sunning himself.

"Keep a sharp eye on those tomato plants and attack *any*thing that travels on six legs or more," I told him. "There may be kitty treats in this for you."

Kojak yawned and twitched a couple of times before lapsing into a cat coma. I guess that was something.

My pickup would be in the intensive care ward if it were human. But it started with no problem. After an imitation of a Chinese New Year's celebration, the engine calmed down. I put the truck into gear and bumped along a rain-cratered sand track past a cranberry bog to the main road a quarter mile away.

Ten minutes later I turned right at the Quanset Beach sign. A line of traffic jammed the narrow beach road. The radio DJ had just played "Hot Hot Hot" by Buster Poindexter, and now he was giving the weather report. "If you think *that* was hot, listen to this." He reported gleefully that the mercury had hit eighty-seven degrees and was still climbing. He wasn't telling me anything I didn't know. The truck cab was like the inside of a sneaker. I punched the radio's off button.

A police cruiser passed, going in the opposite direction. Then the line of cars began to move.

A long, gentle hill sloped down to the tollbooth and the parking lot beyond. I dangled my arm lazily out the window. Sequins of light sparkled on the blue-green Atlantic a quarter mile distant. Low, grass-capped sand dunes swept north and south in rolling ribbons of green and dull brown. The nearer I got to the water, the cooler it became. The salty-kelpy tang of deep ocean permeated the air.

The college kid in the ticket booth checked my beach sticker and waved me into a parking lot as long as a football field. Even with room for nearly a thousand cars, the tarmac was filled solid. The parking attendants pointed me toward a short sand road that curled around the dunes into the overflow parking lot next to the beach buggy check-in shack.

I humped my beach gear across the sun-baked tarmac, following the fragrance of fried clams. The nerve center for beach operations is the administration building, a one-story wood frame structure that houses the main offices, first-aid room, staff locker rooms, showers, and bathrooms. Standing out front, dressed in khaki shorts, jersey, and yellow baseball cap was Charlie Nevers, the parking lot manager. He was talking into a hand-held radio. I asked how it was going. He wiped the sweat off his face.

"Do you *really* want to know? All that rain we've had this summer has made people berserk. Now they're taking their frustrations out on us poor overworked town employees. One of my attendants was almost killed by a lady who yells out, 'I'm a resident and a taxpayer, and if you don't get out of the way I'll run you over.' Then some jerk in a Jeep told one of the girls to fuck off. I threw his ass out of the parking lot. Bunch of high school clowns got into an argument over a parking space and they were going to have a rumble until we kicked their butts out, too. I've scraped three illegal stickers. People are complaining about the greenhead flies, as if we could do something about them. On top of that, MTV is supposed to be filming a video here this week, so every teenager on Cape Cod has been calling us to ask when the hell it is." Charlie shook his head. "Just another quiet day at Quanset Beach."

Two slim young women in their twenties strolled by wearing bathing suits that looked as if they'd both been cut from the same hanky. We gave them a drugstore cowboy leer.

"I know some guys who would kill for this job," I said.

His eyes appraised the women. "Yeah," he said sadly, "but by the end of July I've seen so much skin I get jaded. The most beautiful babe in the world could walk by in a beach outfit out of *Sports Illustrated* and I'd be more interested in her car."

A Kim Bassinger look-alike in a cutaway bathing suit stopped to ask Charlie a question, then ambled off toward the showers.

"I think that young lady was driving a Ford," I said. "Catch you later. I'm going to see Gary."

"I talked to him on the radio a few minutes ago. Ask him about the fight."

"Is that why the cops were here?"

"Yeah. Oops, Waitasecond." His radio crackled. A red Corvette had just blown past the tollbooth without paying. Nevers grinned evilly. "Here it comes. I *love* throwing these bastards out."

He trotted across the parking lot and flagged down the 'Vette. I headed between the administration building and the bustling snack bar and followed a narrow boardwalk mobbed with two-way traffic. The boardwalk widened after a hundred yards into a platform with two park benches on it. I sat down and stretched my legs.

From where I sat, Quanset Beach looked like a huge Bedouin encampment, *sans* camels. Blankets and umbrellas in every range of color spilled down from the edge of the dunes to the water's edge. Waves pounded the beach in a low muffled kettle drum thunder. Black-headed laughing gulls swooped overhead, cackling like lunatics over the blare of boom boxes, the *pok-pok* of paddle games and the shrill piping of children's voices.

Short-legged, droopy-drawered kids wearing T-shirts down to their knees were everywhere, attacking hopeless jobs with feverish energy. Dig a hole to China?

No sweat. Empty the Atlantic Ocean in plastic buckets? Piece of cake.

Older kids in their teens and twenties sprawled lifelessly on their blankets and lazily checked each other out in a laid-back mating ritual. Their burnished skin glistened like polished bronze. Quanset Beach has better name recognition on northeast college campuses than the President. The energy overheated libidos generate in one week at Quanset would run New York City for a decade.

A dragon kite danced fitfully against the milkweed strands in the clear blue sky. The warm sun toasted my face. After a minute, I got up and walked down the slope of the beach to the head lifeguard stand. The white wooden tower was around fifteen feet tall. The stand was roped off from the rest of the beach, as was a corridor to the water. Two paddle boards and other lifesaving paraphernalia lay in the sand.

Gary and another lifeguard lounged above the beach like Assyrian kings surveying their kingdom. I know Gary from softball. We both played on the team sponsored by the bar the locals call the 'Hole, which was fitting, because that's where we finished, in the hole.

I waved. Gary saw me and climbed down. "Hey, Mo, I'm taking a break. Watch that guy swimming way out and give him a blast on the whistle if you have to."

He was pointing at a white face bobbing against the satiny dark ocean beyond the surf line. Nearby, a flock of seabirds swirled like snowflakes. Mo nodded languidly and put the binoculars to his eyes.

"Conditions are right for a riptide," Gary told me. "That guy could find himself halfway to Europe before he knows it."

"Charlie Nevers says you've had a wild morning," I said.

"Yeah, we had two beauts here. Would you believe these guys were shitfaced at ten A.M.? They splashed brew on a woman, so her husband asked, 'Would you please be more careful of that beer?' One drunk says, 'Would you like your head buried in the sand?' and goes after the husband. The wife attacked the drunk with a Padina paddle and we had to bring the cops in." He laughed. "Hell, I'm not complaining. This is still the best job in the world."

"I hate to tear you away from your work, but if you want to look at the outboard, it's in my truck."

He chuckled and said, "I think I can spare . . ." He paused in midsentence.

Gary is about six feet tall, slightly shorter than I am. He has thick brown hair, a mustache, and an easy grin. He's the stereotype of the perpetual beach boy, but he's a consummate pro when it comes to his job. Even as we talked, his trained eye kept flicking toward the ocean. Now he was staring over my shoulder. I turned and followed his gaze beyond the breakers. I saw nothing wrong. Only the head bobbing in the water and the birds dipping and wheeling nearby.

Gary called up to the other lifeguard. "Hey, Mo, pitch those binocs down here." He caught the binoculars and looked real hard through the lenses. After about fifteen seconds he muttered, "Shit."

He handed the binoculars to me and shouted up to Mo, pointing seaward.

"That guy's in trouble! I'll take him."

Mo stood and blew a sharp blast on his whistle,

then barked into a walkie talkie. "Headstand to north and south. We've got a rescue going. Get us some backup."

Gary scooped up one of the elongated rectangular red plastic floats that lay in a parallel row on the sand. A loop of nylon line was attached to one end of the two-foot float. More line trailed from the opposite end. He slipped his arm through the loop and sprinted toward the ocean through the roped-off corridor in front of the headstand.

"Be right back, Soc," he yelled over his shoulder.

He waded into the swirling ebb of the surf. A big wave was coming in. Gary didn't hesitate a second. Just before the wave curled and broke, he dove in and disappeared in an explosion of foam.

The wave knocked him back and he popped into view. He tried again, and busted through the white wall of foam on the second try. Within seconds he was cutting through the water in a blur of powerful arm strokes, rising and falling in the lift of the oncoming rollers.

C h a p t e r 3

Mo scrambled down the ladder. He grabbed a float attached by a nylon line to a red wooden spool. Slinging
his arm through the loop the way Gary had done, he
raced toward the surf.

Two other guards dashed in from stands at the
north and south ends of the beach. They scooped up the
spool, and with each guard holding a spindle, pounded
after Mo. He hit the water running. He was either
stronger or luckier than Gary; he made it through the
roiling breakers on his first try.

I ran to the water's edge and raised the binoculars.
Targeting Gary, I moved the glasses slightly to the right,
past a swirling flock of birds, and squinted through the
curtain of foggy haze hanging over the breaking waves.
A white face bobbed against the dark sea. Arms flailed. It

was a man. I focused in on his face. The man's mouth opened and shut.

Gary was coming up on the swimmer, slicing the water with expert chops of his arms. Only yards away now. Then a few feet. The two men merged. Gary slipped the float belt off his shoulder and put it around the swimmer, then held onto him.

Mo was seconds behind. He reached Gary and the swimmer and all three floated as one for a few moments. An arm shot up and waved like a school kid trying to get a bathroom pass. I couldn't tell if it was Gary or Mo. The two guards handling the spool on shore caught the signal and began to haul in on the line.

Less than halfway to the beach, Gary or Mo signaled again. Two hands went up in a clapping movement.

One of the guards saw the motion. "Guy's unconscious! I'll call the rescue squad. You keep hauling." He sprinted to the headstand and grabbed a telephone connected to the administration building. Another guard took his place.

The rescue had electrified the beach. People abandoned their blankets and crowded the water's edge to watch the unfolding drama.

Gary and Mo neared shore with their burden. They timed the waves, using the ocean's energy to help carry them closer. Almost to the beach now, they disappeared in a tumble of breakers, then broke free and emerged, fighting the undertow, scrambling for footing in waist-high water that tried to suck them back in.

A guard was on each side of the rescued man, holding him by his arms. The lifeline was attached to one of the floats which Mo wore as a belt around his waist. The other belt was attached to the swimmer's waist.

The man was middle-aged, with minimal hair and a paunch. He had thick arms and shoulders. I waded into the surf to help pull him onto shore. As we came free of the water, a woman shrieked. I looked up. Her mouth was open in horror.

What the hell was *her* problem? A second later I found out. There was blood on my hands. Blood on my legs. Blood on Gary and Mo. Blood on the sand. There was blood everywhere, except where it should have been, in the swimmer. It poured off the lower portion of the man's body as if a dozen spigots had been turned on.

We pulled him up a short slope to the crest of the beach and stretched him on a blanket. His mouth gaped, his eyes were glazed and staring, and his face was deathly white. But that wasn't the worst part. His stomach and legs looked as if they had been rubbed against a cheese shredder. The skin was slashed in dozens of places. Handfuls of flesh were missing. His blue bathing trunks were soaked with crimson and sections of cloth were torn away.

A slender woman pushed her way through the crowd and sank to her knees beside the stricken swimmer. She cradled his head in her arms, kissing his pale face and sobbing hysterically. She was talking rapidly in French.

Gary ran up with the first aid kit and applied gauze bandage patches that were soaked in red as soon as he put them on. Face grim, he took a blanket and covered the man up to his chin. Then he put his arm around the sobbing woman and tried to tell her the ambulance was on its way. I don't know if she understood, but it probably wouldn't have made any difference.

The panic was triggered by a fat man with white zinc oxide smeared on his nose. He had elbowed his way through the crowd for a good look, and saw the wounds before they were covered. His eyes connected with his tongue without stopping first at his brain.

"Shark!" he shouted.

The word rippled outward. The crowd became a mob, then a mindless stampeding herd. People grabbed their kids and coolers and bolted for the parking lot as if sharp white teeth snapped at their heels.

The beach instantly became a confused mass of pushing and shoving humanity. I watched the wild disorderly rout in amazement. Within minutes the beach was almost empty of people. Blankets and umbrellas were tossed about as if a big wind had roared through.

Gary was still trying to calm the woman. She moaned and rocked back and forth on her knees. A pair of lifeguards knelt next to the swimmer. One tested for a pulse. My mind did a flashback. Medic bending over a guy who'd been hit by one of the claymore mines the VC turned on us. For a second I thought that's what had happened. This guy must have hit an old mine floating at sea. But that was dumb. There had been no explosion.

A siren wailed. The rescue squad arrived within minutes. Two emergency medical techs piled out of the ambulance and ran onto the beach with a stretcher and their kit. They did a quick pulse check and tried zapping the man's heart with electrodes placed on his chest. Then they lifted him onto the stretcher and carried him up to the rescue truck.

The French lady went with them. The cops had arrived and Gary and Mo were trying to tell them what happened. I walked to the water's edge and squatted in the surf to wash the blood off my hands and legs. When I had rinsed the last of it away, I peered out at the ocean. There was only the endless ranks of waves and a few darting seabirds.

Like Charlie Nevers said. Just another quiet day at Quanset Beach.

Chapter 4

"Offshore wind's moderated," Sam was saying on the phone. "Looks like we might get a day's work in tomorrow. Got to earn some money. Millie broke the bank at the mall."

I smiled at Sam's grumbling. He is the epitomy of Cape Cod thrift. His wife Millie is even more frugal. They probably split a grilled cheese sandwich and a Coke at Friendly's and considered it a big splurge. I checked the tide chart over the kitchen sink.

"High tide's at five A.M.," I said. "Meet you at the pier around four."

"Finestkind. See you down on the shore. I'll be sniffing the breeze."

Sam and I fish from a pretty, steel-hulled tub-trawler named the *Millie D.* We use baited hooks strung on nylon lines hundreds of feet long. Hooking doesn't bring in big catches like gill nets, but the fish are fresher and less damaged, and it's a lot less like factory work. Sometimes we cover expenses; sometimes we don't. We fish mostly because we like the independence and the chance to be out on the water. We gripe a lot, but we wouldn't be fishermen if we didn't.

Like most Cape Cod people, I have more than one job. I dive when someone hires me to find a lost mooring or to check out the underside of a boat. And I have my private investigator's license. I don't do divorces because I don't like listening at motel room doors for heavy breathing. Without wandering husbands or wives to tail, my caseload is lightened considerably. I've located missing lobster pots and runaway kids who haven't run too far. Once I found a lost miniature Schnauzer for a rich summer resident. The Schnauzer bit my hand and the rich lady stiffed me on the payment and flew off to Europe with the dog. Sometimes I even hunt for tuna harpoons.

I don't advertise. People hear I'm an ex-flatfoot who doesn't know when to quit and they seek me out. I'd like to think it's because I'm good, but I know some people hire me because I come cheap. My overhead is low. No office, no high-tech keyhole lenses or electronic listening devices. Just my annual P.I. license renewal fee and a handful of dog-eared business cards that say: **A. P. Socarides. Investigations.** The A is for Aristotle, the P stands for Plato. Most people call me Soc, and I don't discourage them.

Herodotus said circumstances rule men; men don't

rule circumstances. That about sums it up for me. I grew up in a tightly knit, hardworking Greek family in the old mill city of Lowell, north of Boston. I studied the classics at Boston University and didn't do badly; I still translate road signs into Latin or ancient Greek just for the hell of it. I quit college to join the Marines. I survived Vietnam, physically, anyhow, then joined the Boston PD. I made detective and might have stuck with it. But the woman I was going to marry was killed in a car crash that wasn't her fault and my whole life turned upside down.

I heard about the boathouse on a weekend fishing trip with some of the guys from Vice and Homicide. It was part of an old estate that had been subdivided. The boathouse wasn't much then and still isn't, but the location overlooking the bay and distant barrier beach was special. I walked along the edge of the peaceful marsh, smelled the salt spray rose and sedge, saw a pair of snowy egrets tiptoeing in the cord grass in search of minnows, and knew I had found home. I used the money saved to get married as a down payment, scrimped the mortgage out of my cop salary, and volunteered for special detail overtime. I spent every weekend I could at the boathouse patching the leaks in the walls and putting in insulation. I got an old wood stove at a yard sale and hooked it up.

The closeness to the sea had a healing effect. I witnessed the first spring squawkings of the red-winged blackbirds and the return of the striped bass, watched the marsh grass turn to copper in the fall, and saw the scallops being harvested and the bluish plates of ice forming around the edges of the bay. My internal timekeeper became more tied to the seasons' passage than to hands on a clock.

One night I arrested the son of a city politician for hit-and-run. His father was a friend of the mayor's, who appointed the police commissioner. The kid got off. That did it for me. I quit the Department and moved into the boathouse year-round. I met Sam in a local coffee shop named Elsie's. His crewman had left to run his own boat and Sam was having trouble getting a new hand because some of the younger guys thought he was too old. I signed on. Sam took me under his wing and patiently tried to teach me the craft of fishing. In about thirty years, I might know a fraction of what he does.

I still carry a lot of baggage no amount of beautiful scenery can lighten, and I drink more than I should. Which may be why I'm always broke. The IRS doesn't consider self-abuse a deductible expense. Despite my dissipations, I'm in pretty good shape. Fishing ruins your body in the long run, but in between it hardens your muscles better than a Nautilus machine. The toughest part is getting up in the morning. I crawled into bed, set the alarm for three A.M., and turned out the lights.

Sam sucked in a deep lungful of air, let it out, and pronounced his verdict. "Gonna be a good day. On the hot side. Rain coming soon."

It was four in the morning. We stood under the floodlights on the puddled loading platform. The darkened harbor looked like a big hole in the world.

"Sam, you amaze me." I shook my head. "One of

33

those days you're going to have to show me how you do that."

Sam shot me a sly glance and scratched his chin. "If I *told* you, then you'd know, wouldn't you?" He stumped off toward the end of the pier where the *Millie D.* was moored. "What say we go catch some fish."

"Sounds fine to me, Cap." I hurried to catch up.

The minutes before a fishing trip are a delicious time. Your muscles protest and your joints cry out that it's too damn early to be moving, but anticipation crackles in the salty air like an electric current. The morning hush is broken by the scrape of rubber boots on the tarmac, grumpy murmurings, the coughs and curses of sleepy fishermen, boat engines rumbling into life. Expectations are never higher.

Every fishing trip is a treasure hunt, every fisherman a searcher for a big pot of gold. Today you might be the fleet's high-liner, catching more fish than anyone and getting top dollar.

The *Millie D.* was moored alongside the little dock to the north of the fish pier. We climbed aboard, started the engine, cast off the mooring lines, and glided over the limpid waters of the still harbor. Soon we bumped across the washboard breakers that guard the opening in the barrier beach, broke out into the Atlantic Ocean, and set a course so'east.

The eastern sky shifted from black to blue to rose petal pink. Two hours later we were off the elbow of the Cape, rocking in the rolling swells. The air was thick and warm even before the sun lifted off the metallic blue sea into the peach-skin sky. Cobwebby clouds scudded off to the east, the remnants of the rainsqualls that had brushed the Cape that night. It was typical of the crazy weather we'd had that summer.

We set our trawls. While the lines fished, I made coffee and Sam threw a couple of tender cube steaks in a black cast-iron frying pan. He fried them rare and scorched four eggs over easy in steak juice and brown butter. Pure cholesterol, pure heaven. We pulled up a couple of fish boxes for stools and attacked breakfast. In between bites, we talked about the death at Quanset Beach. Sam knew about it. News travels fast in a small town. I filled him in on the details.

"You know more about the sea than anyone, Sam. What could have happened to that guy?"

His brow furrowed. "I've never heard of anyone getting bit by a shark in these waters, but that's the only thing I figure could kill a man."

"I don't know. He was chewed up like he'd gone through a meat grinder. There were a lot of cuts and slashes on his body, and some of his flesh was missing, but nothing bigger than this." I curled my fingers to form a circle about the size of a half-dollar. "That's not my idea of a shark bite, but if it isn't a shark, what is it?"

"Sounds like he ran into an outboard motor."

I shook my head. "There wasn't a boat within miles."

"Humph," he said. He set his empty dish on the deck and pulled his pipe from a pocket. He dug the pipe into an Edgehill tobacco pouch, and touched a match to the bowl. He savored a puff, then pointed the pipe stem toward the ocean.

"Well, there's lotsa things out there that bite. Once saw a man who'd got stung real bad by one of those

Portugee man-of-war jellyfish. Left a heck of a rash on his arm, like somebody whipped him. Your fella would have to get in a school of the darn things to get hurt real dead like you said. You've seen the teeth on a bluefish, but they've never killed anybody so far as I know. Once read a book about a giant squid, the kind that fights with sperm whales. Stingray? Nope. It was some kind of shark, that's my guess, but . . ."

He puffed on his pipe again. He had a far-off look in his frosty blue eyes.

"But what, Sam?"

"Oh, I was just thinking about the ocean, how little we know of it. Heck, I've been hooking fish almost fifty years now. This is my third boat. Sank the first one before I knew what I was doing. I think I've seen everything there is to see. Whales, dogfish, mola-mola, those big flat things with the little mouth and a body that looks like a steamroller run over it. I see the herring come back every year to the stream they were born in, as if they had a map. I've speared eels through the ice. They say eels are born in the Sargasso sea, but nobody can explain to me how they came to the salt ponds. Once I had the dickens scared out of me."

I stayed silent, knowing he would continue.

"Years ago, I fished by myself to save money. I was about five miles east of the old break in the beach, south of the current one. It was night, low fog hanging over the ocean. Well, I looked down and saw something glowing green under the water, moving along like a big Ferris wheel. I tell you, Soc, that one made every hair stand up, like Millie was holding the vacuum cleaner over my head."

"Did you ever find out what it was?"

"Not really. Talked to a few guys. Scientist fellow from Woods Hole said it was probably bio . . . bi-olumi . . ."

"Bioluminescence?"

"That's right."

"That's the sparkle you see in the water sometimes. It's caused by millions of tiny little creatures."

"Don't know about that. Guess what I'm trying to say is that we don't know squat about the ocean. Not by a darned sight, we don't."

We rinsed off our breakfast dishes and went to haul in the trawls. Sam's words ran through my mind. It was hard to look at the green water with its white foam marbling and not wonder what lurked below. I've dived long enough to know what he meant about the mystery of the sea. On more than one dive I've convinced myself something was watching me. I still don't feel comfortable with my feet dangling below the surface. It's probably a genetic residue left over from our ancestors who had to worry big-time about being eaten by something, but it's a real fear, nevertheless.

The breeze that cooled our faces while the boat was underway had died the second we stopped to set trawl. A killer sun beat down on the deck. Its hard rays slow-cooked my head under the Red Sox cap like a burger on a grill. Sweat poured from our noses and chins like rain running off a roof with no gutter.

Sam is tougher than a barnacle on a rock, but he is no youngster. And neither am I. We were gaffing on board fish weighing ten, twenty, or thirty pounds. Fishing is tough work even when the heat isn't pushing ninety. I glanced over frequently to see how he was doing. Sam panted with exertion. I would have liked to quit, but I knew he'd dig in his heels if I suggested calling it an early day.

We set more trawl and took a break in the shade of the wheelhouse. I gulped down a gallon of water to replace what I had lost and squinted up at the pale sun.

"Y'know something, Sam, the old Greeks thought the god Apollo used to ride around the world and that the sun was the blazing wheel of his chariot."

Sam puffed out his cheeks. "Wouldn't mind if Apollo got himself a flat tire."

I chuckled. "It's weird, isn't it, Sam? We complain when the sun doesn't shine, and we complain when it does."

Sam gurgled a swallow of coffee out of his Thermos. "Nothing weird about it, Soc. People are just naturally crazy. Look at us. You think any sane men'd get out of bed before dawn so they could be out here busting their backs on a day like this?"

"Guess you got a point, Sam. But look on the bright side. We've got a waterfront view."

He grinned and removed his trademark tan cap with the long duckbill visor. "We sure got that, Soc. And lots of it." He wiped the sweat off his forehead and glanced toward the fish hold. "We've done pretty good today. What say we head for home after this set? Millie asked if I'd get in early for a change and I'd like to oblige her."

"No problem," I said, trying not to appear too eager.

The last set turned out to be the best. Even with a short day, we'd brought in a good haul. Practically every set had come up with a full catch, mostly cod, some haddock, and a big chunk of pollock. By late afternoon, when we pointed the *Millie D.*'s bow homeward, she sat low in the water from the weight of the fish.

I radioed the catch info into the fish company office at the pier and said we were on our way.

A couple of hours later, we jounced through the cut again and slithered into the harbor. Noisy gulls followed the *Millie D.* like groupies at a rock concert. We were the first boat in and didn't have to wait in line to unload. We pitchforked the fish out of the hold into the loading bucket, then moored next to the pier and got the boat ready for another day of fishing.

The florid orange sun lowering in the western sky augered another hot day tomorrow. The air was even heavier on land. The short walk to our pickup trucks was like a trek across the Sahara.

I was worried about Sam. He looked really beat. During the winter, Sam wears a down vest and flannel shirt with the sleeves rolled up on days that would make a polar bear shiver. He's definitely a cold-weather person; heat does him in. His face looked haggard. Still, I was surprised when he said, "Soc, you don't mind if we take tomorrow off, do you?"

"No problem, Sam. Give me a chance to catch up on a few things."

"Finestkind," he said. "I'll call you tonight and we can talk about the next trip."

"Finestkind, Sam."

Both of us were too stubborn to admit the heat had beaten us.

I stopped at a Cumberland Farms convenience store to buy Kojak some food. He'd sulk if he had to eat the dry stuff. I picked up a copy of *The Cape Cod Times* and scanned it while I waited in line. The banner headline at the top of the front page read: MYSTERIOUS DEATH AT QUANSET BEACH BAFFLES OFFICIALS.

The story said the victim was Jean LeBrun, a forty-two-year-old dentist from Montreal. Hundreds of French-Canadian tourists come to Cape Cod in the summer, and most of them spend their entire vacation at the beach. I ran my finger down the column, looking for an explanation of the death.

The medical examiner said the autopsy showed LeBrun died of shock and loss of blood. Hell, *I* could have told him that. The question was how he *got* that way. The story was pretty accurate, describing how Gary saw the man in apparent trouble. How he was rescued and transported to the hospital. How he was pronounced dead on arrival. I returned the paper to the rack and paid for the cat food.

Kojak heard my truck rattle down the drive and was at the front door to greet me. I fed him immediately rather than endure his pitiful sniffs and reproachful feline glances. Then I peeled off my fishy work clothes and stood under the gloriously cooling spray of the outside shower for about fifteen minutes. I toweled myself dry, got into my denim cutoffs, T-shirt, and flip-flops, popped a brew, and went on the deck. Pleasant Bay was as still as a birdbath. With no breeze to stir their lifeless sails, boats sat as motionless as if they were frozen in time. The purist sailors waited for a breeze. At least one of them had given up and was motoring in.

I looked beyond the beach toward the Atlantic. The Greek poet Homer described the ocean as the source of all. No argument there. Life began in the sea, and people like Sam and me depend on its bounty. But the sea can just as easily spawn death. As it had for Jean LeBrun. If I hadn't been at Quanset, I would have read about him in the paper, come up with some ridiculous theory after a few beers, and promptly forgotten about LeBrun. But I couldn't wipe the terrible bleeding wounds from my mind or forget the sobbing of the woman and the hysteria of the crowd.

*Some*thing had happened out there, but what?

The straggling sailboats had furled their sails and were motoring back. Those without motors would have to paddle their way home. Sometimes it doesn't pay to be a purist.

I went inside and rummaged through the fridge. Just the usual gray-furred penicillin cultures, but nothing fit for human consumption. There was a Baggie with codfish cheeks in the freezer compartment. I defrosted the bag in a pot of hot water and boiled some linguini. I rolled the fish parts in Italian bread crumbs and flour, threw them in an iron frying pan with vegetable oil, added onions and green peppers, and heated up a saucepan of Ragú spaghetti sauce. I opened a cold can of Bud to keep me company while I cooked, and spilled some into the cooking fish.

Kojak's gourmet nose told him culinary history was

in the making. He came over and rubbed against my legs. I scraped some cod and linguini into his white porcelain dish with the kitty face on it and added a little romano cheese. Kojak devoured the fish, lapped the cheese off the pasta, then waddled happily off to lick his whiskers.

The food was okay, but I lost my appetite after a few bites. Reruns of the scene at Quanset Beach kept going through my mind. It was too hot to eat, anyhow. I put my plate on the floor for Kojak, who dashed over as if he were just ending a hunger strike.

I went out to the pickup and drove to the 'Hole. The parking lot behind the bar was packed with out-of-state license plates. Between Fourth of July and Labor Day, the summer crowd takes over and the townies do their drinking at home. The kid checking ID's at the door hardly looked old enough to drink himself. The air inside was thick with loud conversation, and cigarette and kitchen smoke. Little Feat was banging out "Feat Don't Fail Me Now" on the juke. Young shiny-faced tourists with serious tans were playing dating games three deep at the bar. I held a fiver high above my head. The new kid tending bar must have thought I was doing an imitation of the Statue of Liberty because he kept ignoring me. Kojak and a six-pack of Bud were beginning to look pretty good.

I was pondering whether self-immolation would attract the bartender's attention when somebody yelled my name. Gary was waving at me from a corner table. I went over and he pulled out an empty chair. He was with Mo and another lifeguard he introduced as Tony. A passing waitress noticed the desperate gleam in my eye and brought over a frosty beer mug without being asked. I told her to bring me refills at five-minute intervals.

"Sorry I didn't get to look at that outboard," Gary said.

I chugalugged the beer. It tasted wonderful. "You had other things to worry about. You can check out the motor any time."

Gary cupped his chin in his hands and stared at nothing. "It's the first time we've ever lost a swimmer in all the years I've been there."

"That's rough. Anyone figure what killed him?"

He shook his head and gave me a cheerless smile. "All I know is that I was talking to you when I saw this guy in trouble. I'd been watching him because he was so far from the beach. It's something you do automatically. But I wasn't worried. I could tell he was a good strong swimmer. Turned out I was right about that. His girl-friend said he'd been a lifeguard. I look again, and he's stopped. Two reasons why he'd stop. Either he's taking a rest, treading water, or he's got a problem. That's when I grabbed the binoculars for a closer look."

"I remember that."

"He started swimming again, really hard. Then he stopped, threw his arms in the air and went under. He came up and I saw his mouth open. Even at that distance I could tell he was screaming. That's when I hit the water. I had a little trouble getting through the surf, but I was on my way real quick. He was staying afloat. As I got away from the sound of the surf, I could hear him yelling. Shrieking at the top of his lungs, actually."

Mo leaned into the conversation. "Gary's right. I was behind him, and I heard the poor bastard, too. Still gives me the shivers."

Gary continued. "Anyhow, when I got there, just the top of his head was sticking out. I grabbed him by the hair and got the Peterson belt around his waist to keep him afloat. Then I hung on. Mo showed up with the other belt hooked to the towline, and the guys started pulling us in."

"It was a pretty damned impressive rescue, Gary."

He shrugged. "Thanks. Anyhow, guy's unconscious, so we signaled to shore to call the rescue squad. I was still pretty hopeful, going through the resuscitation plan in my head while we rode in. Figured we can keep him alive long enough for the EMT's to get at him. Jesus, Soc. We had no idea he was in such tough shape. I mean all that blood and those slashes on his legs. I think he was gone before I got to him. We hauled a dead body in."

"It was bad, man. I don't ever want to do something like that again. The guy was bleeding quarts, for godsakes." Mo downed his beer.

"Look, guys, you did the best you could."

"Yeah, Soc, I know. It was a picture-perfect rescue. But maybe we shouldn't have let him go out so far."

"Don't blame yourself. Nobody could have done it better. Notice anything else?"

Gary pondered that. "Nothing, except there were a lot of birds hanging about."

"I saw that, too."

He nodded. "The water was all bubbly. I was just

wondering if it had anything to do with the guy being hurt."

The two other guards pushed their chairs back. They said they had to meet their dates. When they left, I said to Gary, "How about a refill on that screwdriver? My treat."

He looked at the glass. "No, thanks, Soc. This is straight orange juice. I'm going to go to a meeting at Town Hall."

"What meeting?"

"The selectmen called it. Everybody's really upset about this thing. Especially the business people. Bad for Quanset's image. Want to come?"

"Think I'll pass."

"You might miss some fireworks. Town Hall wants to hush this beach thing up, but there's no way they can do that. The story's in all the papers. Scuttlebutt making the rounds is the town fathers will try to whitewash it somehow. The park commissioner told me to stay away. Which makes me want to go all the more."

My ears perked up. "On second thought, maybe I will come along. Official interference always brings out the antiauthority tendencies in me."

Gary stood and handed me my ball cap. "Thought you'd say that."

Chapter 5

Town Hall is a hundred-year-old converted schoolhouse on the beach road. The basement hearing room of the rambling white clapboard building doubles as a gallery for the local art association. This month's featured painter was seriously into the Earth Mother theme. The paintings were heavy on the nudes and the nudes were heavy in the thighs. But from what I could see, nobody was interested in art tonight. The crowded room buzzed like a nest of yellow jackets stirred up by a hurricane. Heads nodded, fingers jabbed at chests, and fists pounded invisible surfaces.

The metal folding chairs lined up in neat rows were all occupied, and people jockeyed for standing room. Gary and I elbowed out space between a couple of thunder-thighed paintings and leaned against a side wall.

The five selectmen, actually four men and one

woman, sat behind a long oak table facing the audience. The board's executive secretary was at the far end with a steno pad and tape recorder. At center stage was Stan Roberts. The chairman of selectmen, Stan is a smooth-faced man with a politician's hair-trigger smile. He looks like a poor man's Tip O'Neill. But the only thing he's got in common with Tip is a white mane and a big red nose.

He wore a tan suit and a blue rep tie even though the room was hot and the press of bodies made it hotter, but he wasn't sweating. Maybe he didn't have any glands; I knew he didn't have any backbone. Stan was a retired PR flack in the car rental industry who was smart enough to marry a rich wife. He ran uncontested for selectman and became chairman because nobody else wanted the job. He considers himself a Man of the People.

To his right was Marge Parker, a plumpish woman with a twinkle in her eyes. She was wearing her white R.N. uniform. Beside Marge in a blue chambray shirt and chinos was a middle-aged man who blinked out at the world through thick glasses. Charlie Dumont, a free-lance financial writer. On Stan's left was Mike Spofford, a sixtyish man in a neatly pressed mechanic's uniform. Mike ran the local Mobil station and was respected for his common sense. Next to him, in jeans and T-shirt, his blond beard going to gray, was Deeb Stuart, an aging hippy. He was a carpenter who'd saved his money, bought real estate cheap, and was probably worth a couple of million. He says he's still a flower child at heart, but no one believes him.

Stan glanced at his watch, palm-brushed his side

hair back, and called the meeting to order with a smile he must have practiced in front of a mirror.

"This is something of an unusual proceeding. The selectmen called this emergency public hearing at the request of some concerned townspeople. We didn't have time to post it forty-eight hours in advance as required by the open meeting law, but we did our best to get the word out over the radio stations."

He solemnly lowered his voice. He sounded like a country preacher delivering a eulogy.

"I guess most of you know about the incident yesterday at Quanset Beach, the tragic death of Mr. Jean LeBrun from Montreal. We have Park Commissioner Eddy Fuller here to give us the details." He nodded to a bald man with a white scalp, pink face, and khaki uniform who sat in the front row with his arms and legs crossed. Eddy got out of his seat, hitched his belt up over his pot belly, and faced us.

"Well, there's not a lot to tell you. Our lifeguards spotted a swimmer in trouble. They got him in real quick, and a hell of a job they did, but the gentleman was dead." Eddy was through as far as he was concerned. He sat down.

"Could you tell the folks what was unusual about the accident?" Stan coaxed.

"Oh, sure." Reluctantly, Eddy got back to his feet. "First of all, the accident itself was pretty unusual. Maybe we're tooting our own horn, but our lifeguards are the best on the Cape. They've never lost a swimmer before and we're pretty proud of that record."

I nudged Gary. "He likes you."

Gary whispered back, "Eddy's covering his ass. This is an election year. He doesn't want voters thinking he's hired a bunch of dickheads at the beach."

The park commissioner continued. "Well, they got that gentleman in, but he was cut up real bad, as if—" He paused, realizing he just crawled out on a limb.

"Go on, Eddy," the chairman said.

Eddy shrugged and wiped the sweat off his brow. Knowing Eddy's liking for the juice, I would have bet he was wishing he had a cold beer; I knew I was. "Well, it looked as if something bit him, bit him a lot."

The comment triggered a hubbub. Stan smashed his gavel down like a kid with a hammer and peg toy.

"Thanks, Eddy," he said. "Would Fire Chief Raymond fill us in on what happened next?" Raymond, a skinny guy with a Roman nose and an imposing Adam's apple, got up and read from a sheaf of papers.

"The call came into the station house at eleven twenty-seven A.M. The ambulance was on its way by eleven twenty-nine. EMT's Eldridge and Powell arrived at Quanset Beach at eleven thirty-six and found an individual, male, with serious contusions of the lower body. They applied electrocardiopulmonary resuscitation at the scene, then transported the individual to Cape Cod Hospital, continuing to apply treatment on the way. They arrived there twelve-sixteen P.M., at which time Dr. Frederick Lally pronounced the subject dead."

He sat down. Joe Jordan, the police chief, got up without being asked. The chief is a heavy-set pie-faced man with a perpetual mournful expression. He read in a grim monotone from a notebook in the baroque lingo cops use in the mistaken belief multisyllabic words make them sound smarter than they are.

"Detective Crowell, accompanied by Officer Daley, was dispatched to Quanset Beach. Upon which time they made an examination of the body of a male Caucasian. They determined that the subject's lower body and extremities appeared to be covered with blood, and that he suffered from multiple lacerations, contusions and abrasions. The officers had conversations with approximately a dozen witnesses, but were unable to ascertain as to how these injuries were sustained."

The more people talked, the less they said.

The chief wasn't a bad guy. I coached his kid once in Little League, and the old man got a little overzealous sometimes. But I was getting impatient with this dilly-dallying. Say it in *English,* not in flatfoot talk: The guy was pulled from the ocean bleeding like a sieve and nobody knows what the hell happened.

The chief sat down. Stan said, "I'd like to thank these gentlemen for their concise and informative reports."

I hissed at Gary: "I've read eye charts that were more informative."

There was a sudden lull in conversation and my comment carried. A couple of people smirked in my direction. Stan shot me a dirty look. "The board does not want to downplay this tragedy. We realize it's a good story for the local press, but hope it won't be blown all out of proportion."

He smiled knowingly at Wes Thacher, the editor of the local weekly newspaper. Thacher, a tall lean guy with an unruly mop of snowy hair, sat in the front row, a notebook balanced on his knee. He gave Stan a hound-dog grin.

"You've just heard the facts," Stan continued. "The question now is what to do next? My own opinion is that we should wait for further information before taking action."

Charlie Dumont, the writer in the chambray shirt, cut in. Speaking directly to the audience, he said, "Not all the selectmen feel that way. This board's responsibility doesn't stop with the business community. We've got to think about the taxpayers. The town could be sued for negligence if people are hurt or killed at Quanset. More important, we've got an obligation to the visitors who come here, too. Until we find out what killed that man, we've got to restrict the use of the beach."

The room exploded with angry voices. A red-faced man with a harried expression stood and identified himself as Brad Stomfort, a motel owner.

"Restrict the beach! Are you *crazy?* Quanset is the life's blood of this town's economy. Things are bad enough with the real estate slump. The town can't afford to lose the revenues and neither can the business community. You can't start turning people away from that beach!"

"I didn't say to *close* the beach," the selectman protested. "I said to *restrict* it. Maybe just let people go in up to their knees."

Stomfort went into orbit. "Ridiculous! It's like *admitting* the beach is unsafe."

Stan gaveled the meeting back to order. Marge

Parker, the woman selectman, raised her hand and was given the floor. She smiled and said, "I've been listening to this debate trying to figure out where I'd heard it before. Then I remembered there was a scene just like this in the movie *Jaws*."

Uneasy laughter rippled through the room. "Seriously," she continued. "It's very hard to make a decision based on what we know about this matter so far. We've heard from the park commissioner and the two chiefs, but is there anyone here who was at the beach when this happened?"

Gary raised his hand tentatively. The park commissioner scowled at him. Gary blushed under his tan and stepped away from the wall to face the audience.

"My name is Gary Cozzi. I'm the head lifeguard at Quanset Beach. I've worked at Quanset fifteen years, and have been head lifeguard for the last five. I was the first one to reach Mr. LeBrun. He was cut up real bad."

"Do you have any idea what could have happened to him?" Marge Parker asked.

Gary shook his head. "I don't know what happened, but I do know a lot of children go to that beach. And if we say the beach is safe, it damned well better be safe. I don't want to bring in some kid looking the same way as Mr. LeBrun."

A rumble went through the audience. The chairman rapped his gavel, thanked Gary, and asked if anyone else wanted to speak.

Mike Spofford, the garage mechanic, said, "I'm glad Marge brought up *Jaws*. Everybody here has been afraid to talk about what we've all been thinking. That's the 'S' word. Shark. Is *that* what we're dealing with?"

There was a stir at the back of the room. Mac Mc-Connell, a local skiff fisherman who is not quite as big as a haystack, stepped to the front and turned to face us.

"Christ, that was no shark. I fished these waters for twenty-five years. Seen a lot of crazy things. Most of them have been tourists." Mac's grin was more or less visible through his ginger-and-salt beard. The audience chuckled at the inside joke, breaking the tension. "Sure, there's blue sharks, mako, and dogfish out there, but you'd have to stick your finger in their mouths to get hurt by any of them. And if you're thinking about a great white, forget it. They just don't happen, and if they do, they're too full of fish to bother with humans."

Wes Thacher, the editor, said, "What about blue-fish? The lifeguards had to warn people out of the water a couple of times this summer, isn't that so?"

Gary nodded. "We've done that as a precaution when we've seen schools of blues chasing baitfish in toward shore. A few people have been nipped at other beaches in New England, but we've never had it happen here."

Mac guffawed. "Blues have got more teeth than anyone's got a right to have, and they don't care what gets in their way when they're feeding. But you could go swimming offshore every day of the summer, Wes, and you'd have about as much chance getting killed by blues or sharks as that newspaper of yours has of voting Republican."

There was laughter again.

A man in a turquoise LaCoste shirt got up. "Seems to me we're jumping to conclusions. We keep talking about sharks, like we know this for a fact. Next we'll be saying it was piranha. Couldn't there be another explanation? I've seen the way the surf rips the gravel off the bottom and whips it around. Maybe this guy got hurt when they dragged him through the surf."

Eyes turned to Gary again. He cleared his throat. "I don't think so. If that were true, I would have been cut up the same way."

LaCoste Shirt persisted. "But we can't rule it out entirely, can we?"

Gary shrugged.

Stan Roberts interjected, "This board still has to decide what to do. Our lifeguard friend tells us he's been out there fifteen years and nothing like this has ever happened. Whatever it was must have been a freak accident. We may never know what caused it. But based on past experience, I'd bet it would probably never happen again."

"Probably!" The exclamation came from a statuesque woman across the room. Stan Roberts knew her. "Mrs. Talbot," he said.

The woman strode to the front, not waiting for an invitation. She wore white shorts and a navy polo shirt emblazoned with a logo that said *Quanset Beach Sailing Camp.* She had blond hair going to white, intelligent blue eyes, and was probably in her sixties, but it was impossible to tell. She was one of those lucky people whose face doesn't fall into a sagging ruin as they age.

"For those of you who don't know me," she declaimed in a rich voice, "my name is Tillie Talbot. I run the sailing camp up on the bluff that overlooks the public beach. The camp's been in my late husband's family for fifty years. Since that poor man died yesterday, my phone hasn't stopped ringing. I've done nothing but talk to worried parents and assure them their kids are in no danger. My business will be hurt as much as anyone's, probably more, if word gets around that we've closed the beach. But I agree with Gary. I'd rather close Quanset down if there's a chance of a single child being hurt. I'm urging the selectmen to act."

"We *intend* to act," Stan said defensively. "That's what we're here for."

"Good. Then what harm would it do to close the beach to swimming just for a few days until we have some expert opinion as to the cause of that poor man's death? Then we can make a decision based on hard information, not just a lot of guesses whether it's sharks or octopi." Tillie Talbot directed a scornful glance at the guy in the LaCoste. "Or even gravel."

There was a scattering of applause, and a tall man in his midthirties rose. He wore a white polo shirt, white slacks, and white Gucci loafers. He faced the audience and identified himself as Fred Costello, president of the Board of Trade.

It was a little like Quasimodo telling the Paris rabble that he was a hunchback. Everybody in town knew "Fast Freddy," especially the cops who busted him in the 1970's when he stole a load of confiscated dope from a state police warehouse. Freddy had used an alcoholic state police sergeant as his inside man. The staties were embarrassed and wanted the case wrapped up quick and dirty. The state cop went to the slammer for a few months and Freddy got a suspended sentence, a light fine, and a hundred hours of community service. Freddy survived the cruel and inhuman punishment, then cut his ponytail and beard, bought a three-piece suit and a Mercedes, and went into the real estate business.

The local businessmen regarded him as a pariah at first, but they conveniently got amnesia about his past when he started spreading the greenbacks around. Freddy the felon became Freddy the public-minded citizen.

"I've listened to both sides here," Freddy was saying. "And it's again reaffirmed my decision to move to this town. This is grassroots democracy in action. I agree wholeheartedly with Mrs. Talbot. We can't take any risks with the guests of this community. Quanset Beach must be closed."

The guy in the LaCoste shirt jumped up again.

"I've got a fourteen-year-old son who practically *lives* on his surfboard at Quanset. If I thought he or anyone in my family were in any kind of danger, I'd vote to shut the beach down in a minute. But nothing in what we heard calls for the kind of drastic action that could damage business. We've already been hurt by the crummy weather that's hit us every weekend. Now we get a few sunny days and you want to tell the tourists they can't cool off. Listen, folks, if Wes Thacher wants to be there tomorrow with his camera, we'll all go for a nice long swim to show everybody the beach is perfectly safe. We'll even pack a picnic lunch."

Several people started talking at once. Stan Roberts sternly gaveled them to silence.

"I think we've heard representative views from both sides," he said. "I'd personally be opposed to making a decision that affects a great many of our citizens on such short notice. I'm going to move that we table the question of the beach closing until the board's regular meeting next week. And that we place it on the agenda for discussion pending the receipt of further information. In the meantime, we'll stand in recess, so anyone who wants to add to the record can stop by and see our executive secretary, Barb Schneider."

The motion was seconded. The "ayes" had it. The gavel came down for the final time. People surged out of the suffocating heat of the room. Gary and I were walking across the parking lot when Eddy Fuller broke from the crowd and came over. The park commissioner grabbed Gary by the arm. His face was twisted in anger. "I told you that you weren't needed at this hearing."

"It was my responsibility to be here. I'm the head guard."

"You *won't* be the head guard if you pull crap like this." Eddy wheeled and stalked off.

Gary watched him and shook his head. "There goes a dedicated servant of the people. Aren't you glad you came?"

"Ain't grassroots democracy grand? C'mon, give me a ride back to the 'Hole. I'll buy you a beer and we can talk about the influence of the Greek city-state of Pericles's time on New England town government."

Gary grinned bleakly. "If it's okay with you, maybe I'll just take the beer."

A woman's voice was calling. "Gary, wait up a minute."

Tillie Talbot, the camp owner, was walking fast to catch us.

"Hi, Mrs. Talbot," Gary said. "Nice to see you."

They shook hands and Tillie Talbot said, "I just wanted to thank you for speaking out tonight, but you may have made a few enemies. As you saw, some people don't agree with you."

"Thanks for the warning, Mrs. Talbot. By the way, this is my friend Soc. He was at the beach when the accident happened and saw the whole thing."

Tillie Talbot had a firm handshake. She also had a very warm smile. "I don't think we've met before."

"I spend a lot of time fishing," I told her.

Gary said, "Don't let him fool you. Soc's being modest. He may be a fisherman, but he's a private investigator, too, and a damned good one."

Mrs. Talbot fixed a curious eye on me. "Maybe we should investigate some of the Huey Longs who think they own this town. Gary, I had planned to bring my kids to the beach this week for an overnight, but I may have to call it off. If word got back to the parents, my camp would be empty in a few hours. Well, good night. Nice to meet you, Soc."

She shook hands again and strode off in the direction of her car.

"Nice lady," I said.

"Yeah," Gary answered. "Damned nice. I've gotten to know her pretty well through the years with the kids coming down to use the beach. Her husband was a terrific guy, too. She's been working like a beaver to hold that camp of hers together since he died a few years ago, but it's been touch and go. This stuff at the beach won't help."

I clapped him on the back and gave him a gentle push in the direction of the Jeep. "I'll tell you what *will* help. That beer."

Ten minutes later we were sitting at a table at the 'Hole. I was hungry and ordered a stuffed quahog. Gary was staring into his glass, his mouth set in a hard line. "The damned fools. They don't know what they're dealing with out there."

"You got any guesses?"

"Hell, no, but I'll tell you something, Soc. I've never been scared on a rescue. There isn't time to be. You just launch yourself into the ocean and keep paddling. All that hard training and drill comes into play. It's a real rush, the most exciting thing you've ever done, and it makes all the boring hours cooking in the sun worth it." He took a sip of his drink. "There was something I didn't say tonight. Maybe I should have."

I signalled for another beer.

"Soc, I had the eeriest feeling when I was swimming out to get that guy. I didn't see anything. Just the birds whirling around. But it was as if someone turned on the cold water. I got scared. I'm still scared. I think that if I'd arrived a minute sooner, they'd be looking for a new head lifeguard. There was something out there, Soc, something *hungry.* I could feel it."

The hairs prickled on the back of my neck. "Any idea what it was?"

He shook his head. "Not a clue. Here was this guy, down here with his girlfriend. He's out there swimming, having a good time. Then, *wham.* He's chopped liver."

I put the fork down and pushed the ketchup-covered quahog away. My beer came. I asked Gary if he wanted an encore on his drink.

"No, thanks. I have to get up early tomorrow. It's supposed to be a hot day. Lots of people going to be coming to the beach."

"Worried?"

"Yeah, Soc, I am."

And to tell the truth, I was worried too.

Chapter 6

Kojak woke me up before the thunder did. His sharp ears had picked up the approaching celestial artillery. He crawled under the sheets with me and began snoring. I extracted all seventeen pounds of coon cat and put him at the foot of the bed. He expanded the way cats do, taking up most of the bed until I was squeezed into a corner. The full force of the thunderstorm hit later. It had been a summer of extremes. Hot and cold. Rain or sun. Nothing in between. No wonder the merchants and motel owners were nervous. I fell asleep listening to the distant thunderboomers. Once again, Sam's nose had been right.

I got up around nine. I fried three eggs and dropped them onto a pile of Hormel corned beef hash with lots of ketchup. The air coming off the bay through the sliders had a scrubbed scent after the night's rain. I fed Kojak, checked my tomato garden, found more leaves gone, but no sign of the invading worm, then got in the pickup and drove to the fish pier.

I puttered around on the *Millie D.* for part of the morning. Then I got a load of frozen herring out of the big freezer on the pier and took it to a bait room where I chopped it into cubes a couple of inches long. I stuck the bait on hooks and coiled the trawl lines carefully in the plastic tubs. This was one of the most important parts of tub-trawling. When the trawls are set, the line flies out of the tub in a blur of hooks through a metal chute and into the water. One bad coil and the lines snarl like a plate of linguini. It takes hours to untangle the mess.

At lunchtime I broke off work and drove over to Elsie's restaurant. I asked Elsie what was in the surf-and-turf special. She said it was a sandwich, half bologna, half tuna. I figured I couldn't go wrong, but it doesn't pay to underestimate Elsie. The bologna tasted like cardboard and the tuna was drier than old sawdust. Elsie could put Weight Watchers out of business.

After lunch I baited more hooks, then stored the tubs in the freezer so the bait wouldn't spoil. The boats started coming in with their catches, tailed by squadrons of squawling gulls. By mid-afternoon, the fleet was lined up in the cove, waiting to unload. I kibbitzed a while, then went home and popped a beer. I sat on the deck, looking out at the low-lying brindle of the distant barrier beach, and thought about the hearing the night before. Common sense should have told the town fathers to close the beach until someone had some answers. But even small-town selectmen are political animals, and it was no surprise they caved into the demands of the business people. I hoped their decision didn't backfire. I drained the beer, went inside, and picked up the phone.

My finger hovered over the dial. Question: How do you call a woman you haven't talked to in months? Answer: Quickly, without thinking, before you change your mind. I punched out a number in West Barnstable and listened to the rings, half hoping nobody was home. A voice answered. No getting off the hook today.

"Hi, Sally, it's me," I said.

She didn't answer right away. I held the phone a couple of inches away so she wouldn't blow out my eardrum when she hung up.

I should have known Sally had too much class to slam the phone down or tell me what a jerk I was. "Soc? What a nice surprise." I had my ear cocked for sarcastic nuances, but she sounded as if she really meant it. "How have you been? I've missed you."

I thought of her chestnut hair and the blue eyes that tilt on the color spectrum toward the marsh heather that grows wild along the edge of the sea.

"I'm fine. I've missed you, too."

"You wouldn't know it," she said with a note of good-natured skepticism. "Every time I talked to you, you were busy. So I stopped calling. And waited for you. And waited. Then I got tired of waiting."

I was squirming like a school kid. "I'm sorry. You know how it is. You don't call someone for a long time. Then you're embarrassed to call them because it's been such a long time."

"I'm not just *some*one, Soc," she said softly.

Sally had a way of cutting through my smoke screen.

"I know, Sal. That's why I'm even more embarrassed. I called you with an ulterior motive."

"You really know how to sweet-talk a girl, Soc."

"You'll have to admit an ulterior motive is better than none at all."

"I can tell you better after I hear what it is."

"Okay, here's what I have in mind. If you're not busy, how about having a drink with me? Something cool at someplace even cooler. How about Tugboats?"

"Sounds good. I'm roasting here even with all the windows open. In about an hour?"

"I'll meet you there."

I hung up and went into the kitchen. Kojak was sitting in front of his dish like Oliver Twist in the workhouse. I sighed and spooned some Nine Lives prime grill into his dish. Kojak knows what a guilt-ridden sucker I am, and he's a real pain when he's in a sulky mood. Conscience soothed, I showered and shaved, changed into jeans, Top-Siders, and an aquamarine polo shirt, and set off to Hyannis.

Sally was much nicer than I would have been in her place. There was no logical reason under the sun for me to have put her off all summer. She was beautiful, intelligent, and charming. A man would have to be addled not to want to spend every living minute with a woman like that. Sam was right. Fishermen *are* crazy. And I must be crazier than any of them.

.   .   .

People who don't know any better think Hyannis is like Hyannisport, where the Kennedys have their summer houses. The port is actually a high-toned affluent suburb, and Hyannis itself is like a small city, even though technically it's a village. In the summer, the roads are clogged with bewildered tourists. Crossing Hyannis was like going through an automotive meteor shower. Sally had a shorter distance to come from the north side of the Cape. When I pulled up to the restaurant, her red Honda was in the parking lot.

I climbed the stairs to a second-floor deck that overlooked Lewis Bay and Hyannis Harbor. Sally was waiting at a table near the bar. She wore white pleated shorts and a bluish-purple tank top. The color went well with the dusky Neapolitan complexion she had inherited from her Italian mother and the eyes passed down by her Celtic father.

I kissed her lightly on the lips and apologized for keeping her waiting. She said she had only arrived a minute earlier herself. We ordered two margaritas straight up with no salt. We danced conversationally around each other like a couple of flamenco artists. She asked me how my fishing and detecting were going. I said I was doing fine and asked after her job. Sally is the head dolphin trainer at a Cape Cod aquatic park called Oceanus. She said it was fine, and asked how my family was. I said they were fine and asked how Huff and Puff, her trained dolphins, were.

"They're both fine. Froggy, too," she added. Froggy was a beluga whale who has a voice like a kid with the croup.

"Say hi from me. Tell them I'll come by with a fish someday."

"I will, but I'll tell them not to hold their breath waiting." She took a sip of her margarita, watching my reaction above the rim. The zinger was lobbed in nice and easy from the outside, but Sally got her point across.

"I said I was sorry for not calling you."

"Apology accepted, but it still doesn't explain why I haven't seen you for months. Is it something I did or said?"

"Of course not. Would you believe me if I said I was busy?"

"No."

"Would you believe me if I said I didn't know?"

"Yes." Sally was perceptive as well as beautiful. "I would believe that more than anything. That doesn't mean I like it any better. No one likes having somebody they care a lot about treat them like a stranger. Okay. That's my tongue-lashing. Tell me about your ulterior motive."

Glad to change the subject, I described the injuries I had seen at Quanset Beach, and filled her in on what the instant experts had to say at the public meeting.

"Your specialty is marine mammals," I concluded. "Do you know of anything that could inflict that kind of damage?"

She was frowning. "I can't think of *any* marine mammal that would hurt a human being."

I looked across Lewis Bay. The big black-and-white island Steamship Authority ferry was cruising slowly out of the harbor, its rails lined with passengers bound for Nantucket.

"A couple of people have suggested sharks," I said without enthusiasm.

"Obviously you don't buy that."

I shrugged.

"Well, sharks aren't my specialty, but I know a little about them from working around the people at Oceanus. From the wounds you described, I'd say no. A shark digs its teeth in and shakes its head, yanking out a mouthful of flesh. That's why even a small shark bite can be dangerous."

"That leaves us with the gravel theory."

She shook her head emphatically. "Sounds rather farfetched."

"I agree."

The smell of food cooking came from the kitchen. "This is lousy timing, considering our topic of conversation, but that smells terrific. Are you hungry?"

"Famished. I'm in the mood for fish and chips."

I signaled the waitress. "It's as good as done."

The sun sinking in the cloudless western sky was bright orange. Tomorrow would be another hot day. A faint zephyr breeze had sprung out of the southwest and after dinner we cooled off even more with lime sherbert. Then Sally ordered Campari and soda. I recalled that we drank Campari on our first date and she was pleased I remembered. The tables around us were starting to fill. Sally suggested we have another cooler at her apartment.

I followed her in the truck to an old carriage house behind a manse on the north side of the Cape. Sally's apartment was on the second floor. She made us rum coolers and we sat on the deck sipping our drinks. The sky went from purple to black over Cape Cod Bay, and fireflies made flickering sparks in the velvety darkness. As the light faded, tiny gnats came off the marshes to feed, and we moved inside to the sofa.

We talked some more until there didn't seem to be anything else to talk about. Keeping her eyes on me, Sally brushed her hair back. With her other hand she reached out and touched mine. "I'm glad you called."

I took her hand and ran my fingers up the silky smoothness of her arm. It was impossible to be close to Sally without succumbing to an irresistible urge to reach out and touch her. "I'm glad I called, too."

She smiled. "I had an ulterior motive in seeing you."

"What was that?" Sally was the least devious person I knew.

"This." She leaned over and kissed me.

I folded her in my arms, feeling her warmth, using my lips and fingertips to explore the nooks and crannies I had come to know so well. Our arms and legs entwined. We rolled off the sofa, hitting her carpet with a thud. We broke into laughter and didn't stop until the tears came. It was what we needed to break the conversational dance we had been performing all night. We left a trail of clothing all the way to the bed. We made love, dozed off, made love again in the pleasant lazy way that comes after the first rush of desire. We fell asleep with our legs and arms playing pretzel.

The clock radio awoke me. The radio announcer was the same hyper DJ I had listened to in the Quanset Beach traffic line. This morning he was urging listeners to identify the rock group for two free dinners at a local

Italian restaurant. I mumbled into my pillow that the band was Dicky Do and the Don'ts. Sally kissed me and murmured, "Gosh, you're old." I never did find out if I was right. It took a moment to disentangle, but we got up finally and showered together to save water. Then she was off to a marine mammal symposium at the New England Aquarium in Boston. I said I would call her, which sounded awfully lame. She smiled knowingly, kissed me on the cheek, and was gone.

I stopped off at Elsie's on the way home. The eggs were underdone, the bacon was carbonized, the toast was buttered cold, and the coffee tasted like Rustoleum. On the whole, though, Elsie's cooking was improving.

From Elsie's I went home. Kojak inhaled his breakfast, burped like a longshoreman, looked toward the screen door as if the thought of going out passed through his mind, then twitched a couple of times and headed for my bed. I fooled around at the boathouse and thought about Sally. Around eleven o'clock I headed to Quanset Beach.

You never would have known a swimmer had been chewed to death two days earlier. The tollbooth attendants were taking parking fees as fast as they could. Even so, traffic was backed up for miles on the beach road. I eased the truck into a corner slot and walked across the parking lot to the snack bar, then along the boardwalk to the benches. The beach looked the same as it did the last time I was there. Kids running around with plastic shovels and buckets. The noise of paddle games and boom boxes. The rainbow colors of umbrellas and beach towels.

The surf had moderated considerably in the last

twenty-four hours. Everybody was in the water, from kids to old folks. They waded, swam, splashed, or simply stood up to their knees or their waists just beyond the foam where the waves broke onto the slope of the beach.

The only thing different was the lifeguards. In normal times, the guards would have been watchful, but relaxed, leaning back in their chairs, chatting as they let their eyes wander over the beach and ocean. Today, they were wound as tightly as clock springs. Gary and Mo angled forward in their seat like a couple of greyhounds before the starting bell. Gary looked as if he was trying to crawl into his binoculars. He was so intently scanning the water that he didn't see me at the foot of the tower.

"Hey, Gary," I yelled. "How's it going?"

He lowered the binoculars and waved. He told his partner to keep a sharp eye out, then climbed down to the beach. We shook hands.

Gary has a tough time not smiling. His mouth just keeps snapping back into a shallow U no matter how hard he tries. But there was no mistaking the edge in his voice.

"It's going okay, so far. The guys are really pumped up. Especially with all those people in the water."

He tensed as if he had seen something and stared toward the ocean. I did the same. After a few seconds, he relaxed, but his eyes scanned the sea like the beam of a lighthouse.

"You can't keep people from swimming," he went on. "That's what they come here for. He puffed out his cheeks. Everybody seems to be having a good time except us. I'll be glad when the day is over. It just seems unreal."

I knew what he meant. There was something in the air, as if the molecules in the atmosphere were stretched thin. Maybe I was just picking up Gary's worry vibes. I told him to hang loose. We shook hands again and Gary climbed back onto the stand. I followed the smell of frying clams to the parking lot, got in my truck, and headed home. The farther I got from the beach, the less jumpy I became. Still, anxiety sat in my stomach like a rock.

I drove up to my house and all thoughts of Quanset Beach faded from my mind. I had other things to think about.

Chapter 7

A gleaming snow white Cadillac Allante blocked my drive. The word PIZZA was on its license plate. Kojak sat on the front doorstep. His eyes were narrowed to slits and the whiskers on his coal face were turned down in a classic sourpuss. I said hello, but he ignored me. Water was running in the kitchen. A slim figure in a black dress was at the sink, her back to me. She turned and smiled. Light glinted off the gold in her front tooth.

"Hello, Aristotle," my mother said. "I do your dishes from this morning."

They were actually the dishes from yesterday or the day before. I went over and put my arm around her slim shoulders. "Thanks, Ma. This is a big surprise, seeing you here." Actually, I was stunned. My mother almost never leaves Lowell, where the family business is. "Is everything okay at home?"

She plunged her hands back into the soapsuds. "Sure, sure," she said dismissively. "Everything is good, Aristotle."

The screen door to the deck opened and my brother George came into the kitchen. George is a couple of inches shorter than I am, and a few pounds heavier. We both have dark brown hair and olive complexions, what I like to describe as a *strong* nose, and a mustache, but the similarities end there. My hair is over the collar, I wear a gold earring, and my idea of formal wear is a clean pair of socks.

"Hey, Soc, how's it going?"

"Fine, George, you look great." He had on beige, pleated-front slacks, a white shirt unbuttoned at the neck to show off his gold chain and crystal pendant, and tassled brown leather loafers. He grinned and gave me a brotherly bear hug and a thump between the shoulder blades.

"Thanks. You, too." He patted his stomach. "Trying to work off the gut at the health club, but it's a losing battle."

"It's an *impossible* battle. I know what a great cook Maria is. How is she, and the kids?"

"Good, Soc, good. Come up and see us some time."

"I will." I glanced at my mother at the sink. "It's sort of a shock to see you and Ma here."

"Yeah, well, it's a shock to me, too, Soc. I got a business to run, after all."

George still resents the fact that I bailed out of Lowell to move to Cape Cod and play beachcomber, while he stayed home and helps my parents run Parthenon Pizza, the family business.

I ignored the subtle dig.

"You probably should call the next time you visit," I said. "You lucked out today, but I'm usually fishing this time of year." He wasn't the only one who worked.

"Yeah, I know." He lowered his voice. "I told Ma that, for Godsakes. But she was anxious to get down here. Probably thought you'd run for it if you knew she was coming. Christ, if you were out fishing she would have hired a boat and gone looking for you. You know how she is."

"Yeah, George, I know."

To understand the subtext of one brief brotherly exchange, you have to know a little about my mother. Ma was born on the island of Crete, which explains a great deal about her. Like others from her rocky homeland, she is by turns proud, critical, brusque, and uncommonly kind and generous. She is also stubborn. It is a quality, which, with my father's industry and Athenian entrepreneural spirit, had much to do with building Parthenon into the premier frozen pizza company in New England.

George has a family, and now that my parents are older, he pretty much runs a multimillion dollar business. I am an ex-Marine who has seen combat, and worked the toughest neighborhoods of Boston as a cop. We are considerably over twenty-one. Yet both of us become twelve-year-old boys in the presence of my mother. With George, it's a question of propinquity; a large percentage of the killing schedule Ma still puts in at the bakery is devoted to telling him what to do, and he has simply wearied and given in. With me, it's a little more complicated.

My mother wanted her firstborn son to be a professor and thought naming me after a couple of long-dead philosophers wouldn't hurt. She is a curious combination of pragmatism and superstition and to her this was perfectly logical. She became convinced she made the right decision as I grew older and I began to remind her in appearance of her grandfather Nikos, a passive, peace-loving farmer who became what they call a *pallikari,* or warrior, and cut a swath through the Turkish army occupying Crete. It was a noble cause, but she never got over the fact that her beloved *papou* had blood on his hands. After I defended George in a schoolyard brawl and sent a couple of kids to the hospital, she renewed her push to steer me into peaceful pursuits. But Nikos's genes were too strong. I left college to join the Marines. The rest, as they say, is history.

"Two minutes, Aristotle," my mother said over her shoulder. "First I finish the dishes."

She scrubbed a dented aluminum saucepan as if she were going to put her hand through the metal, then held the blackened bottom up to her face like a mirror. I cook on the high-heat, quick meal principle, and the pot had lost its reflective qualities many scorchings ago. She shook her head, put the pot in a rack, dried her hands on a dish towel, folded the towel, hung it neatly on a hanger, then came over and stood on her tiptoes to give me a peck on the cheek.

"Come," she ordered, cheerily, "we sit outside. It's a nice day."

George and I tagged behind my mother like ducklings. We went onto the deck and she surveyed the boats dotting the bay.

"So beautiful," she said. There was a nostalgic gleam in her gray eyes. "The water reminds me of the harbor at Heraklion back in Crete." She frowned. "But this *house*, Aristotle, you must do something about this house."

The boathouse suits me fine, but I'm not the fastidious person my mother is. Spill a drop of water and Ma will catch it on a sponge before it hits the floor. She *irons* her sheets and pillowcases. And you actually *can* see your face in her dishes.

"I put the cat outside," she was saying. She shook her head in disgust. "The dirty animal sleeps on your bed." Now I knew why Kojak looked annoyed. He gets irritated even when *I* kick him off the bed. Hoping to avoid a review of my housekeeping skills, I changed the subject. "It's great seeing you and George. You're sure everything's okay with the family?"

She brushed the sand off a deck chair and sat. "Yes and no, Aristotle. Your father and sister Chloe are good, but you remember your cousin Alex?"

My mind's eye went up the trunk of the family tree, ran out to dead end on a couple of branches, and fixed on a handsome, dark-eyed kid in his teens.

"Of course. His father is Uncle Alexander, who teaches at MIT. His mother is Aunt Demeter. She's an account exec with a big Boston ad agency. They've got the house in Weston."

A glow of pleasure lit my mother's face. Zounds, she was thinking. He actually knows who his family is. She would probably dedicate a new stained glass window to the church to thank God for the miracle.

"Your cousin Alex is a good boy. Very smart. But he's getting into trouble now."

"What kind of trouble, Ma?"

"He leaves home and . . ." She seemed at a loss for words and turned to brother George.

"He's running around with a bunch of assholes, Soc."

She pondered his description and decided that for the time being she couldn't improve upon it in Greek or English.

"What George says is true. Alex has bad friends, and he doesn't listen to his parents any more."

"I'm sorry to hear that, but I'm not sure what it's got to do with me."

George laughed. "It's easy, Soc. You're Alex's idol."

Ma cut him down with a withering glance. He looked like a kid who had just been caught swearing in church and mumbled something about taking a walk. He was probably going to sneak a butt. My mother doesn't like him smoking.

"What George says is true. Alex doesn't study in school. He is very smart, but he says he doesn't want to go to college. He doesn't listen to anyone. He tells his mother and father that Aristotle never finished college and he's doing okay."

It had been years since I'd seen Alexander and Demeter. Alex was their only kid. They lost a daughter when she was very young, and had lavished all their attention on Alex, a cute raisin-eyed little charmer. They gave him everything he wanted. Too much, in fact, and in their suffocating love they ended up spoiling him.

Alex and I got along okay. The first time he tried to bullshit me I'd cut him off at the knees, and I think he appreciated that because he'd stick to me like glue whenever I saw him at family gatherings. We'd toss a ball around and gab about sports. He liked the idea that I had left the family and gone my own way. He seemed no different from any teenager. Vain, self-centered, egotistical. Maybe a little more obnoxious than average. Other than that, not a bad kid. Just screwed up from having to fill the vacuum left by his sister's premature death.

I felt sorry for Alexander and Demeter. They've had some rotten luck. But youth counseling wasn't my line.

"Gee, Ma, I'm pretty busy fishing. I'm not sure I can get off the Cape to see him."

It's always a mistake to underestimate my mother. She was ready for my pitch and bunted it back to me for a base hit.

"No problem, Aristotle," she answered with a golden smile. "Alex lives on Cape Cod this summer with his friends. Not too far from here," she added, in case I didn't get the point.

Aw, jeez. Snookered. "What do you want me to do, Ma?"

"It's like George says, Alex will listen to what you say. You *must* talk to him, tell him to go home, go back to school and study hard. Make him *ezgenis,* Aristotle."

She used the Greek word meaning 'well-mannered.' It also meant being 'civilized,' in the tradition of Greek culture. Which was pretty funny, when you considered that the only reason I might have any influence over Alex was because he envied my uncivilized lifestyle. Alex was a smart kid. He'd see through the hypocrisy right away.

78

Do as I *say,* Alex, not as I do. But what the hell. What Ma wanted, Ma got. This seemed like a small thing, talk to a kid. How much time could it take?

"Okay, Ma, I'll do my best."

She smiled and patted my knee. "I know you will, Aristotle." She rose and smoothed her black dress. "Well, we must get back to the bakery. Papa is all alone."

There must have been at least fifty people working at Parthenon Pizza the last time I was there, but I knew what she meant. She and Pop were a team. She called for my brother. George came around the corner. He had the guilty look of a kid who's been caught smoking cornsilk behind the barn.

"George, give your brother the address. Then we go back to Lowell." She kissed me on both cheeks and went into the kitchen for a last inspection tour.

George handed me a slip of paper from his pocket. "Good luck," he said. "You'll need it. This kid's a real winner. If it was up to me I'd let him twist in the wind."

I held the paper out. "Be my guest. I've got plenty to do without playing Father Flanagan to a juvenile delinquent."

"Naw, Ma would go bonkers." He gave me a rueful grin. "She has to come all the way down here to talk to Aristotle. *Aris*totle will know what to do." George has a real sibling problem because he feels he's underappreciated by my parents, who still favor their wayward older son. What makes it worse is he's right.

"Look, George, this isn't exactly a case of the folks laying a Prodigal Son feast out for me."

"Yeah, I know, Soc. Sorry. I've been working too

hard. Then she yanks me out of the bakery to play chauffeur."

We walked out to the Cadillac. "You ought to take some time off, George. Maybe come down here without the family. I'll take you fishing for blues and stripers. We'd have a blast."

The idea must have appealed to him because he smiled. "Yeah, you know something, I think I'd like that. Thanks."

"Think about it. I'll call you soon and we can set a date. And say hi to Maria and the kids."

"I will. Don't be a stranger. Come up some time for dinner."

"I could use some Greek soul food. It's pretty slim pickings on Cape Cod. Mostly lettuce with feta on it and the gyros are sliced meat loaf."

Ma was already sitting on the passenger side, her hands folded in her lap. "How is your friend Sally?"

"She's fine. I just saw her. She asked about you and Pop."

That pleased her. She reached out and touched my arm. "Bring Sally to see us some time. Poppa and I like her. She's a very nice girl."

"I'll be sure to do that, Ma."

"Good, Aristotle. You need a woman in your life." She glanced at the house and sighed meaningfully.

George started the engine, and they were out of the driveway in a cloud of dust. I watched until the Caddy disappeared around a bend. Kojak slunk from the garden where he'd been hiding. I picked him up and patted his dusty head until he made a creaking sound that is his version of a purr. Then I brought him into the house and gave him some kitty snacks and a saucer of milk. He perked up after that and headed for my bedroom.

I put the address George gave me on the kitchen table and cracked a cold beer. What the hell could I tell this kid? Stop running around with these bums, dude. Go to college, dude. Do what your mother and father tell you to do, dude. Chill out, dude. Did kids still call each other dude? Christ.

I let my eyes roam around the boathouse. Okay, so the braided rug was worn and unraveling. The overstuffed green flowered sofa sagged in the middle and didn't match the purple tweed wing chair. Spiderwebs hung from the corners, but their owners helped control the fly population. Black tufts of Kojak fur had attached themselves to most surfaces. The boathouse smelled like a fish tank, but that went with the water view. Place wasn't bad, I thought. So it wasn't ready for a spread in *Architectural Digest*. I went outside and looked at the shingles. They were brown and curled like toenails needing to be cut.

Suddenly inspired, I climbed in the pickup and drove to the Mid-Cape Home Center. I bought a course of white cedar shingles and a box of nails, then stopped by the package store for a six-pack of Bud. Back home, I used a crowbar to strip the old shingles off the northeast side, facing the garden. This side takes the biggest beating from the winter weather. I started nailing on the new shingles. The work was hot, and I had to make another beer run, but the gratification was instant. By late afternoon, blond shingles covered a good part of the side. The rows were more or less parallel. I was admiring my work when the phone rang inside the house. Gary was on the other end of the line. I barely said hello before the words tumbled from his mouth.

"Soc," he said. "It's happened again."

Fifteen minutes later I was at Quanset Beach. Two police cruisers and the park commissioner's truck were angled in front of the administration building. Beach staff, park department people, cops, lifeguards, and kibitzers milled around in the parking lot. I asked a young parking lot attendant where Gary was and she pointed inside. Uniforms crowded the beach manager's office. Eddy Fuller was on the phone. The park commissioner looked as happy as a beached haddock.

Gary was in the hallway talking to two uniformed cops. He said he'd be free in a couple of minutes and suggested I wait in the lifeguards' locker room at the back of the administration building. I sat at the scarred metal table where the guards take their lunch breaks and pawed through an old *Parade* magazine. Gary came in, flopped into a chair as if the energy had been drained out of him, and stared at me. His tanned face was ashen.

"How bad was it?" I asked.

"Could have been worse. We just heard from the hospital emergency room. Kid's going to live. He'll have scars on his leg the rest of his life, but at least he'll *have* a leg."

"What happened?"

"It was a surfer this time. Town kid named Joe

Simmons. He's about eighteen." Gary slammed his fist on the table. *"Damn!* We should have been watching the surfers' beach."

The surfers had their own beach beyond the north headstand away from swimmers.

"You can't keep an eye on everybody in the water, Gary."

"I guess so." He said it without conviction. "We thought we were home free. Everything was okay at the protected beach. Then one of the surfers came running up from the north stand. He's screaming bloody murder, pointing out at the water. Joe Murdock checks with his binocs, and sure enough, one of the surfers is in trouble. The guy seemed to be on and off his board. Joe called the headstand to tell us a rescue's going on. Then he hit the water with his paddle board. Joe reached the kid in a few minutes. Simmons is lying belly down on his board. He's half conscious by then, but he's hanging on for dear life. Joe gets him to shore. Meantime, I've called the rescue squad. The kid's leg was a mess. The EMT's did their best to stop the bleeding and shipped him off to the hospital."

"Did anyone see anything?"

Gary rubbed his face wearily. "Not really. A couple of his buddies said he was resting on the board with his legs in the water. Then all at once they heard him scream."

"Anything else?"

He was silent a moment as if he didn't really want to admit what he was about to say. "One guy remembers there were a bunch of birds whirling around."

"How about the surfer? Did he see what grabbed him?"

"He wasn't in any shape to talk. He'd lost a lot of blood. They'll ask him later, I guess. Soc, what the hell is going *on* out there?"

"I wish I knew, Gary. I wish I knew."

"C'mon," he said, wearily. "I've got something to show you."

I followed him down the hall to the first aid room. "Cops are supposed to pick this stuff up later." He reached into a closet that had bandages and splints on the shelves and handed me part of a neoprene wetsuit. "This is the bottom to the kid's wetsuit. The EMT's sliced it so they could work on him."

Someone had cut the wetsuit leg off around the thigh, but more interesting was the area from the shin down to the ankle. It was in shreds, tattered like a court jester's wattles.

I fingered a tatter. "Looks like it got caught in a lawn mower."

"That's not all." Gary removed a navy wool blanket from a yellow plastic surfboard leaning against the wall. One of the three stabilizing fins was missing from the board's bottom and part of the left rear side had been chewed away. I knelt down and brushed the sand from the ragged edge.

"This plastic is tougher than steel. You'd need a lot of pressure to gouge chunks out of it this way."

Gary nodded. "Well, what do you think?"

I stood up. "Unless you can prove somebody did this with a chain saw, I think you'd better close the beach."

"Way ahead of you. I kicked everyone out of the water. I've put a call into the selectmen to make the closing permanent, or at least until this thing is cleared up. I should hear from them any minute."

"While you're waiting, how about showing me where this happened?"

Gary told Charlie Nevers he'd be on the beach and to call him on the hand radio if they needed him. We left the administration building and walked north along the snow fences that edge the parking lot and protect the fragile dunes. About a hundred yards from the building, we cut through the dunes on a narrow boardwalk.

Half a dozen surfers in their late teens were hanging around the north lifeguard stand. Some still had their wetsuits on, but nobody was surfing. They all looked disconsolate until Gary told them their buddy was going to be okay. Gary and I continued past the wrack line of seaweed down the sloping beach until our toes were almost in the foaming edge of the surf. He pointed to a spot around two hundred feet out into the water. I borrowed his binoculars and strained to see through the lenses, trying to project my eyeballs under the hard jade surface of the sea. Nothing was amiss. All I saw was the mesmerizing ranks of inbound waves.

Someone hailed us. A young guy was walking fast in our direction. A Pentax 35 mm camera dangled from a strap around his neck and he carried a narrow tan notebook in his hand.

Sand walking is tough and he was puffing like The Little Engine that Could when he reached us. "Hi, Gary," he said between breaths. "How are you doing?"

"Been better. How are you, Don?"

"Busier'n a one-legged man at a kick-ass contest."

Gary's old smile flickered. "Don, this is my friend Soc. Don Rollins from the *Gazette*."

Rollins had a wide, corn-fed face, and big blue eyes that blinked behind thick glasses. He was built like a college football player who went off training after missing the final cut. He wore a Hawaiian shirt that was tight around the shoulders and gut, baggy chinos, and Keds high-top sneakers.

I've run into a lot of newspeople. Basically, reporters and P.I.'s do some of the same work. We both go around asking people dumb questions they don't want to answer. The good reporters are easy to spot. You can almost see them wagging their tail when they sniff a hot story. Rollins looked as if he'd just escaped from the pound. We shook hands and Gary asked if Rollins had heard anything out of Town Hall.

"Yeah," the reporter said. "The selectmen are polling each other over the phone, trying to decide whether to close the beach. Apparently, some members of the board still aren't convinced."

Gary exploded. "Goddamnit, how many bleeding bodies do they have to see?" He started back across the beach. I followed. Rollins straggled behind us, pausing on the way to click off shots with his Pentax. The voice of Charlie Nevers crackled over Gary's radio.

"Gary, you'd better get back to the AB."

"What's going on?" Gary asked.

"Can't tell you on the radio," Nevers replied.

We hustled back to the parking lot and Gary went into the administration building. Rollins said he was going to check his office. He went toward the pay phone outside the administration building. A minute later, Gary and Nevers burst out the front door and headed toward the red beach patrol truck.

"C'mon," Gary told me.

"What's going on?"

"Pop Squires called in from the beach buggy booth. A guy in an ORV just drove up all excited."

I trotted to keep up with them. "Excited about what?"

"You're not going to believe this, Soc. There's a body on the beach."

Chapter 8

Rollins sensed the urgency in the air with that special radar good reporters seem to have. He slammed down the pay phone and sprinted after us. Gary tossed me a set of keys. "These are for my Jeep," he said. "You guys can follow us down."

He raced to the beach patrol truck, a big ketchup-colored GMC four-by-four, and clambered in with Charlie Nevers. I slid behind the steering wheel of Gary's Jeep and Rollins hopped in on the passenger side. Bubble light flashing, the patrol truck crossed to the far end of the parking lot and, with us close behind, drove off the blacktop onto the sand road through the dunes to the beach buggy shack.

The patrol truck pulled up next to the shack. Gary and Charlie got out and went over to Pop Squires, who was talking to a thickset guy wearing a refrigeration company polo shirt, plaid shorts, and a Detroit ball cap. Parked nearby was a recreational vehicle, one of those aluminum houses on wheels people use to overnight on the beach. A woman and two small kids sat in the RV's cab. The guy in the plaid shorts was waving his arms and pointing toward the beach. They talked a couple of minutes, then he and Gary got in the patrol truck with Charlie Nevers.

They took the sand road that runs behind the dunes. A few hundred feet from the check-in station, the hard-packed ruts ended. I shifted into four-wheel drive, the fat tires bit into the soft sand, and the Jeep lurched forward.

Keeping a loose grip on the steering wheel, I let the tires follow the ruts left by others, easing in and out of the potholes. Steady as she goes. Lead-foot the gas pedal, and you'll destroy your shock absorbers and hammer your head against the roof. If you're driving a big heavy truck like Gary, you can get away with it. He humped through the moon-crater holes like a Sherman tank. The lighter Jeep bounced from bump to bump.

Rollins was trying hard not to fly out of his seat. He clutched the roll bar with one hand and held his Pentax down on his chest to keep the camera from jumping up and smashing him in the face.

"Sorry!" I yelled. "I don't want to lose him."

"That's oh-k-kay. I d-d-didn't need these fillings anyway." He smiled grimly and got a tighter grip on the roll bar.

After driving about a mile, the pickup spun left

onto a spur track. I followed. Moments later, the track broke through the dunes and we were driving along the flat upper part of the Atlantic beach. The ocean pawed the beach in low easy breakers.

The outer beach stretches a dozen miles to the south, forming a natural oceanfront highway. Before four-wheel drive, people came out in Model A Fords, and later converted bread trucks into primitive off-road-vehicles, or ORVs. The beach buggies used to race along the hard-packed lower beach just out of reach of the water. They were banned to the upper level after a buggy ran over and almost killed a woman partially buried in the sand.

On hot summer days the beach looks like an extension of the Mid-Cape Highway. But even with the traffic you can carve out your own slice of waterfront property. Here it's less crowded than the public beach to the north at Quanset. Dozens of self-contained vehicles or smaller Jeeps and Toyotas draw up to the crest, facing the Atlantic like cars at a drive-in movie. People lounge in their beach chairs within arm's reach of their beer coolers. Some stick fishing poles in sand sockets, but it's mostly for effect.

A half-dozen ORV's were clustered together the way they do sometimes for a communal barbecue. The patrol truck slammed to a stop, spraying sand, and we parked beside it. Rollins was slightly green around the gills, but he was a true newshound. He spilled from the Jeep, camera and notebook in hand, adjusted his thick glasses, and charged toward the group.

The menfolk had assumed command and the

women were busy trying to keep curious kids back. The crowd parted to let us through. The center of attention was under a worn baby blue woolen blanket with a pink hem.

Technically, this was beach patrol territory under Charlie Nevers's jurisdiction. Charlie is trained to handle a heart attack or apply CPR in the course of his patrol duties. But he sensed this was different and hesitated as if he wanted somebody else to make a move. Gary obliged him. He reached down and pulled back the blanket. A hacking sound came out of his throat. "Oh, jeezus!" he groaned.

I don't think Gary expected what he saw. I know I didn't. I was still thinking about the man killed at Quanset. Bloodied, and dead, but still a human being. Not like the bloated thing that grinned up from the sand at us.

Every city cop sees a floater at least once in his career. People jump off bridges, or murderers use the harbors and rivers as body dumps. But you never get used to a body that has been in the water. The exposed areas of skin were mahogany, almost black. Fish and mollusks had gone to work on the neck and face. Nature's way of recycling, I guess. The mouth gaped open in a grotesque circus parody that told me why I never liked clowns as a kid. The eyes were empty sockets. There were some shreds of whitish clothing on the body. The skin on the hands that hadn't been nibbled away was just starting to flake off. It's tough to calculate without factoring in water temperature, but I figured the guy had been in the water no less than two weeks.

The thing gave off a strong, almost sweetish dead-fish odor. Some of the ORV people had got too close. Judging from the retching I heard behind me, they wished they hadn't. A sight like that sticks with you. So does the smell. Gary seemed paralyzed. I had seen enough.

"Cover it up, Gary," I said.

"Yeah," he said, and quickly drew the blanket over the face. "God," he whispered hoarsely. "I never expected it to look like *that*."

He backed off and put his hand on Charlie's shoulder. "Radio the AB. Tell them we've got a body out here and to call the cops. I'll talk to some of the people."

Charlie turned and ran to the truck. His face was the color of a lime rickey. Rollins didn't look too good either. He had raised his camera up to his chin and it stuck there when Gary pulled back the blanket.

I tried to cheer him up. "Say cheese," I said.

He said, "Jeezus."

Gary was talking to the man in the plaid shorts. I went over and listened.

"I'd been fishing all morning," he was saying. "Had two poles in the water. Didn't really care if I caught anything, just having a good time sitting in the shade of the truck having a brewski. Checking out stuff with my binoculars. Wife is in the RV making lunch and the kids are building a sand castle. I notice something rolling around in the surf. Damn gulls are flying around like vultures. I get nosy and walk down to take a look. Christ, there it is. I run back and get a blanket to cover it up so the wife and kids won't get upset. Then I drive up to the beach buggy booth and have the guy there call you." His voice cracked. "God, I've never seen anything like this before. Hope I never do again."

Eddy Fuller arrived, looking even more unhappy than ever. Rescue people and cops showed up next. The medical examiner was on his way.

Gary said he'd have to hang around. Rollins was busy interviewing witnesses. Gary asked me to drive Plaid Shorts back to his RV. On the way, I listened to the guy go through his story three more times before I dropped him off at the beach buggy booth where his family waited.

When I got home I pounded more shingles onto the boathouse to keep my mind off the face on the beach. I was expecting Sam to call. When I didn't hear from him by eight o'clock I called his house. Millie answered the phone. She didn't talk very much, which was unlike Millie, and turned me over almost immediately to Sam. He said it looked like a fish day tomorrow. He apologized for not calling me and said he'd explain later.

I flopped onto the couch with a bag of stale Cape Cod potato chips and watched TV until I conked out. It was nearly midnight when I woke up, got undressed and went to bed.

I lay on my back and stared at the ceiling. Two corpses. One new and one old. Both within a couple of days of each other. Separated by a short distance. Formless questions nagged at me. Images of bloodied swimmers and grinning, skeletal floaters haunted me. I slipped into a fitful sleep. At four A.M. Stevie Nicks came on the clock radio. I got up, dressed and went to meet Sam at the fish pier.

The day wasn't as hot or muggy, and we didn't

sweat bullets the way we had the last time. Sam looked drawn, but he said he felt fine. Other than that, he didn't talk much. Fishing was good. We pulled the last of our trawl lines and headed back to port. Sam, who was at the wheel, finally unloaded what was bothering him.

Lighting his pipe with more than the usual ceremony, he said, "Millie and I had a talk last night." Puff, puff.

I nodded.

Puff, puff. Sam was clearly uncomfortable. "She got all bent outa shape 'cause I took too much heat the other day. I'll admit my brains were a little broiled, but that was some hot weather, you'll have to admit that."

"Heat took me down, too, Sam."

He gave me an appreciative nod. "Sure, anyone would have suffered working all day under that sun. Still, no excuse to give up my boat."

"Is that what Millie wants you to do?"

Puff, puff. Angry now. "She wants me to think about staying shoreside. Build skiffs or fix outboards, something like that."

"What do you want to do, Sam?"

He shrugged. "Want to please Millie. But jeeper's crow, Soc, I can't give up fishing. I know I'm not getting any younger, and I complain a lot, but most of it's talk, you know that."

"Hell, Sam, you've quit regularly at least once a day every year I've known you. What did you tell Millie?"

He puffed. "We compromised. She wants me to go to a doctor. Made an appointment to see Doc Smithers for a physical tomorrow, so I guess it won't be a fish day.

I guess she's right. I'm not feeling myself, so I said I would see what he said, maybe he'll give me some vitamin pills. It was the only way I could get her to let me go fishing today."

"Maybe it's a good idea to have a physical anyhow."

He scowled. "When was the last time you had a doctor look at you, Soc?"

"Back when I was a city cop."

"Humph," Sam said triumphantly. He took a last puff and knocked the pipe against the side of the boat to get rid of the ashes. "We had some pretty good fishing today, didn't we?"

"Yeah, Sam," I said. "Pretty good fishing."

I was worried about Sam. His leathery face had looked wan and the wrinkles around his eyes seemed deeper than usual. He must still be worn out from the hot day. I know I was. His disagreement with Millie had to be weighing on him. They rarely argued about anything. I couldn't blame Millie for being worried. Tough old salts like Sam seem as ageless as the sea that shapes them. It's hard to remember they're as human as anyone else.

Millie knew her husband inside and out, but there was a side to Sam she'd never know unless she had seen him, looking hypnotically off at the rim of the world, sun sparkle from the waves reflected in his clear blue eyes, a beatific smile on his wide mouth. Sam had a mistress. The sea. *Thalassa,* the ancient Greeks called it. Deep down, I'd bet Sam hoped that when he died, the ocean would fold him in her briny arms.

Chapter 9

The late afternoon sun was slanting through the clean-limbed locust trees as I drove up to the boathouse. Kojak heard my truck exhaust popping off and was at the door to greet me with a broadside leg rub. I opened a can of 9-Lives super supper and put some frozen chicken legs on the hibachi and basted them with Open Pit regular barbecue sauce. I showered, changed into cutoffs and T-shirt, and whipped up a batch of *tzatziki,* a dip made of yoghurt with ground garlic and cucumber. I ate out on the deck. The chicken legs were a bit charcoaly, but delicious. I scooped up *tzaziki* with pita bread. I set my dishes on the floor for Kojak to wash and popped a beer. On the way home, I had picked up a copy of the *Gazette.* I spread it out on the kitchen table.

The lead story under Rollins's byline was banner

headlined: ANOTHER MYSTERIOUS ATTACK AT QUANSET! A sidebar story said the selectmen had closed the beach temporarily. That was nice of them. Another brief item reported the unidentified body found on Quanset Beach. I shook my head and folded the paper. Crazy.

Rollins had done a thorough job covering the story. He detailed the second attack at Quanset and tied it to the death of the Canadian tourist. The story on the body that floated ashore yesterday had little to offer. No cause of death. No ID.

A bold-faced headline over the boxed story in the lower right-hand corner of page one caught my eye. DOES PIRATE CURSE HANG OVER QUANSET? The story was bylined by the *Gazette*'s editor, Wes Thacher. The article was about the Quanset pirates, a jolly and sodden bunch of cutthroats who'd captured a merchant vessel off the Cape in the early 1700's. The pirates got into the cargo of Madeira wine and were staggering drunk when the ship got caught in a storm and was driven ashore near Quanset Beach. Some of the prisoners drowned.

Like the boozer who walks away from a head-on car crash, the pirate crew had the luck of the inebriated, and survived. To celebrate their good fortune, the pirates stopped at a tavern, were nabbed by the local posse, and were shipped to Boston. An admiralty court found them guilty of piracy and murder. Four were hanged. I'd read the story before, probably in the Chamber of Commerce booklet.

The *Gazette* added a new twist. A local historian

named Del Huggins claimed Jack Graff, one of the condemned pirates, had cursed the townspeople who captured him. Moments before Graff took the short drop to eternity, the pirate swore his death would be avenged by misfortune from the sea. He was either a good prognostician or a canny calculator of the statistical odds of calamity happening if you waited long enough. Disaster had struck the Quanset Beach area at least once a generation thereafter. A devastating smallpox plague was carried to shore in the wreck of a plague-ridden schooner. Fifty years later, a storm wiped out half the old village. Then a German U-boat shelled a local fishing trawler and sank it with heavy loss of innocent lives.

I put the paper down and shook my head. The scuttlebutt must be flying around town in the wake of these stories. I grabbed my Red Sox cap, got in the pickup, and drove to the 'Hole, hoping to pick up some gossip. A squad of bushy-faced regulars in work clothes and ball caps had captured a corner of the bar. They were defending it against greater numbers of tourists by sheer beer-belly bulk alone. With the beachhead secured, there was no contest.

I joined the party and signaled the bartender for a draft. The frosted mug slid down the bar with its foamy head more or less intact. Several arguments were going on simultaneously. With the dull roar of conversation and the jukebox's throb, it was hard to get a fix on a single debate. But one word kept popping out again and again. *Quanset.* Everybody was an instant expert.

Hoppie the Sunoco station mechanic was having a fiery debate with a tuna spotter named Hal.

"No *way* is it sharks," Hoppie was saying. "No effing *way.*"

"Then what the hell is it?" Hal called derisively. "Fucking piranha?"

"Makes more sense than sharks."

I butted in. "Has anyone heard how the Simmons kid is doing?"

"He's okay, Soc," said Hoppie. "They saved his leg. He'll need more surgery later on, I hear, but he'll be surfing again. If he wants to."

"Did anyone talk to him about what happened?"

"One of the kids who works part-time at the garage is an EMT. He was at the hospital when the cops were talking to Simmons. The kid said he never saw what hit him. One second he's paddling along, waiting to catch a wave. Then wham, his leg feels like it's gone in a meat grinder and gets half chewed off."

Hal's face lit up in triumph. "Right. Just like a shark would do it."

Mac McConnell stood nearby. I hadn't seen him since the selectmen's hearing. He was listening intently, but taking no part in the argument. That was strange. Mac is the consummate know-it-all. The more he drinks, the more he knows. But not tonight. His sun-scorched face was impassive. His mouth, ever ready to offer an opinion on any subject in the universe, was clamped shut on an unlit cigarette. He caught me looking at him and jerked his head toward the tables.

"Can I buy you a beer, Soc?"

"Sure thing," I replied, wondering what had gotten into him. Mac never bought *any*one a drink. He signaled the bartender and two mugs came our way. We carried them over to a corner table. The young couple occupying the table had finished eating and paid their bill, but they were taking their time leaving. Mac stood over them, smelling of ripe sweat and booze. They took the hint and quickly gathered up their things. Mac creaked into his chair, sucked down half the mugful of beer and squinted over his ferocious beard at me.

Mac is as tall as I am and twice as wide. The parts of his body that see the sun, like his blunt, pugnacious nose and massive hands, are as red as a boiled crab. He wears soiled jeans, a dirty T-shirt, and a tan hunting cap that's so stained it looks camouflaged. I think they're the only clothes he owns.

Mac was a town kid, son of a son of a fisherman, as Jimmy Buffett would say. He could have scratched out a living on the clam flats, like his old man, but he got off the Cape, went to college, and put himself through law school with the money he made fishing summers. He got his law degree, had his picture in the local papers, bought a suit, got a haircut, hung out a shingle, and after a law practice that lasted almost as long as the blink of a judge's eye, he dumped it all and went back to fishing. I don't know how Mac would have been as a lawyer, but he was one hell of a fisherman.

"Saw you at the selectmen's meeting the other night," he said. "What did you think?"

"I think the surfer kid who got his leg half bitten off would be a lot happier if the selectmen had closed Quanset."

He chuckled sourly and took another swig, leaving

a trace of beer foam on his untrimmed lip. He paused thoughtfully, then squinted at me over his ferocious beard. "You've done some diving, been on the water fishing a few years now. You've got more brains than those guys yapping at the bar. What do you make of it?"

"Hell, I don't know. I've heard a few theories, but every one has flaws in it. I'll have to wait until somebody comes up with solid evidence before I form an opinion one way or the other."

His eyes drilled into mine. "Something I've got to tell you, Soc, but you've got to swear not to get it around, especially to that gang up there." He jerked his head toward the bar where his buddies were gathered.

I shrugged. "Tough to keep secrets in this town, but nobody will hear it from me."

He looked around as if the sugar bowl on the next table were bugged, then hunched his wide shoulders forward. "You know how I fish, Soc. Skiff fisherman. Scallops, flounder, stripers, lobsters. Whatever's in season. I fish alone to keep costs down and because nobody will work with me."

Mac had tried charter boating. Every time a customer lost a fish, Mac took it as a personal assault on his reputation. He'd threaten to toss a customer overboard if another striper wriggled off the hook. He yelled at too many charters, and word got around. Most people didn't want to pay big bucks to go fishing with Attilla the Hun. His business petered out, and he turned to the solitary craft of skiff fishing.

"I've seen your skiff," I said. "If she were a woman, I'd propose to her."

He beamed like a proud father. "Yeah, she's a real honey. Twenty-two-foot ocean-going hull, real solid, new seventy-five-horsepower Johnson outboard. I don't think anything about taking her through the cut, even in the winter."

When Mac gave up his law practice, most local people respected his decision. They knew Mac wanted the freedom he wouldn't find in an office. But the same people who didn't blink an eye when he went back to fishing think he ought to be in a padded cell for going through Quanset Cut no matter the time of year. Barely a couple of hundred yards wide, the cut is the passageway between marsh-edged Quanset Harbor and the Atlantic Ocean. It may be the trickiest piece of water, per linear foot, in New England. It's about a mile north of the bathing beach, a meeting of treacherous and ever-changing shoals, currents, tide, and surf. In the summer, it can be tricky. In the winter, it's just plain deadly.

"The last time I tried going through the cut, I ended up wearing my boat for a necktie, and that was in the middle of August."

"It's a tough little stretch of water, especially when you're loaded with fish," Mac acknowledged, "but it's the quickest way to get out to the fishing grounds." He sipped more beer and went on. "Last few days I've been heading out late, staying out all night to fish for cod, then coming in in the morning. Catches have been pretty good. You know how it's been since the storm. You get a few swells, but otherwise the water's been like glass. It's really pretty just sitting out there jigging. I was watching the house lights on the bluff overlooking the beach, letting my eyes get half shut, when Blackstone started to make a fuss."

Blackstone was Mac's Labrador retriever, named after the great British jurist.

"What kind of fuss?"

"First he bared his fangs and started growling and barking at nothing. Then he went silent and shivered like he was freezing. I'd been almost dreaming. My eyes blinked open. It was as if a sliver of time had gone by and I missed it. I looked out over the water. Didn't see anything unusual. Just the skiff setting real easy in the waves. But I had this feeling I wasn't alone. I realized I'd been holding my breath. I let it out. That's when it happened." He shook his big head. "All hell broke loose. My jig lines all went crazy, jerking up and down and snapping against the boat. The skiff started to rock. I don't know if it was from the jigs or me jumping around, yelling bloody blue murder and trying to figure out what the hell was going on. I thought I heard something thumping against the bottom of the boat, but I'm not sure now whether it was just me knocking stuff around. Then I saw it."

"Saw what, Mac?"

"Christ if *I* know, but I'll tell you what it looked like. It was like a big shiny thing, maybe ten, twenty feet across, moving through the water real close to the surface."

"What did you do?"

"What the hell did you *think* I did? I started the fucking motor. Thank Christ it was new and kicked in right away because I would have run home on the wave

103

tops. I got out of there in a hurry. Didn't even pull my jig lines in. I let them drag til I got through the cut. When I got back to my mooring I pulled them up." He shook his shaggy head again. "There was nothing there."

"You mean no bait?"

"I mean no bait, no line, no hooks in most cases. I had a fish on one. He would have been a big steak cod. Everything was gone but his head. His body was just plain chewed off behind the gills. Poor bastard's eyes were staring at me."

I pondered Mac's story. Finally I said, "Mac, I don't want you to take this the wrong way, but were you drinking that night?"

Mac glared at me as if I had just asked him if the Pope lived in Rome. "Of *course* I was drinking," he roared. "I *always* drink."

I spread my hands.

Mac leaned on the table until it almost buckled with his weight. "No fucking way, Soc. There's a difference between drinking and being so pissed you get the d.t.'s. I was mellow maybe, but not drunk. Look, you've been diving for a long time and fishing a few years. What do you think it was?"

"Maybe it was a tuna with the moonlight reflecting on the scales."

"Naw," he said with an unbelieving grin, "if this was a tuna, I'm a sardine."

Mac was definitely not a sardine. We sipped our beer silently. Finally Mac said, "You know me, Soc. Big mouth. Know-it-all. But this one's got me stuck. I'm scared to go out fishing at night now."

"About where did all this happen?"

"Off Quanset Beach. Quarter mile maybe. Am I going nuts?"

I stared at him for a moment, thinking about the attacks on bathers, the dead body in the surf.

"Maybe we're *all* going nuts, Mac."

That was as far as it got. We had a couple more pops. With the big secret off his chest, Mac was back to his old self. He burped a lot and he told me how the Red Sox, the White House, and the Federal Reserve could solve each and every one of their problems. I promised at least three more times not to tell anyone his story. We went back to the bar where the townies were still holding the fort. Since I was my own designated driver I decided to leave while I still could.

Mac's story must have made me jittery. I was walking from my truck to the boathouse with my eyes up at the sky picking the constellations out of the heavens. Something brushed my ankle. I almost jumped as high as Orion's belt. It was only Kojak. We both went in the house and crumped out on the couch. I told Kojak about my day. He told me about his. The telephone rang.

"This is Tillie Talbot out at the Quanset camp. Do you remember me from the hearing the other night?" Her voice was crisp and businesslike.

"Of course, Mrs. Talbot. What can I do for you?"

"Gary said you were a private detective. Is that true?"

"I do some private investigative work."

"Good. Could you come to my camp tomorrow morning? Is ten convenient?"

"Ten is fine with me, Mrs. Talbot."

"Splendid. See you there."

I hung up, wondering why a kid's summer camp needed a private detective. I was still wondering when I slipped under the covers and fell into a beery sleep.

Chapter 10

The Quanset Beach Sailing Camp was at the end of a hard-packed clay road that turned to dirt after a few hundred feet and skirted a lush marsh before yielding to scrub oak and pine forest on both sides. The road went past a double-ended dory that spilled over with red and white impatiens. Someone had painted a *Please Drive Slowly* warning on it. The camp was a complex of tennis courts, horseshoe pits, and open-sided lean-tos with bunks for four. Noisy flocks of kids dressed in identical tan shorts, white T-shirts and blue ball caps traipsed around with counselors who looked barely older than their charges. Others roamed through the trees like young dryads and fauns. Preteen boys and girls played Robin Hood on the archery course and some arrows were actually hitting their targets.

I parked by an oversized log cabin with an *Office* sign out front. Some boys and girls sat on the wide steps intently practicing sailors' knots on short lengths of manila line. I got out of the truck and started toward the door. A red-haired boy who looked like a young Mickey Rooney blinked behind coke bottle glasses and demanded, "Sir, do you know how to tie a bowline?"

"I could tie one in my sleep." I took the line and pushed the tip through the appropriate loops, my eyes shut, telling the little story they use to teach a bowline. "Okay, the rabbit comes out of its hole, goes 'round the tree and back into the hole. Voilà, a bowline, one of the best knots ever invented."

"Wow, that was totally *awe*some."

Tillie Talbot came out of the log cabin onto the porch, trailing campers like a mother hen. She was comforting a sobbing boy who hung on her waist. She clucked effusively over a gimp key-holder a girl made in a crafts class, turned the unhappy boy over to a counselor, and gently brushed away the other campers competing for her attention.

"Mr. Socarides. Nice to see you. Please come on into my office." She held open a heavy wooden screen door. I stepped into a large room filled with wooden tables and benches that were bolted to the floor. A stout white-haired man in a chef's hat told Mrs. Talbot that the grocery truck hadn't arrived with food for lunch. She called him Leon, advised him to improvise, then asked another counselor to take all calls for her. We walked down a hallway into an office. She offered me a deck chair and seated herself behind a heavy oak desk. The office walls were covered with photos of smiling campers and camp staff. The pictures were dated; some of them went back several decades.

Tillie leaned back in her chair and took a deep breath, then removed her glasses. She let them hang by a strap around her neck and rubbed her eyes. Thirty years ago, Tillie Talbot would have been stunning. Now, probably in her midsixties, with age wrinkles on her neck and elbows, her skin darkened from the sun, excess pounds around her waist and thighs, she was merely beautiful. She replaced the glasses and saw me inspecting the photos.

"That's Captain Bill, my late husband," she said. Tillie indicated a man with a rugged build and a wide pleasant face who appeared in many of the group shots.

I pointed to the smiling woman who stood at his side. "And this would be you?"

She nodded. I was right. Tillie Talbot in an earlier day was a knockout.

"Bill's parents started this camp. They gave it to us as a wedding present. We've run it every summer. We both taught at Amherst College. That's where we met, in fact. The camp was a terrific break from our professorial duties. There's nothing like fresh air and the screams of some city child who's just seen his first garter snake to clear away the stuffiness of academe. We both loved to sail. Bill designed our own class of sailboats. That's a picture of one on the wall. He died three years ago."

"I'm sorry to hear that."

"It was a blessing, really. Cancer doesn't just kill you. It strips you of human dignity. Bill was an incredibly robust man. But he was just a bag of bones at the end. He was grateful to go."

"You've run the camp alone since then?"

"I've administered it, but I've had a great staff. Old Leon, our chef, has come back every year. I don't know what I would do without him. And the counselors have been wonderful. Bill made me promise to hold onto the camp as long as I was able." She lifted the mound of paper on her desk and let it fall. "Sometimes I wish deathbed promises had never been invented, but I do love running this place. Bill and I never had any children. The kids who have gone through here have been our family."

I glanced at the photos again. "It must be a very large family by now."

"Enormous, but I'm afraid it will come to an end soon, even if I could keep going on forever."

"Why is that, Mrs. Talbot?"

"This is the age of specialization. Camps that can't move with the tide are going down the drain. How's that for a mixed metaphor? The parents pay a lot to send their kids here, but it pretty much just covers the cost of operation. You don't make a great deal of money after taxes, insurance, upkeep. It seems the only way a camp can keep afloat these days is by specializing in something. Hockey. Soccer. Computers. Languages." She sighed. "What's wrong with us, Mr. Socarides?"

"Pardon?"

"Whatever happened to our capacity to just *enjoy* our childhood? Why should a child have to spend a summer day working when he or she could be out on the water doing something absolutely worthless and fun like sailing? This is a time for children to build up the memories that will sustain them later in life. Are they going to look back fondly to those wonderful days they spent at camp in front of an IBM computer or sitting around parsing the verb *être?* My God, what a dismal prospect."

"I'm all for worthless fun. Where do your campers come from?"

"Geographically, most are from Eastern seaboard cities. Boston, New York, Washington. Their parents have two things in common. They want their kids out of their hair and can afford to send them here. The kids bond with others whose parents don't want them, and can't wait to come back next summer. Many return later as counselors. We often have inner city children here on scholarships. I wish we could afford to have more."

"You must have a good time, even with all the work."

"Oh, I *do,* Mr. Socarides. Since I've retired from teaching, my summers at this camp have become even more important to me. I'll run it for as long as I'm physically and financially able. Which is why I called you."

"I hope you're not looking for a counselor; I never could learn to wind gimp."

She smiled. "To be honest, neither could I. The kids give their useless parents useless gimp key rings. Serves them right. But don't sell yourself short. I saw you show that boy how to make a bowline. I'd bet you'd make a fine sailing instructor."

"Sounds good, but you didn't ask me to come by to teach a course in marlinespikeship."

She studied me for a moment, then nodded somberly. "You're right. I'd like to hire you for something more pressing. I'd like you to help me save this camp."

"I'm afraid I don't understand, Mrs. Talbot."

"Then come with me." She spoke in the firm but gentle way she talked to her campers. We left the office and took a path to the edge of a bluff overlooking a narrow beach. A long boat pier extended into a small cove that emptied into the ocean through the cut. Across the cove, sunlight glinted off the cars in the Quanset Beach parking lot.

She swept her hand in the air. "It doesn't take an appraiser to see this camp is potentially extremely valuable real estate. I've got twenty acres of prime land, most of it waterfront. I've had dozens of offers from developers to buy it. The vultures started circling shortly after Bill died."

"You're still here, so I'd guess you chased the vultures away."

She nodded, her eyes on the water. "Fortunately, the camp has been able to break even up to now. But this year may be different. The property has been reassessed and the taxes have gone up. I've been plagued by state and town inspections and had to make some expensive improvements. I've even had some of Bill's sailboats vandalized. Still, I thought we might be able to muddle through. The incidents at the beach in the past few days changed all that."

"You said at the hearing the other night that you'd been getting calls from worried parents."

"Four campers have already been taken home by their parents. I thought that would be all, then the *Ga-*

zette came out with that silly pirate's curse story. Have you read it?"

"It sounded like one of the stories you see in the supermarket tabloids. Bermuda triangle. Loch Ness monster. Bigfoot. It sells papers, I guess."

"It did more than that. It was on the six o'clock national news last night. Any parent who hadn't heard about the beach tragedies would know about them by now. Look, honey, did Tom Brokaw say Quanset Beach? Mi*God,* that's where little Mamie's at camp."

A sense of unease gnawed at my gut like a hungry mole. "I can't say I blame them. I was at Quanset when the swimmer was killed. This thing worries me."

"It worries me a great deal, too, Mr. Socarides. The children have been forbidden to go anywhere near the beach and I've given orders to my counselors. My main concern right now, however, is with human predators. Let's go back to the office and have some iced tea."

As she was pouring me a tall glass she asked, "Do you know Fred Costello?"

I took my glass. "I know who he is."

"Then you must know *what* he is."

I nodded. "One of those vultures you mentioned?"

"Good, you *do* know him. Then this will be easier to explain. Mr. Costello has been this camp's most persistent suitor. He's made several offers, all of which I have refused. Yesterday he made another offer. Curiously, it was much lower than the previous ones."

"Costello must be aware you're having a tough year."

113

"I think he's more than aware. I think he's got something to do with it."

"You could be right, but there's nothing illegal about making an offer to buy someone's property."

"Of course, but I think there's a pattern to some of the official harrassment I've experienced this year."

"Are you suggesting undue political pressure?"

"Frankly, I'm not sure what I'm suggesting. But the fact that Mr. Costello shows up on my doorstep after each incident strikes me as more than coincidental."

"Anything's possible, I suppose. But how do you think the beach attacks fit in? You don't think somebody staged them just to get their hands on your land?"

"No, of course not. I think that whatever attacked those people was a natural phenomenon. However, I wouldn't put it past some people to use a natural event to try to force me off my land."

She pulled open a drawer in the wooden desk and extracted a thick manila folder which she spread open on her lap.

"These are all stories about the camp over the last several months. Most are from the *Gazette*. The only one remotely favorable was a feature story about the demise of the old Cape Cod sailing camps. It may have been a hint. The rest is about the safety and sanitary inspections and so on. Title Five sanitary code violations. Fire safety violations. Water violations. I've had to put in a whole new septic system. It cost me thousands of dollars. I've even had federal immigration people here looking for illegal aliens! I'm surprised they didn't arrest Leon. He was born in Germany. This latest batch of stories has to do with the attacks. They manage to mention their proximity to my camp in one way or another."

"You think the newspaper's part of this pattern you mentioned?"

Her face crinkled in amusement. "I think I know what's going through your mind right now. There's a little voice back there saying, 'This lady is paranoid.' "

"Just because you're paranoid doesn't mean they're not out to get you."

The smile she flashed me must have made men's knees weak decades ago. "I couldn't have said it better. I was beginning to wonder if I was starting to see a conspiracy behind every bush. That's why I called you. I've lost any perspective I might have had. I'd like you to look into this whole thing. Then you can tell me whether I'm going crazy. *Please,* Mr. Socarides, I need help desperately." Her eyes were pleading.

I shrugged. "I never give guarantees of success."

She pulled out an envelope and handed it to me. "This has five hundred dollars in it."

I gave the envelope back without opening it. "Look, Mrs. Talbot, let me size this thing up free of charge. If it looks like there's something to it, then I'll take your money."

"That's very generous of you, Mr. Socarides."

"Let's just say I'm doing a little work on behalf of a client who's treated me pretty well."

Her brow wrinkled. "I don't understand."

"I came down here with my brains scrambled from Vietnam, cop work, and a personal thing that didn't work out," I told Tillie Talbot. "I found there's nothing like the sea breeze blowing in one ear and out the other to cool off an overheated brain. I've seen too much of the Cape plowed under and blacktopped to make room for condos, strip malls, and subdivisions. You can still find marshland or beach that's so beautiful it will take your breath away, but it's becoming harder all the time, and I'm a lazy guy. Once the land is gone, it's gone forever. So if I can save a piece of this place, I'm glad to do it."

Tillie was smiling. "I'm very grateful," she said. "There's one other thing. Mr. Socarides seems so formal. May I call you by the nickname Gary used when he introduced us the other night?"

"I'd be insulted if you didn't."

"Good, and I'd be pleased if you called me Tillie."

The office door flew open. The young counselor in charge of the phone flew in.

"Sorry to bother you, Tillie. The grocery store just called and said their truck broke down and they can't make the delivery—"

Tillie sighed and straightened her shoulders. "All right. Bring the camp pickup around and we'll go into town and pick the food up ourselves." She turned to me. "Would you like to come for lunch, Soc? Dining at Camp Quanset is quite an adventure."

I thought about being in the same room with a hundred wired and hungry kids.

"Maybe some other time," I told Tillie Talbot.

Chapter 11

Fast Freddy Costello is the American success story. In a few short years he went from conducting business in a darkened bar booth to a turreted Victorian mansion on the beach road. The shingles gleamed with antique yellow and red paint and the trim glistened in the sun. A sign out front said QUANSET REALTY & CONSTRUCTION, the company Costello owned. The shiny new look was fine, but I remembered what Aristophanes said: *You can't teach a crab to walk straight.*

I had exchanged my faded jeans, ball cap, Bud Light T-shirt, and Nike cross-trainers for tan poplin chinos, a navy polo shirt, and Top-Siders. The L.L. Bean look. Nonthreatening, all-American, practical, Waspish. Just the thing to wear to a real estate office.

I parked the truck out of sight around the corner

and walked to the office. I gave the friendly receptionist my name and asked to see Mr. Costello. A minute later, an outstretched hand came out of the office trailing a blinding white smile for which Freddy must have paid a dentist a couple of grand.

In his druggie days, Freddy could have passed for a tall Charles Manson. Straggly long beard, patched jeans, and tie-dye shirts. It was the kind of warmed-over 60's look that customs agents learn about in their profiles in crime class. On Cape Cod, it was no big deal. The Cape has always tolerated eccentricity. The way you dress and look is your business. But clothes tell a lot about a man. Now Freddy was a walking billboard for what the Chamber of Commerce coined a Wonderful Way of Life. Since going legit, Costello shopped at Louis's instead of Levi's. Today he wore lime pants with blue whales swimming on them, and a tie with pictures of little Cape Cods knotted under a button-down blue oxford weave shirt. A gold tie clip was made in the shape of a sailboat. The object was a jaunty nauticalness, I guess, but it made me seasick. I think I preferred the Manson look.

He showed me into his office, indicated a comfortable chair, and sat down behind his desk, still smiling.

"Socarides," he said thoughtfully. "I've heard the name and I've seen the face."

"I live in town. Maybe you've seen me at Le Bayside Bistro." Le Bistro is an upscale bar that sells thimble-sized glasses of beer for three dollars. I went in once to use the bathroom.

"That must be it," Freddy said. "I do a lot of business lunches there." He leaned back in his chair and sized me up with a lazing lizard look. I would have bet a stuffed quahog that he was trying to guess the thickness of my wallet.

"Well, Mr. Socarides, what can I do for you? Looking, selling, or building? This is a great time to do business. Interest rates are almost rock-bottom. No telling how long they'll stay that way, though."

The essence of American capitalism. Put a little fear into the prospective customer. Car won't start in the dead of winter? Worried about bad breath? Afraid you'll be up all night with a cold? Buy our product and you'll be okay. I knew damn well real estate was flat and you could practically name your price. But to hear Freddy tell it, you had to move fast before the next guy beat you out. He almost had me convinced.

"Actually, I'm here for a friend. Tillie Talbot."

I let Tillie's name sink in and watched his reaction.

"Tillie," he crooned. "Great lady. How is she?"

Funny question to ask about somebody you had talked to just a day earlier.

"She's fine. As you know, Tillie's had a lot of buyers interested in her camp property. She's not sure what to do about the offers. She asked my advice. Your name came up frequently in our conversation. I thought it would be worthwhile to talk to you."

He gave me a big bad wolf smile. Freddy had an easy charm enhanced by the large, almost feminine brown eyes that looked out on the world from under carefully trimmed bangs and blow-dried hair. He was pushing forty, but he had a boyish innocence that probably appealed to some people and fooled others. His skin

119

was too smooth, too soft, as if someone forgot to add the hardener when his features were being formed. His face had none of the lines that mark a person's character for good or bad.

He looked at me through the round metal-rimmed granny glasses that had replaced the punk shades he used to wear when he was moving agricultural goods.

"It sounds as if Tillie has finally decided to sell. I'm glad to hear that."

I made a long cast and placed the bait in front of Freddy's nose.

"It's something she's certainly *thinking* about, but she hasn't made a final decision. Hell, you know how women are. . . ."

He nodded knowingly. Freddy and I were on a fast track to some serious male bonding.

"I'm really glad to hear she's asked someone for help," he said. "Tillie's a great woman, smart and independent, but there are a lot of unscrupulous developers out there."

"That's funny, I told her the same thing."

"I just wish she'd taken my earlier offers. The real estate market is glutted, and the banks got burned by a lot of commercial paper. They're real cautious about lending money for development these days."

"What happened to the lucrative real estate market of five minutes ago? Is financing going to be a problem for you?" I asked.

"Hell, it's a problem for *every*one. But let's face it. That camp is a prime piece of property. The last of its kind. Every piece of waterfront on the Outer Cape has been subdivided or made part of the National Seashore. If Tillie wants to wait long enough, prices will come up. That could be years off. I can afford to sit on the property, but I don't know if Tillie can. The camp must be a financial drain on her."

"She's had a tough year. Problems with state and town inspections, apparently. This business at Quanset Beach isn't helping."

"You're talking about the attacks on those people. Isn't that just incredible? I couldn't *give* away beachfront property near Quanset."

"Tillie told me about your last offer."

"That's just an indication of what's happening. For a while, every real estate guy in town was drooling over that camp. As I said before, the value is down. It's simply a question of supply and demand. My offer is the best she can get. I have to figure in the price of what it would cost to subdivide that land. Some of it is marsh we wouldn't be able to build on. Then there's the cost of roads, running in utilities, and so on. The regulatory process is prohibitively expensive these days. All that had to be figured in."

I nodded. "I don't know if price is that important to her. She's concerned about what would be done to that land. The camp has been in her family for years. She'd be more inclined to talk to a local person who would develop it properly, which might not be the case if she dealt with some faceless off-Cape corporation."

He nodded sagely. "That's exactly what I said to her."

"Then you'd be the sole buyer?"

"I'd be the *primary* buyer. I'd make sure my investors were all people with a love of the Cape."

I smiled eagerly. "That *is* reassuring. I'll be sure to pass it on to Tillie. It could make a difference." I looked at my watch and started to get up. "Well, I won't take any more of your time."

"That's quite all right. Let me give you my card." He came around the desk and pumped my hand, firmer and longer than the first time. "Thanks for coming in. I'm available to answer questions for you or Tillie any time you want."

"That's kind of you. I'll let Tillie know I talked to you."

He walked me to the front door. We shook hands again. "You said you lived in town?"

"Yes, I have a little place on Pleasant Bay."

"Is that so?" He grinned. "Let me know if you want to sell it. But enough business. . . . I don't know if this would interest you, but I'm throwing a cocktail party at my place tonight. Around six. I'd love to have you come by if you're not busy."

I paused long enough to convince even me I was mentally consulting my crowded Filofax calendar. "I'd be delighted," I told Freddy.

"Wonderful." He asked his secretary to tell me how to get to his house. I walked back to the truck and drove aimlessly around town, trying to digest what I had just learned. Not much. The part about the investors was interesting. I wondered who they were. Freddy said they were all people with a great love of Cape Cod. Even if it were true, it wasn't something that would make me giggle with happiness. Men love a beautiful woman, but that doesn't prevent some of them from trying to take advantage of her or even worse. I wondered if Rollins had picked up any gossip on his reportorial rounds. It was worth a try, I decided, and pointed the truck in the direction of the *Gazette.*

The newspaper was in a one-story, shed-roofed white clapboard building across from the Masonic Hall. I asked the receptionist if Rollins was in. He came to the lobby a minute later wearing a lopsided grin.

"Good timing," he said, brushing sand off his sneakers. When he straightened, he shoved his glasses up his nose. "I just got back from Quanset Beach. Guess what?"

"High tide was on time?"

"Naw," he said in his midwestern nasal twang. "Another body floated ashore today."

That *was* news. "The ladies at the tourist info booth are really going to have a good time with that. Where did it float in?"

"Just south of the first one."

"Any ID on either one of them?"

"Naw, it was pretty much like before. Coast Guard is trying to get a trace on what was left of the clothes, but the stuff was pretty far gone and they're not too hopeful. Medical examiner says the first guy drowned. There was no evidence of external injuries and he figures the body was in the water around ten days to two weeks." Rollins shivered. "I've covered car crashes and fires, but this is the worst. That freaking beach is becoming a morgue. C'mon out back."

He led the way through the art department to the newsroom. A couple of reporters were working the phones and a copy editor was going through a story on a word processor. We went through a door into a tiny room lined with filing cabinets that I guessed was the paper's morgue.

"Those bodies had to come from somewhere," I said. "Does the Coast Guard have anything to say about a possible wreck?"

"They've been checking. This is interesting. An oil spill was reported on the south beach a few days ago. But no ships or fishing boats are reported missing. Sound funny to you?"

"Absolutely hilarious. There's something else I wanted to ask you about. I was talking to Tillie Talbot. She says the state and town inspectors have been spending so much time at her camp she may enroll them in a sailing class."

"Yeah. Poor Tillie." He ran his hands through his hair and sighed. "They've been on her ass big-time over health and sanitary violations."

"Tillie thinks someone with political clout has been trying to turn the heat up so she'll sell her property."

He pondered that one briefly. "Fast Freddy Costello?"

"Then it has entered your mind."

"Tillie told me about Fast Freddy's offers. It was just a logical conclusion."

"What do you think?"

"It's possible. Freddy's an ex-felon, which would put him in the company of most of our state politicians. I'm not sure Town Hall is pure as the driven snow either. Like they say, money talks and bullshit walks."

"In Freddy's case does it talk and walk?"

"I tried checking around. I don't have a lot of time to do investigative reporting, but I couldn't find any evidence. To give the devil his due, Tillie had been putting off improvements she probably could have made. The violations at the camp were real."

"Were they any more real than the violations that get overlooked from time to time in a small town?"

He smiled weakly. "Not really. I could give you the names of a half dozen businesses that are breaking the rules. Laundromat, couple of restaurants. No one at Town Hall is killing themselves to enforce the law in those cases. It's been selective with Tillie. I'll be the first one to admit that."

"Tillie says the *Gazette* has been leaning on her."

Rollins peeked out the open door to see if anyone was within hearing range, then bent forward and gave me a big grin.

"You aren't trying to get me fired from this high-paying position, are you, Soc?"

"She just mentioned that the *Gazette* had given her a lot of ink lately."

"She's right. I talked to Wes about that. He just gave me the story about people only wanting to read bad stuff about the *other* guy. But . . ."

"But what?"

"Well, there were a couple of things. On the beach

stories I wrote, Thacher inserted lines that said the attacks took place not far from the Quanset Beach Sailing Camp. He said he was just trying to pinpoint the location for the reader. He's really been involved in the story since it broke. Even covered the selectmen's hearing. What the hell, it's his paper. Maybe he was just bored sitting in that office writing editorials all day. That's probably why he did the pirate curse story."

"I noticed his name on it."

"Yeah. I was grateful as hell he didn't put my byline on the damned thing. Thacher actually came out of his office rubbing his hands. You'd think he'd just gotten the scoop on JFK's assassination, for chrissakes."

"Maybe your boss wanted to have some fun."

"Look, Soc, I like to have as much fun as anyone. God only knows, it's the only reason I stay in this business. It's certainly not the pay. And I'm not above writing a little fiction with my tongue in my cheek. If you can't inform them, entertain them, my pop used to say. Except that this dumb piece was absolutely incendiary."

"It wouldn't be the first time a newspaper reported fiction as fact."

"I would be the first time *this* paper did. Do you know anything about Wes Thacher?"

"Only that he's run the *Gazette* since papyrus was invented."

"Even before that. Thacher's one of the most well-respected country editors in the country. He came out of Harvard, Columbia Journalism School. His books on community journalism have seduced more than one sucker out of a metro city room into small town newspapers. Me, for instance. I came all the way from Indiana to work here. My father was a newspaperman, too. He respected the *Gazette* tremendously."

"I hear a 'but' in there."

"This paper used to be an institution. Everybody in the news business knows its reputation. They use it in journalism schools as an example of the best in newspaper writing. A paper that practiced the craft of newspapering the way it should be. Now let me ask you something. How many really hot, courageous investigative stories have you seen lately in the *Gazette*?"

"I don't get the paper every week."

"Okay, then I'll tell you. None. Nada. Zero. It's as if the wind's gone out of Thacher's sails. He used to fight against uncontrolled development. Now the paper is nothing but a mouthpiece for the businessmen in this town. It's become the worst thing a newspaper can be, besides dull or timid; it's become coerced by its advertisers."

"Times change, people change."

"I agree, but there's more to this pirate curse. I got curious and started asking questions. I talked to people at the Mass state archives and the Massachusetts Historical Society. They dug into the old records of the pirates' capture and trials. The stuff's pretty well documented. Nobody ever heard this story."

"Are you saying the story is a fake?"

"I don't know what I'm saying. This whole thing has me bummed out. Maybe I should get out of newspapering and go into public relations."

"Don't do anything rash. What's Huggins say?

He's the guy who provided him with the historical data."

"That's another funny thing. I've tried to talk to him. He says he's too busy and there's nothing he can add."

"Humph. That's odd. Town historians are rarely shy about sharing their knowledge. Where does Huggins live?"

"At the end of Joshua's Hill Road. Pretty little full Cape house." He eyed me. "Are you going to talk to him?"

"Maybe, after I finish the task at hand. Where's your story going from here?"

"Not sure. The state's sending down a marine biologist to look into the attacks. I talked to her by phone. Wouldn't tell me a damn thing. You would have thought I was asking her about the Manhattan Project. Lessee, our esteemed selectmen are still looking for their balls. Marge is the only one on the board who's got *cajones.* The merchants are howling that they're ready to go on food stamps. And the Coast Guard's following up on those floaters. If you've got any ideas or leads, I'd be happy to hear them. No, let me change that, I'd be *ecstatic.*"

"I'm low on my ecstasy supply, but I'll let you know if I hear anything."

Rollins tilted his head and gave me a shrewd look. "Gary told me you're a private eye. Maybe we can work a deal. You tell me what's going on, and I'll tell you."

"I'm a great believer in the simplicity of the barter system. Keep in touch."

We shook hands. Thacher walked by the morgue and gave me a curious glance. Rollins caught it and said, "If Wes asks, I'll tell him you were a witness I was grilling on this beach story."

I said that was fine and asked if I could use the morgue. Rollins showed me the system and left me alone. I opened a filing cabinet drawer, pulled out three fat dated envelopes labeled *Quanset Beach Sailing Camp,* and opened them. The yellowing clips went back about fifteen years. The early stories were puff pieces about the sailboat Tillie's husband designed, the camp's history and sailing regatta winners. The second envelope had more of the same. But half-way through the clips in the third envelope, the tone of the stories changed.

The camp began attracting more official attention than a toxic waste dump. Tillie was cited for violating the building code, the health code, the electrical code and plumbing code. Everything except the Morse code. That was just the *town* stuff. She'd been called before several state boards to defend her license. It was a wonder she was still operating.

I pushed the envelopes away and wrinkled my nose. A smell like the clam flats on a hot day at low tide emanated from the articles. The basic gospel of town government is: don't make any more work for yourself than absolutely necessary. Enforce the law for your fellow townspeople with an easy hand. Tread lightly, unless the violation is blatant and harmful, there's a complaint, or the violator is from out of town.

Then there was the state. The Commonwealth of Massachusetts has all kinds of enforcement bureaus, but their indifference is legendary. A lot of these inspection offices are dumping grounds for political hacks who think endorsing the back of their paycheck is a week of work. Something beyond normal government machinery was driving the enforcement directed against the Talbot camp.

Wes Thacher went by the open door, glanced at me, then came in to introduce himself. "Don tells me he's been talking to you about the Quanset Beach incident. Thanks for coming in."

"You're welcome. Glad to help."

He saw the clips and envelopes on the table and raised an eyebrow. "I see you're interested in the Quanset Beach camp."

"I have a friend who's looking for a summer camp to send his kid." I tapped the envelopes. "Looks like Tillie's had a rough time in the past year."

Thacher shook his head. "Damn shame. Tillie runs a terrific camp. But it's showing its age, and the regulators are a lot tougher than they used to be. I can vouch for that. We have to be careful as hell what we do with all the chemicals we use in our darkrooms."

"I remember the old *Gazette.* You've made a lot of changes."

"It was either change or die. I'm afraid the days are gone when you could run your newsroom out of one pocket and the ad department out of another. I have the only typewriter left. C'mon, I'll show you around."

I followed him into a large room where half a dozen people sat behind two ranks of computers. There was the buzz of telephones and low conversations.

"This is our composition department. The ads and editorial copy are typeset here." In the next room, pages were being laid out on angled tables. "It all comes together here in the art department. This is our next edition." We watched the ads and news stories being pasted up for a few minutes, then he led me into the press room. He waved his hand like a father pointing out his new offspring. "Got rid of the old press and brought in the four-color offset. It's made a big difference in the kind of services we can offer."

"All this equipment must have cost you a bundle," I commented.

"You don't find this stuff in a Cracker Jack box. We'll be paying the bank back for a long time at their usual usurious interest rates. We expanded just before the bottom dropped out of our prime advertising source, the real estate market. But I think the risk was worth it. A good community newspaper means a lot to a small town. It stimulates the economy, and it's what you need to make a democracy function."

"Thanks for the tour."

"Thanks for listening to me expound on grassroots journalism."

We shook hands and he headed back to his office. I put the Talbot clips in a box for refiling and pulled the envelopes labeled Costello, Fred. I slid the clips out and glanced at them. Most of them were about Costello's community service. There was nothing about his drug bust. It was as if Freddy had always been an upstanding citizen.

Scraps of waxed paper that had been cut from the

ads and stories the newspaper art department was laying out were stuck to the soles of my sneakers. I absent-mindedly removed them as I pondered the missing clips. Finally, I decided there was nothing more I could learn at the *Gazette.*

A short while later, I was back at the boathouse. I admired my shingling job, then went inside to use the phone. Mildred answered at Sam's house. She said Sam wasn't home, that he had gone for tests at Cape Cod Hospital.

"Nothing serious, is there, Mildred?"

"No," she said, but she didn't sound as if she were convinced. "The doctor just thinks it's a good idea be-cause of Sam's age."

"I'm sure everything will be fine. If he's not too cantankerous, maybe he could call me when he gets home."

Mildred laughed. "He was cantankerous when he left for Hyannis, but I'll have him call you anyhow, Soc."

I hung up and shook my head. Medical tests tend to find conditions you didn't want to know about. While I had the phone in my hand I dialed Sally Carlin's num-ber. I was engaging in a bit of dishonesty. I knew Sally would be at work, but this way I could always say I had tried to call her. I don't know what it was with me and Sally. Maybe some of the brain cells that let one human being connect with another had been damaged. She was beautiful, intelligent, and just plain nice. Even my mother and father liked her. Uh-oh. Speaking of family stuff. There'd been so much going on I'd put wayward

Cousin Alex on the back burner. Ah, hell, I'd tend to it later. I hadn't figured out what to say to the kid anyhow.

My brain felt battered. I felt like doing something non-intellectual. I put up shingles until I started hitting fingers more often than nails, and I knew it was time to get ready for Costello's party.

C h a p t e r   1 2

Two young car valets were working the white gravel horseshoe driveway in front of Costello's house. They saw me drive up in the pickup and flipped a coin. The loser came over and got behind the wheel.

"This is one of those high-compression racing engines," I told him. "Don't be surprised if the engine takes a minute or two to stop when you turn off the ignition."

"Figures," he grunted, and flipped the bird to his buddy who was sliding into a nifty silver Porsche. He muscled the shift lever into grinding gear, and moved the pickup around the corner of the garage where it wouldn't devalue the property.

Costello's house sat on a low hill overlooking a salt pond rimmed by clusters of dark-needled cedar trees.

The place was an eclectic combination of *Gone with the Wind* antebellum plantation, Charles Addams Victorian, and Cape Cod shlock. The builder had gone crazy with towers, gables, and miniature windmills and the house itself was slightly smaller than a blimp hangar. The house had created quite a stir in town. Freddie's neighbors could forgive his felonies, but not his bad taste. They had tried to stop construction. They signed petitions, sought injunctions and writs of mandamus, and wrote letters to newspapers, but all they did was enrich a platoon of lawyers. Casa Costello stood as a monument to Freddy's rise in the world.

A wide staircase swept up between curving balustrades to a spacious veranda and a doorway overhung by a Colonial pediment and flanked by Doric columns. Guests milled around and guzzled champagne offered by handsome young men and women in black slacks and white shirts and bowties. I lifted a glass of bubbly from a passing tray, drank it faster than Dom Pérignon should be drunk, and followed the stream of guests through the double front door.

The high-vaulted ceiling in the entryway would have been nice for a bishop's domicile, but here it was only a reminder that money doesn't buy class. A wide doorway led into a formal dining room with whitewashed walls and heavy, dark wood Mediterranean furniture. The thick-legged mahogany table in the center of the room had more food on it than at a medieval wedding.

I queued up, grabbed a plate, and for starters heaped it with shrimp, Swedish meatballs, rare roast beef, deviled eggs, smoked salmon, turkey, Danish ham, stuffed mushrooms, and more shrimp. Then I went through the French doors at the rear of the room onto a flagstone patio that wrapped around a kidney-shaped swimming pool.

A steel band that looked as if it had just stepped off the boat from Montego Bay was playing Calypso on the far side of the pool. Softly metallic notes of "Maryanne" wafted as lightly as helium balloons on the warm night air. A honey-blond Nereid in a cutaway swimsuit dove into the pool and swam underwater in a flowing ripple that shattered the reflected shimmers from Japanese lanterns into sparkling watery shards. She got out at the other end and wrapped herself in a towel, far too quickly for the men who were watching her and not fast enough for the women.

I walked down a shallow flight of steps and navigated my way around the pool to the bar. The bartender was a friendly and efficient Boston College law major who stuck a cold frosty bottle of Sam Adams in my hand. I found a place to sit away from the crowd on the low flagstone wall around the patio. Behind me, a carpet of freshly-mowed grass swept in a gradual descent to a bluff that dropped off into a salt pond. I took a deep breath and let it out. The breeze smelled of cigarette smoke and barbecue, ocean and marsh, perfume and cologne. But mostly, it smelled of money.

From my vantage point, I had a good view of the crowd. In a small community, you get to know the local faces even if you don't know the names behind them. I only recognized a few. I polished off the food and beer.

After ten minutes, I was on my way to the bar for another Sam Adams when a figure in a vanilla polo shirt, white duck pants, and black Chinese slippers detached itself from a knot of chatting guests and grabbed my arm.

Fast Freddy gave me a banana-shaped grin. "So *there* you are. Glad you could make my little get-together." He'd been sampling the Dom Pérignon, too.

I glanced around at the crowd and estimated there were at least a hundred people in view, and probably another fifty in the dining room and on the veranda.

"Quiet, intimate gatherings are hard to resist. I was just enjoying the view."

"Pretty awesome, isn't it? I got this land off an old fisherman who bought it years ago as a wood lot. Six acres on the water. Every real estate guy in town tried to buy it, but the old bastard wouldn't deal with anyone locally. I got a straw from out of town, the fisherman sold it and went to Florida with all his money. He probably had a heart attack when he found out the land was transferred to me. What do you think of the house?"

My eye traveled along the two-and-a-half story crescent-shaped monstrosity. "I've always liked traditional Cape Cod."

"You probably heard about the trouble I had building it. I added a few geegaws like the phony windmills just to piss the neighbors off. The blades run by electric motor. C'mon, let me introduce you around."

He led the way back to the terrace and gave me rapid-fire intros to at least two dozen people whose names I forgot immediately. He told me not to leave before talking to him again, then swirled off to greet more arriving guests, leaving me with a dinosaur from the Jurassic period who wore a neon green blazer over cranberry slacks, and his wife, who was spilling out of a silver lamé dress. She was a buxom redhead about twenty years younger than he was, and they both had that Naugahyde skin people get from winters in Florida and summers on the Cape. He learned I lived on the Cape year-round and asked what I did in the winter. I said in the summer there's fishing and fornication and in the winter there's no fishing. He was hard of hearing and didn't understand, but his wife let out a whoop of laughter and dug her nails into my arm so hard that it hurt. Her husband doddered off and she started filling me in about her cosmetic surgery.

More familiar faces were showing up around the pool. Wes Thacher stood talking to Stan Roberts, the chairman of selectmen. They broke off their conversation and Stan left to stalk voters. I told the redhead I'd love to hear more about liposuction but I needed to have a word with my stockbroker. I walked over to Thacher and said hello.

Thacher looked like Central Casting's version of a country editor, and he hadn't discouraged the image. He was dressed in tan cotton slacks that were pouched out around the knees, a thrift shop light pinstripe gray seersucker jacket, blue button-down Oxford weave shirt and a striped navy and red bow tie. His hair was snowdrift white, in need of a trim. The horn-rimmed glasses were the perfect finishing touch.

"Good to see you again, Mr. Socarides. I meant to

ask you today, what do *you* think happened at Quanset Beach?"

"Someone died. That's all I know. I read something in the *Gazette* about a pirate curse."

Thacher's eyes twinkled. "You'll have to admit a pirate curse makes as much sense as anything."

"I dunno," I said, getting into the game. "I was sort of leaning to a Loch Ness monster theory myself."

"Then you should tell that lady over there." He gestured to a woman in a sensible blue dress who had just come through the French doors onto the terrace. "I'll introduce you."

He took me by the elbow and led me across the patio. The woman was about thirty-five and attractive in a schoolmarmish type of way. She smiled and said, "Hello, Mr. Thacher. Nice to see someone I know."

Thacher looked around. "Pretty boring crowd. Most of these freeloaders probably don't even know Costello. They came for the free food. Like me. Diana, Mr. Socarides here is one of the more interesting guests. He was on the beach when the Canadian man was killed the other day. He's got a theory about the beach attacks."

She had short black hair and hazel eyes, and lips that were full and sexy and prissy at the same time. She gave me a finger brush that passed for a handshake. "Diana Trumbull. I'd be interested in hearing your theory, Mr. Socarides."

Thacher said with a straight face, "Mr. Socarides thinks it's the Loch Ness monster."

"Really," she said, arching an eyebrow.

"I was making a joke," I explained.

Thacher was practically busting a gut trying not to laugh. Diana Trumbull's stare had turned icy. "I don't think the death of one person and the maiming of another is any kind of joke." She turned back to Thacher. "Thanks again for filling me in today. It was a great help."

"Just remember that the *Gazette* gets the exclusive when you solve this mystery."

"You'll be the first to know."

Thacher spied someone across the terrace. "Excuse me, Diana, I've got to go stroke one of my big advertisers. Nice to see you again, Mr. Socarides. We'll talk more some time." He had an easy smile that made me grin even though he'd set me up for a lecture from Miss Trumbull. Left alone with me, she shifted uncomfortably from one foot to another and gripped her shoulder bag as if she had just heard there were purse snatchers in the area.

"Do you live in town?" she said, to be polite.

"Yes. I'm a fisherman. And you?"

"I work for the state Division of Marine Fisheries."

"How do you know Thacher?"

"My boss put us in touch. They're friends."

"Any ideas on what's really biting people at the beach?"

"It would be premature to speculate," she said frostily. "I just arrived today."

"Of course," I said. Our conversation was really percolating. "I'm going to get another beer. Can I get you something at the bar?"

"No, thanks." She might as well have added: *Drop dead, Bozo.*

I don't expect every woman who meets me to swoon at my feet, but for some inexplicable reason, Miss Trumbull was bordering on the hostile. I didn't know what her problem was, but outside of my normal curiosity, I didn't care. I said it was nice to meet her, and headed for the bar. Costello caught me midroute and drew me aside.

"There's somebody I want you to meet." He took me by the arm to where a half dozen people were clustered like acolytes around a tall, gray-haired man.

"This is former Lieutenant Governor Jack Olney." Costello said it with pride, as if he were showing off a new golf club. "Jack, this is Mr. Socarides."

The last time I saw Jack Olney's high-cheekboned face was in a news photo carried by *The Boston Herald*. The picture showed Big Jack, all six foot five of him, walking down the State House steps for the last time after a bare-knuckled political career that had seen him rise to within a pulsebeat of the governor's chair.

Olney was known as the enforcer in the Great and General Court of Massachusetts, where he'd been Speaker of the House before going on to lieutenant governor. He kept the rank and file in line with a firm hand. Bills died or flourished at his whim. Committee chairmen were appointed or demoted on his say-so. Those who bucked Big Jack were given offices in closets. He could kill a raise for a judge who balked at hiring his cronies. He might have been elected governor if the Republicans hadn't started saying in public what was whispered in the back halls of the State House: Jack Olney was as corrupt as an old log. Kickbacks from big money public works programs. Bribes. Appointments for sale. Pension scandal. Olney knew the law enforcement dogs would be yapping at his tail if he stayed in the race, so he withdrew his candidacy and faded into the background until the investigators and press turned their attention to other bent officials, which Massachusetts breeds like termites.

Olney enveloped my hand in his and gave me his famous vote-grabber's grin. His calculating eyes were hard as jade. He turned to a youth in his late teens or early twenties who was standing next to him.

"This is my son Steve." Olney's son was a blond kid with a square jaw and a James Dean pout. Steve Olney's face had none of the longshoreman toughness of his father's except around the eyes. He kept his hands in his pockets.

Freddy said, "Mr. Socarides is the friend of Tillie Talbot's I was telling you about, Jack."

Olney's grin turned positively wolfish. "Mrs. Talbot is a lovely lady," he said in the sonorous tones one of the columnists at *The Boston Globe* said was an affected rip-off of Mayor James Michael Curley. "Some of my friends have sent their children to her camp and they thoroughly enjoyed the experience."

"Jack owns a great house not far from here," Costello interjected. "In fact I found it for him."

"Yes, it's a beautiful place," Olney said. "Do you play tennis, Mr. Socarides?"

"Not since the mice chewed the strings on my racket."

Olney guffawed. "Well, perhaps you'll get it restrung and come over some time for a match."

Olney had been searching the crowd with his eyes

as we talked. He must have seen who he was looking for because he shook hands once more and said, "Nice to meet you, Mr. Socarides. You and young Fred here will have to come by for drinks."

Costello watched him go like a Red Sox fan in the presence of Ted Williams. "Jack's a good guy to know. He's got more connections on Beacon Hill than the State House plumber."

"Is he one of the major investors you were talking about?"

It had been just a guess, but Costello's eyes narrowed. "Let's just say Jack sees the Cape's potential. Look, I have to schmooze with some guests who just arrived, but I want to talk to you again some time about the Talbot camp. Maybe we can do lunch. I'll give you a call."

He clamped my shoulder and shook my hand at the same time, then walked over to the French doors. Three new guests had just come onto the patio. The slender young woman wore a sleeveless saffron jumpsuit that set off the velvety darkness of her skin. She was on the arm of a man with rusty hair and beard who wore a short-sleeved safari shirt and matching slacks. Close behind them was a squat, powerful-looking man with close-cropped hair. He was dressed in weightlifter's baggy pants and T-shirt.

The woman was exotic by Cape Cod standards and the two men had a toughness about them that was out of sync with the other guests. Costello led them around a corner of the house and out of sight.

I listened to the steel band and moseyed around for

a few more minutes picking up conversations about golf or tennis or real estate or how the kids and grandchildren were driving them out of their minds and affecting their golf and tennis games. The redhead in the silver lamé dress waved and headed toward me. I wasn't in the mood to discuss tummy tucks. I grabbed two cold bottles of Sam Adams and walked to the front of the house. The car valets were sitting on the steps having a smoke. I gave them each a Sam Adams. "You've got to be careful not to get dehydrated."

They gratefully accepted the beers.

"Thanks," one said. "It's hot as hell out here."

"My pleasure. Figured it was going to be a long night for you."

"No problem," the other kid said. "Costello pays us pretty well, the tips aren't bad, and we get to drive some pretty nice wheels even if it's only for a few yards."

"That reminds me. I'm looking for my pickup. Just give me the keys. I'll understand if you don't want to bring it around."

The kid who had taken the truck originally must have felt guilty, especially after I'd brought him the beer. He scrambled to his feet. "I'll show you where it is." We walked toward the garage.

I said, "I was wondering who those people were who just came in. Pretty, dark woman. Guy with a red beard and a friend who looks like he does free weights."

"You noticed her, too? Wasn't she something? Costello told us they'd be coming and to treat them nice. He said they're some kind of TV film crew he rented a house to. Supposedly doing something on that stuff that's been going on at Quanset Beach. Here's your truck."

The pickup was hidden in the shadows cast by a wide-spreading big-leafed catalpa tree.

"You should get that motor fixed fairly soon," the valet said. "She stalled on me a couple of times, then kept running for about five minutes after I switched the key off. Sounds like it could be the timing."

"These Ferrari engines are all kind of temperamental." I gave him a fiver to cover the humiliation of having to drive the pickup. The motor coughed a couple of times, then caught. I drove off, wondering if I'd gotten anything out of Costello's little barbecue beyond a beer buzz and a case of heartburn.

An eight-by-ten manila envelope hung from the nail on my front door. I don't have a phone answering machine and the nail functions as my message center. I pulled the envelope off the door and went inside. Kojak came out of the bedroom blinking his eyes. I threw the envelope on the kitchen table and gave him a handful of kitty snacks before he knocked me over with his hungry affection. Then I settled into the overstuffed couch and called Sam.

This time he answered the phone. "Been trying to get you, Soc." He paused. "Got a little problem about tomorrow. Doc wants me to take it easy until the tests are in."

"Is everything okay?"

"Oh, sure. He says don't worry, but it's best not to take chances, in case something's wrong with my ticker. I think the whole thing's a bunch of hooey, but I've got to keep Millie happy. You want to see if the Eldridge kid's free and take the boat out tomorrow?"

"I can't, Sam. A case just came up."

"Oh, that's too bad. I mean, that's good about a case. Give you a chance to use your brain instead of your back."

"I'll call you tomorrow to see how you're doing."

"Finestkind, Soc. I'll be here."

I hung up and stared into space. Shit. Now they were looking at Sam's heart. I didn't even want to *think* of the possibilities.

I strolled out on the deck. As I gazed at the yellow lights glowing in the houses along the bay, thoughts tumbled over in my mind. I went inside to a hall closet, pulled out a chart, and unrolled it on the kitchen table. The map showed Cape Cod's big bent arm swinging in a great uppercut into the Atlantic Ocean. I studied the chart, then called Gary, told him I'd heard a second body was found, and asked where it landed.

"Just south of the protected beach," he said.

I pondered that. "Gary, you going to be around tomorrow? I need a ride down the beach."

"No problem. Come by around ten. I'll be at the administration building hiding from all the TV crews that are running around since that pirate curse story came out and the bodies started floating ashore. I'm trying to keep the lifeguards busy at the same time. I don't know how much more snow fence we can put up."

"Anything else that's new?"

"Just that the state's sending down a marine biologist to check things out."

"I know. I met her tonight at a cocktail party."

"Leave it to you to find a new woman in town. What's she like?"

"Pretty. Probably quite competent."

"Oh, that's good. The competent part, I mean. Maybe she'll be able to help."

"Maybe." I told him I'd see him tomorrow and went back to the chart. The telephone rang.

"Soc," my brother George said, "Ma wants to know if there's anything going on with Cousin Alex."

"Tell her I'll get to it tomorrow, George. I promise."

"I hope so, pal. She'll take it out on me, Pop, and Chloe. You're safe down there on the Cape." There was reproach in his voice. Big brother hiding out in the dunes again.

"I promise I'll do something tomorrow," I said, with irritation I instantly regretted. Hell, I didn't blame George for chafing under my mother's demands. I tried to make amends. "Don't forget to think about going fishing with me."

"Sure, Soc. I don't know when I can make some time, though. Between work and Maria and the kids . . ."

"That's okay, George. We'll do it sometime."

I said goodbye and hung up, wondering if George and I would ever really get to know one another as people, or if we really wanted to.

I went to the fridge, foreboding in my gut because I was sure I was out of beer. The can of Old Milwaukee I keep for emergencies was tucked in back. I sat at the kitchen table and spotted the envelope that had been tacked to my door. I slit the envelope open with a kitchen knife. Inside was a single sheet of white writing paper. Typed on it was a message that sounded like something out of Huckleberry Finn.

Indian Rock. 8:00 AM tomorrow. Leave message at number below if you can't make it. J.F.

I'll be damned. I smiled. Then frowned. Then smiled again. I didn't need a crystal ball to predict life was about to get even more interesting.

C h a p t e r   1 3

Captain Edward Penniman was a whaling captain who became the richest man in town, and didn't mind advertising his wealth. He built a French wedding-cake house on a hill in Eastham and put a whale's jawbone archway over the front walk to let people know he made his money the hard way.

The taxpayers of America bought the Penniman house when the feds took the property and nearby Fort Hill as part of the Cape Cod National Seashore. The Seashore has built a small parking lot that services a network of nature trails. Around seven-thirty the next morning, I left the truck there and followed a dirt path through a locust grove and along the edge of grassy hills that rolled down to the great marsh. About a mile distant, ranks of breakers advanced against the dunes of the outer beach.

The morning stillness was broken by a distant buzzing. I looked east, over the ocean. A black speck moved against the blue sky. The speck became a dot, sprouted wings, and grew into a twin-engined red-and-white Cessna. The plane circled lazily overhead, cruising low over the fields like a hungry marsh hawk, then turned and headed back toward the ocean. I watched it shrink to a dot, and started walking again.

The path entered a sun-dappled, red cedar thicket and broke into the open after a couple of hundred yards. I was on Skiff Hill. Here, the National Park Service has put up an open pavilion with a roof shaped like a coolie hat. The interpretive station is near a fifty-foot-high cliff that overlooks the great marsh. The boggy archipelago of salt meadow grass islands and mudflats stretches off to the outer beach where Henry Boston wrote about his stay in the Outermost House in 1926.

Protected by the roof was Indian Rock, a boulder about the size of a flattened Volkswagen. Its surface was scarred by deep cuts made by the Indians who used the rock to sharpen their stone axes and bone fishhooks. It made a good seat. Across the marsh, herring gulls dipped and wheeled like shreds of paper borne on the wind. Common terns whipped by in nervous bursts of speed. In the stillness, it was easy to imagine loin-clothed braves stalking game or enemies, arrows tipped with horseshoe-tail barbs poised for quick release.

"Penny for your thoughts," a voice rumbled.

John Flagg had come up quietly behind me. I knew he was delighted at catching me off guard and that behind the mirrored aviator sunglasses his eyes were dancing with mirth.

"The price for thoughts has inflated to a dollar," I told him. "But if you must know, I was thinking about Indians skulking around in the briars."

"You've been watching too many John Wayne flicks on the boob tube."

It was good to see Flagg. A year had passed since I last talked to him. You could never be sure where he was. John's life had been a long journey since he left the Wampanoag Indian community of Gay Head on Martha's Vineyard more than two decades ago. We had met in Vietnam. He was a 101st Airborne paratrooper who had gone over to counterinsurgency, and I was in the Marines. Ours was an unlikely friendship, a hard-drinking wiseass Greek kid from a prosperous family in an old factory city and a teetotaling dirt-poor Native American from a tiny island town. But we had some things in common. We were both from Massachusetts. We both hated the war. And we both had caught our feet on our ancestral roots. I was trying to escape my heritage. Flagg was trying to find his. Now he worked as a troubleshooter for a small and obscure spook-for-hire federal government agency whose name doesn't mean anything because it changes so frequently.

He was dressed in navy blue suit trousers, black shoes buffed to a spit shine, a starched white open-collared shirt that was having a hard time containing his broad shoulders, and a conservative gray tie. His blue-black hair was longish over his ears.

I pulled his terse note out of my pocket. "You're getting absolutely loquacious, Flagg."

"Wrong. Let's take a walk."

He led the way onto a path bordered by cattails.

151

"Where have you been keeping yourself, Flagg? It's been almost a year since we worked on that case together."

"Yeah, the killer whale caper. I've been around. How's Sally Carlin, the nice dolphin lady? She get smart and dump you yet?"

"Not yet, but I'm working on it. How's Annie?"

He grinned proudly. "Little sister's doing great. Still making pottery. Her stuff's getting into galleries in Boston and New York now. Fetching good prices. Says she'd like to hear from you sometime."

Annie and I had been lovers. It might have been a good thing, but she got hit by the fire of the personal war Flagg and I had waged against each other. By the time we called a truce, it was too late. It could never be the same between Annie and me. I still felt guilty about it. I mumbled something about giving Annie a call.

"She'd like that," Flagg said. He stopped and looked off toward the ocean where the sun was climbing into the sky, then turned back to me. "Reason I got you here, Soc, is I could use your help with a job."

"What kind of help, old friend? Topple a government? Mine a harbor? Or go undercover at Hedonism Two?"

"Not even close. I need a diver who can keep his mouth shut."

"You don't last long underwater if you can't keep your mouth shut. Is this a government assignment?"

The Cessna I had seen earlier was approaching from the sea. It made a wide circle once more over the fields. Flagg watched until the plane headed toward the ocean again.

"Can't say right now," he said.

I shook my head. Flagg wore secrecy like an insurance man wears a three-piece suit. "Let me guess. National security again?"

"Something like that."

"What would I be diving on?"

"Can't tell you that, either."

"Okay, can you tell me *where* it is?"

Flagg gazed off toward the hills. "Picked up one of the folders they print for people using this trail. Did you know this used to be all Indian land? They had houses all over these hills. Champlain came by, and everything was going great until his guys accused an Indian of stealing a copper kettle. There was a big fight. One of the French sailors got killed."

"I know my local history, Flagg. The white man wins in the end. He gave the Indians diseases they couldn't handle. It was the original unconventional warfare."

Flagg gave me an odd look. "Funny you should say that, Soc." He started walking again. "You know," he said with a chuckle, "we got even with those Francos and Anglos. We gave you guys tobacco. Pretty soon, no more white man."

"I'm really glad you got me up here so we could take this pretty nature walk while you laid your revisionist Wampanoag history on me, my friend, but I have the distinct feeling you're stalling me."

He stared at me. My face was reflected in his sunglasses. "This could be a tough job. I wanted to sound you out."

"We've known each other since Vietnam, Flagg.

Comrades in arms, remember? If you need help, just ask."

He held his stare another moment, then said, "I'm asking."

"Okay, you got me. Can you tell me when this thing is going down?"

"Depends."

Flagg was doing his tight-lipped spook-out. "Depends on *what,* for godsakes?"

There was a rumble overhead. The Cessna had come in again, low enough for me to see the pilot's face even if I couldn't make out his features. Flagg waved. The pilot waved back and the plane waggled its wings.

"Depends on *that,*" Flagg said.

"Friend of yours?"

"Could say so. He's got a gadget that can read the ocean bottom from the air. Saves a lot of time. When he finds what he's looking for I'll let you know."

A thought came to me. "Couple of bodies have come ashore lately. They have anything to do with what you're not talking about?"

"Maybe," he said after a moment. He started up the path to the parking lot. "I left my car at the top of the hill. Where are you parked?"

"Over by the Penniman house."

"You still got that old pickup?"

"I'm attached to it for sentimental reasons."

"I like a man who's not afraid to be sentimental. Need a lift?"

"No, thanks. I'll walk. I need the exercise."

"I'll call you. You still fishing?"

"I'm off for a few days. Sam isn't feeling well."

"Sorry to hear that."

"Me, too."

We shook hands and parted. Flagg climbed to the Fort Hill parking lot, covering the distance in the loose-legged shamble that belied his quickness of foot. I cut across the fields. The grass was deeper than it looked and hidden briars caught at my sneakers. By the time I got back to the pickup, Flagg was gone. I leaned against the fender and tried to make sense out of the past few days. First the nastiness at Quanset Beach. Then the bodies. Finally, Flagg appearing like a magician's assistant in a puff of smoke. Connected? It was too farfetched on one hand, too coincidental on the other.

One thing was as certain as the tides. Flagg was attracted to trouble like a moth to a flame.

Chapter 14

Cousin Alex lived in Little Taunton, a working-class summer colony settled in the 1940's and '50's by Italians from an industrial city near Boston. The old ethnic flavor has faded, but you can still get great pasta at the neighborhood restaurants, and stroll on Squadrilli Way and Angelo Road. The Osterville yacht club set wouldn't be caught dead in Little Taunton. I'd be the first to admit it has its tacky side. But the place has a festive charm you don't get in the high-toned locales.

I turned north off Route 6A, the Old King's Highway, and drove toward Cape Cod Bay until I came to a close-packed collection of summer cottages. The address George had given me was a flat-roofed beach house on a dirt road that ran parallel to the beach. In the drive was a new black Camaro, a shiny silver Toyota 4Runner, and a white Honda CRX. I went up to the front walk and rang the bell.

A stocky guy answered the door. His chin was half-shaven, as if it needed fertilizer to make it sprout. His short forehead was separated from small eyes by a single bushy brow.

"I'm looking for Alex," I said. "Is he here?"

He twitched. "Who are you?"

"I'm his cousin. Who are you?"

"I'm Chili."

Chili looked like a fun guy, so I said, "If you're chilly, why don't you put on your long underwear?"

Chili just stared at me. His face twitched and his hands twitched. He was making me twitch. He wiped his nose with his knuckles. "Wait here," he said, and shut the door in my face.

A minute later the door opened again. Alex stood there. He looked as if I were wearing a Gumby suit.

"Soc," he said. "It *is* you."

I pinched his cheek. "In the flesh, Cousin Alex."

He grabbed my hand and pumped it. "God, I thought Chili was kidding when he said my cousin wanted to see me. C'mon in."

The door opened into a run-down living room furnished in the plastic and wood Danish modern furniture popular about the same time Peter Fonda made *Easy Rider* twenty years ago. Alex led the way through the kitchen and onto a deck. Chili slumped in a plastic chair drinking a beer. I bet myself he was trying to figure out my long-underwear comment. Stretched out in a chaise longue in a string bikini was a skinny strawberry blonde with breasts too big for her anorexic body. A black-haired guy sat in his bathing suit under the umbrella of a patio table. A cordless phone and a notebook lay in front of him. No one moved. It was as if I had stumbled into a kid's game of statues.

"Hey guys," Alex said. "This is my cousin Aristotle. Everyone in the family calls him Soc." He glanced my way to see if it was okay to use my nickname.

I went over and shook hands with the woman on the chaise longue. She was just over drinking age, and would have been attractive if she let her bleached hair go naturally brown, got rid of the corn row braids, and filled out her pinched features with a little more flesh. Her nostrils were red and inflamed. Summer colds must be going around.

"I'm Tanya. Nice to meet you." She had a pretty smile.

The guy at the table came over. He was a clean-cut kid who looked like an ad in an Exeter Academy brochure. He smiled disarmingly and extended his hand. "I'm T.J. Nice to meet Alex's cousin. Would you like a beer?"

"No, thanks, I usually don't start drinking until after nine in the morning. Nice spot you've got here."

"Thanks. We got a pretty good deal on it for the summer."

Alex came over and put his arm around my shoulders. "This is so incredible, Soc. How did you find me?"

"I was talking to my brother George the other day. He mentioned you were on the Cape for the summer, so I asked for your address. I was in the neighborhood and thought I'd stop by. I haven't come at a bad time, have I?"

"God, no. I never thought *any*one from my family would come to visit me. But I'm glad it's you. My cousin here is one mellow dude," he announced proudly.

Alex had grown a half foot since I saw him at the last family wedding. He was a tall slim kid with long arms and legs. He had thick dark brown hair, a boyish oval face, and a smile that always seemed out of place with the sadness in his large gray eyes.

The phone on the table rang. T.J. picked it up and glanced at Alex.

"Why don't you show Soc the beach," he said. It was more than a suggestion.

"Let's take a walk," Alex said, grabbing my arm. We stepped off the deck onto the sand. "Man, it's been ages since I last saw you at that dopey wedding. How's it going? You still catching fish?"

"Trying to. The fish don't always cooperate."

"Yeah, but that's so cool, Soc. I've always admired you, the way you thumbed your nose at the rest of the family and went your own way."

"I didn't exactly thumb my nose at them. My parents are great people. I love and respect them. I had to march to a different drummer, but that doesn't mean I don't regret it. I regret it lots of times."

"Maybe. But you did what you wanted."

"Looks like you're doing what you want to this summer. Are you working?"

He paused to pick up a smooth flat stone. "I've got a thing cleaning restaurant kitchens."

"What about your friends? They cleaning kitchens, too?"

"Yeah, we all are."

"The restaurant business must be good. A waterfront cottage costs a bundle."

The beach was crowded with families. Alex found a place where nobody was swimming and skimmed the rock into the water. It bounced six times.

"We've been pretty busy, and we split the rent so it's no big deal." He grinned. "Besides, we're all rich kids. You still in the boathouse?"

"Yup. Me and Kojak the cat."

"That place is totally awesome, Soc. Will you leave it to me in your will?"

"You'll have to share it with Kojak."

"No problem. He's pretty awesome, too."

"How're your folks doing?" I said.

His smile faded. "Okay, I guess. I haven't talked to them in a while."

"Yeah, I know what you mean. Ma is always after me to call her more often. How was school last year?"

He laughed. "It was *fine*, for me. I dropped out a couple of months before the semester ended."

"Too bad. How come?"

"I was just tired of everybody ragging my ass. It's bad enough I've got my parents on my case without my teachers doing it, too."

"Think you'll go back?"

He frowned in thought. "I don't know."

"What are you going to do after the summer? A lot of the restaurants you're cleaning will close for the season and the local job market goes flat in the winter."

The grin returned. "Maybe I can help out on your fishing boat."

I grabbed his arm. "Pretty scrawny, but I can use you as lobster bait. Give me a call."

We headed back to the cottage. T.J. was off the phone and kissing Tanya's skinny neck. Chili still twitched in his chair. The phone rang again. T.J. picked it up. He told the person on the line to wait, then came over to shake hands with me.

"Sorry we didn't get to talk. I'm trying to get some figures to make a bid on a job."

"Maybe next time. Good luck with your kitchen cleaning," I said.

He thanked me, stepped off the deck with the phone, and walked down onto the beach. Out of earshot.

"Guess I'll head for home," I said.

"Sure you can't stay a while longer?" Alex was being polite but his heart wasn't in it. He seemed nervous at my being there and I had a good idea why.

"I've got some errands to run. Maybe I can drop by another time. See you, Tanya. Take it easy, Chili."

She gave me a desultory wave. Chili glared.

Alex led the way back into the house. I stopped in the living room and patted my shirt pocket. "Say, I didn't drop my sunglasses out there, did I?"

"I don't know, Soc, I'll go and look."

He went back onto the deck. I only had a few seconds. There was a phone and an answering machine on a side table next to the sofa. I lifted up the answering machine. On the bottom was a label printed with a three-digit security code. Good, one of those models that allow calls to be retrieved from an outside phone. I memorized the numbers and replaced the machine. Then I went back to the kitchen and knocked on the slider. Alex stood on the beach near the deck. I pointed to the sunglasses in my hand.

"I'm getting senile, I guess. They were in another pocket. Sorry."

My cousin walked me to my truck. I ran my hand over the 4Runner's gleaming fender. It was the model with all the works, the one that went for more than twenty grand.

"Nice wheels," I said. "T.J.'s?" Alex nodded.

"I'll give you a call some time. We can toss a football around or shoot some hoops."

"Yeah," Alex said. "I'd like that."

We shook hands quickly, then Alex walked briskly back to the cottage. I got in the truck, drove down the street, made a quick U-turn, and parked where I could watch the front door.

I sat in the truck for half an hour. The cab was like a pressure cooker, and the heat didn't improve my disposition. I've got a stubborn streak when I'm angry, so I waited another ten minutes. A black-and-white Datsun pickup came toward me and pulled into the driveway. The driver and another guy went up to the front door and were admitted. They were out in less than five minutes and took off.

Damn! I slammed the palm of my hand against the steering wheel. The little jerk. Phone calls. Expensive cars. Nostrils irritated by nose candy. Dope deals were going down in the cozy little cottage by the sea, and my dumb cousin was in the middle of it.

I started the truck and headed back to Route 6A. How had Alex hooked up with this bunch? He could be a pain in the butt, but he'd never been in any major trouble. Was he just rebelling against his successful parents and life in general? Hell, I didn't know. My mother was right to worry about Alex. But she was wrong about his friends. These weren't bad boys, they were *very* bad boys.

Chapter 15

Two TV station vans with satellite dishes on their roofs were parked in front of the Quanset Beach administration building. The press had succeeded in prying Gary out of hiding. A couple of women reporters had him pinned up against the building wall and were trying to jam their microphones down his throat.

I beeped the horn. Gary broke off the interview and came over to the truck. The reporters pounced on a young lifeguard who didn't seem to mind the attention. Gary was a different case altogether.

"God, am I glad to see you! Those people are relentless."

"Remember what Andy Warhol said about everybody being famous for fifteen minutes?"

"Yeah, well, I've had my quota of fame. Let's go for

a beach ride. There's something I should tell you, though."

Diana Trumbull stepped out of the administration building. Avoiding the reporters, the marine biologist walked over to the beach patrol truck.

"Miss Trumbull?" I asked Gary.

He nodded. "She called after I talked to you and said she wanted to go on the beach. Figured I'd take you both out at the same time."

"It's no problem for me." I grabbed my chart and a notebook, got out of the pickup, and walked over to where Diana Trumbull waited.

"Nice to see you again, Miss Trumbull."

She didn't bother to hide the faint amusement with which she regarded me. "It's Mr. Socarides, isn't it? The fisherman with the Loch Ness monster theory."

"I'm leaning toward giant blood-sucking sea leeches today." I climbed into the back of the truck and perched on a fiberglass toolbox. "I'll ride out here and get some fresh air while Gary brings you up to date. Hey, Gary," I said, "could you do me a favor and keep track of our mileage on the odometer?"

"Sure thing," he replied. He got in and cranked the engine, then drove onto the beach between the snack bar and the administration building. A minute later, the truck lumbered to a halt at the tide line. I stayed aboard while Gary and Diana got out and walked to the water's edge. Gary gestured toward the sea; she took notes.

Except for the BATHING PROHIBITED signs posted all over the place, it was an ideal summer day. Sunny, with puffball clouds pasted onto a flat blue sky. A few people strolled along the edge of the surf just out of reach of the waves, but you could tell by the way they kept checking the water that they weren't comfortable. Almost no kids were around. Those that were, dug holes in the sand near the dunes, far from the water. Lifeguards watched from their towers like prison guards eyeballing the inmates. An unreal stillness hung over the sand.

Gary introduced Diana around to the guards. She took more notes, then they got back in the truck and we drove off the beach across the parking lot to the beach access road. Squadrons of the greenhead flies strafed us. I tried to swat them with my cap and keep my seat on the toolbox, which wobbled ominously each time the truck hit a pothole.

The greenheads lost interest after we left the road behind the dunes for the track that went along the ocean. Except for a couple of beach buggies a half mile distant, this beach was empty.

The truck stopped and Gary read off the mileage to me. We had gone .7 miles from the parking lot. Chart in hand, I walked down the sandy slope to the water. The green sea was serene. Wavelets lapped at my sneakers. I marked an X on the chart to locate my position, drew a rough diagram in my notebook, and went back to the truck. Gary was telling Diana how the first body had been found. She was listening to him and watching me. Minutes later, we were underway again. A quarter mile to the south, Gary stopped once more.

"This is where the second body came ashore," he said.

Again, I walked to the edge of the surf and marked an X on the chart and in the notebook. Diana peered over my shoulder. She wore a nice perfume.

"Mr. Socarides, I'd like to apologize for the other night. I was rather abrupt with you. I just want to explain—"

"You don't have to explain." Actually, I had wondered what made her fly off the handle.

"No, it would make me feel better," she said. "You see, I'd been working for months preparing a report on the big outfall pipe that's going to carry treated sewage into Massachusetts Bay. I was close to completing my job when they pulled me off the project. It's a controversial issue and I suspect it was because my report was unfavorable. I know *this* is an important assignment, but I wasn't happy at being yanked away to look for sea monsters. I took my frustration out on you. I'm sorry."

"I don't blame you for being upset. No apology needed."

"That's nice of you." She glanced at the scribbles in my notebook. "May I ask what you're doing?" she said politely.

"The current runs south along this shore. That suggests the bodies came from northeast of here. Since there's nothing out there but ocean, they probably came from a ship. There was an oil spill a bit south of us, but no shipwrecks have been reported. I'd guess that if you were able to compute the tide flow and how long the bodies were in the water, you might be able to come up with a rough estimate as to point of origin."

"Hmm," she said. "May I ask why you're doing this?"

"Just curiosity. As a scientist, you would appreciate that."

"I also appreciate precision and the ability to base conclusions on solid facts."

"Does that mean you're never open to empirical data?"

She paused to ponder the challenge. "That depends. Do you have any?"

"Maybe. Feel like hearing a story?"

"Everybody likes a story."

Gary was scuffing along the beach stuffing plastic flotsam into a garbage bag. He seemed in no hurry to leave. I plunked my butt on the sand. After a second's hesitation, Diana sat down beside me. I unrolled the chart and spread it out between us.

"I have a friend, a local guy who's been fishing these waters since he was a kid. You could blindfold him and he could find his way home by the sound of the water under his keel or the wind against his skin. It's a sea sense all the old-timers had. People don't need it now because of the high-tech navigational gear that's available. A landlubber like me can come into the fishery and buy a black box that will tell me where I am, how fast I'm going, how deep the water is, and where the fish are, all at a push of a button."

"I'm sure you're every bit as competent at what you do as your friend." Diana was being patronizing, but I let it pass.

"The other night my friend was fishing off Quanset

Beach." I tapped the chart with my finger to show the spot off the inlet. "He was alone in his skiff about here. Quiet night as he describes it." Having set the stage, I told her Mac McConnell's story.

She didn't say a word until I was finished. Probably spellbound.

"You *did* say your friend saw a glowing blob in the water after something ate his fish."

"That's what he told me."

Crimson patches appeared on her cheeks. She managed to get the corners of her mouth up in a smile, but she was straining every muscle in her face. Her hazel eyes flashed with anger.

"Thank you for that wonderful story," she said evenly. "I'm sure you'll have a lovely time telling your friends on the waterfront how you suckered in the know-it-all marine biologist and put her in her place."

"Miss Trumbull."

"For your information, I *saw The Blob.* The original was much better than the remake."

She got to her feet and stalked back to the truck. I shook my head. Diana Trumbull was a very sensitive lady. She was right about the movie, though; the remake stunk.

I went back to my chart, marked X's where the Canadian tourist and the surfer had been attacked, and transferred the information to my notebook. The attacks were directly off Quanset Beach, maybe a few hundred feet apart. I enclosed them in one circle. Then I drew another circle showing where Mac got scared out of his sneakers. Mac had been more due east and a little south. The bodies had come ashore to the south of the parking lot. I circled the two sites as one. I drew lines with my pencil and connected the circles.

I stared at the triangle made by the intersecting lines and nibbled my lower lip.

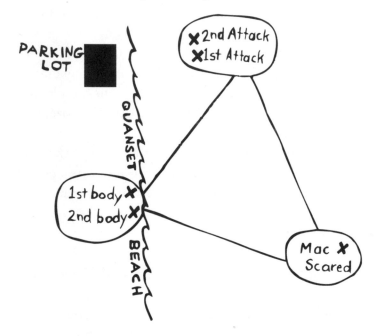

A black-and-red GMC Blazer was coming along the beach track. It stopped next to Gary's truck and the dark-skinned woman I'd seen at Costello's party got out, followed by her two male companions. I rolled up my chart and climbed the slope of the beach. Gary gestured for me, so I rambled over.

"Hi, Soc, I'd like you to meet these folks. They're doing something on Quanset Beach for British TV."

The bearded man grinned broadly and stuck his hand out. "I'm Nigel Eden, the producer for this motley crew." His upper-class English was as crisp as a scone. "This is my assistant, Solange Tournay, and my cameraman, Jack Morgan."

Eden was a compact man, with the muscular ruggedness of a mountain climber. He had curly reddish-blond hair and a beard that was so short as to be an afterthought. His big horse teeth were too many and too large for his mouth, but the equine effect was softened by the overpowering friendliness of his grin. He was like one of those incredibly fit British gentlemen back in the days of the Empire, adventurers who took on bloodthirsty Fuzzy-Wuzzies or desert sand storms armed with jovial equanimity, a bottle of quinine water, and a Jolly Good Show.

We shook hands all around. "I think I saw you at Fred Costello's party," I said.

"Mr. Costello was kind enough to invite us. We met Miss Trumbull there, but I don't remember you."

"I left early. Are you with the BBC?"

"We're free-lance," Eden said. "We do mostly unsolved mysteries for British and American TV. Bigfoot, UFO's, Noah's ark. Tabloid stuff. I'd be the first to admit it's trash journalism. But it pays splendidly. And it *is* rather fun."

"What do you think of our Quanset Beach mystery?"

"Fascinating. We're thinking of naming it Cape Cod's Blood Triangle as a send-up on the Bermuda Triangle. It would be nice if we could find a gigantic magnetic vortex or sunken city just off the beach here. A missing squadron of World War Two Hellcat planes in mint condition would be lovely, too."

"Nothing would surprise me."

"That's good. Unfortunately, we don't have a great deal of visual material outside of this splendid beach. We did speak to the young fellow who had his leg injured. We have some wonderful footage of that interview. And we saw the historian who filled us in on the pirate curse. Now we're talking to witnesses like Mr. Cozzi here."

"Soc was on the beach the day the man was killed," Gary told them. "You may want to talk to him."

"Mr. Socarides thinks it may be the Loch Ness monster," Diana interjected, a malicious gleam in her eye.

"Oh, really?" Eden didn't blink. "We've done Nessie a few times. Personally, I hope they never find the old girl. She's been a prime source of some smashing stories."

"Actually I'm more partial to giant leeches," I said. "I'd be glad to talk to you, but I don't know if I can add anything to Gary's account."

"Perhaps you and Miss Trumbull would like to come by some evening for cocktails? We could do an interview."

"I'm afraid it would be premature. I have nothing to offer right now," Diana said crisply. "I just started my investigation and I wouldn't want to speculate."

"I understand completely. Later, perhaps. Mr. Socarides, maybe we can lure you. We're renting the Dwight place on Quanset Bluffs. Mr. Costello found it for us."

Eden looked at his watch. "Well, it's been very nice chatting, but I suppose we shouldn't waste the daylight. We hoped to film a few shots of the beach. What do you think, Jack?"

Jack didn't look as if he was thinking about anything. His wide mouth was locked in a straight line, his watchful deep set eyes yielded nothing. His face, with its pale skin stretched tight across high cheekbones, had the hard bony look of a skull mask. His hair was cropped to a military nubble against his head. He wore a T-shirt with an extra wide neck hole, and baggy zebra striped weight-lifter's pants.

He nodded, opened the back of the GMC, and took out a camera, then followed Eden who had walked down to the water with Gary and Diana. He moved with that rolling swing of the shoulders free-weight lifters get from packing more muscle on the deltoids and thighs than the human body was meant to carry. Cops call it "joint physique." Guys get it when they've got nothing to do but lift weights and write their defense attorneys.

Solange and I were left alone and I had a close-up chance to study her as well. She was as slender as a blade of salt marsh grass, but she had the athletic figure of a ballet dancer, with long firm legs, and narrow but strong-looking shoulders. Her black hair was cut short and spiked on top in gentrified punk style. She had bottomless dark eyes, a small nose, a wide mouth with perfect lips, and cinnamon skin.

"Have you been working with Nigel and Jack very long?" I asked.

"About a year," she replied, her voice low and mellow. She too spoke with a British accent. Her pronunciation was soft-edged, unlike Nigel's, whose words were punched out with the cold precision of a die-cutting machine.

"It must be interesting work."

"It has its moments. And you?"

"I'm a fisherman."

"That must be interesting, too."

"It has its moments."

She smiled. "You don't *really* think this is a Loch Ness monster, do you?"

"I was joking with Miss Trumbull. She failed to see the humor."

Solange gazed off at the waves breaking onto the beach. "I think I understand. Maybe she's frightened. I look at the ocean and it takes my breath away, it's so beautiful. But at the same time, I can't help thinking what a place of death it is."

"You can say that about almost any spot on earth. It's a dangerous world. The ocean will generally treat you right if you respect what it is. It can't be taken for granted."

"Is that what happened to that man who was killed? Did he take the ocean for granted?"

It was my turn to look for augeries in the surf. "No. He was just swimming, doing what thousands of people do all the time. But I see what you mean. There was no reason that should have happened."

Nigel Eden was calling. Jack had put a camera on a tripod and they were swiveling it around. Solange extended her hand. "I have to go. Drop by and see us." She smiled. "We could talk about fishing." Her fingers brushed mine.

"I'll certainly try."

Minutes later, we were bouncing on the beach road. Back at the administration building, I told Gary I'd check in with him later. I got in my truck and headed out of the near-empty parking lot. The carnival atmosphere had vanished, along with the people. The sun was still bright, and the sky unclouded, but the beach had become a sinister, unfriendly place. What had Nigel called Quanset Beach? Cape Cod's Blood Triangle. I thought of the three-sided diagram I had drawn. Although the day was warm, I shivered.

Chapter 16

I popped a beer, went out on the deck, and wondered why I was spending so much time on this Quanset Beach thing. I had other stuff to worry about. I was supposed to find out who was trying to take Tillie Talbot's camp away from her. My fishing partner was having hospital tests and talking about retiring. I had to make a civilized person out of my jerk cousin or face the wrath of my mother. Flagg was trying to recruit me for a secret salvage job that was probably over my head in more ways than one. And I had been treating a lovely lady as if she were a street person panhandling for a dime.

I felt suddenly weary, as if the weight of the world were on my shoulders. The weariness turned to self-pity. I was starting to enjoy feeling sorry for myself. Kojak came out onto the deck, sat directly in front of me, and stared. *Nothing* is more intimidating than a hungry cat staring at you.

"*Et tu,* Kojak?" I got out of my chair and went inside to feed him.

The sun was falling down the sky and taking some of its heat with it. I strolled out to the garden. The worm had struck again, big time. More plants were stripped. Anger welled up inside of me. This guy has got to go. I peered under some leaves. I was sure he was watching me. No sign of the little creep. I turned to check my shingling job. Not bad. None of the shingles had fallen off the house. The new shingles made the old ones look even worse. I went into the shed and got my hammer, nails and more shingles.

As I hammered away, I thought about Tillie Talbot. There was a pattern there, as faint as an old spiderweb, but still a pattern. The harassment began after she told Fred Costello to take a hike. Fred knew a former lieutenant governor, who would certainly have the connections to make Tillie's life miserable. Money, power, and influence were not static forces. They had to *flow* somewhere from somewhere. It was just a question of throwing a few wood chips into the stream and watching where they went.

Tap-tap. The broad-headed shingle nails sank easily into the soft wood.

Costello admitted he wanted Tillie's land. But why? Sure, it was a choice piece of property, but in the turgid real estate market it could turn out to be a white elephant. It might make a good long-term investment. In the meantime, a developer would have to lay out a bundle before the property was in any kind of shape to offer to rich people with deep pockets. After the boom-to-bust times of the eighties, most banks were reluctant as hell to lend money to speculators. I couldn't figure it. Unless Tillie's camp sat on top of an oil field.

Tappity-tap. I nailed up another row of shingles.

I switched mental gears. Cousin Alex. He wasn't a bad kid. Spoiled and pampered, and a little naive, but he didn't fit in with his hard-assed buddies. This was a tough one. I had leverage to use on him. He envied my lifestyle, but I would get nowhere telling him to do as I *say,* not as I do.

The telephone rang. I laid the hammer down and went inside the boathouse. Mac was on the line.

"You doing anything tonight?"

"I've got nothing planned. What's going on?"

"I went fishing again last night."

"Fishing? You've got a lot of guts going out after what you told me."

"Pure necessity, Soc. Figured I'd better go damned soon or I'd never set foot in a boat again. It's like getting back on a horse after you fall off. Mostly, I got pissed off at myself. Hell, it's *my* ocean too. I've been working the water since I was a kid. That's a lot of sweat equity, and I'm not going to get scared off. Besides, it's either fish or go back to lawyering. Now, *that's* dangerous. Hell, they'd find me dead of boredom with my nose in a tort case. Anyhow, to make a long story short, I went out again and saw something."

"The glowing blob?"

"Jeez, Soc. Keep your voice down. There's nobody listening, is there?"

"Just my cat and he's unconscious."

"Okay. No blob this time. Something completely different. Pretty hard to describe. I'd rather show you, let you form your own opinion. I'm going out around eleven. Can you come? I keep my boat at Crowell's Landing."

"I'll be there," I said.

I showered and changed into fresh jeans and a T-shirt. Then I threw some lettuce into a bowl with a can of tuna, Caesar salad dressing, black olives, and feta cheese. After dinner, I got in the truck and headed toward Little Taunton, parking once again where I had a view of Cousin Alex's house.

The night was warm. People young and old strolled the narrow streets. Music and laughter spilled from a half dozen backyard barbecues. The scent of charcoal-grilled steaks and burgers made my mouth water. This wasn't such a dumb place to run a drug operation. In a quieter neighborhood, Alex and his buddies would have attracted attention. Here they were just another bunch of young guys out to have a good time.

Half an hour passed. Nothing stirred at the cottage. I left the truck and walked onto the beach from the parking lot, climbed over a stone jetty, and headed toward the backside of the cottage. The beach was deserted. A second later, I learned why. With no breeze to blow them away, a million no-see-ums had come off the marshes. Since I was the only edible thing in sight, a cloud of the ravenous little insects swirled around my head. Slapping my arms and face like a hand-jive artist, I trotted up to the deck behind the cottage.

The blind was up at the big picture window. I

peeked in. Alex and his friend Chili sat on a couch watching MTV. T.J. paced back and forth with the cordless phone stuck in his ear. I moved closer. No sign of the girl. T.J. grinned and put the phone down. He clapped his hands and did a high-five with the other two guys. Then he stuck a flower-patterned baseball cap on his head and pointed to the TV. Chili got up and turned the set off. They must be getting ready to leave.

I cut through the side yard to the pickup. Just in time. Headlights lit up the driveway. The 4Runner backed out and drove down the street. I got on its tail, staying fifty yards behind. The Toyota joined the sluggish line of cars on the Old King's Highway and headed west to Yarmouthport, then across the Cape to Route 28. Traffic was heavy and I had to cut a few people off. They leaned on their horns and gave me a one-fingered salute.

On Route 28, the 4Runner pulled into the parking lot of a sports bar. I parked where I could watch. Chili went into the bar. Minutes later, he emerged with a skinny bearded guy.

The beard crossed quickly to a white BMW, opened the door, shut it, walked over to the Toyota, and got in with Chili. The dome light flashed on and for a second I saw Cousin Alex in the backseat. The bearded guy stayed less than five minutes. Then he got out and went back to the BMW. Both vehicles started their motors.

I followed the Beemer onto Route 28, a congested strip of fast-food joints, motels, and discount retail outlets. A few minutes later, the white car turned off into a minimall and parked outside a liquor store. The bearded guy went over to a late model dark blue Ford van with smoked windows. Somebody in the Ford opened the door and the bearded guy got in. I drove by, praying my pickup wouldn't take that second to pop off. Interesting. The van had an official blue state license plate.

Uh-oh. Cousin Alex and his buddies were being set up. The scenario goes like this: The cops suspect dope deals are going down. An undercover cop makes a small buy. A surveillance team watches. The narc races to a mobile lab. The stuff is tested to make sure it's the real thing. Next, the cops set up a major deal. This time they make the collar. They've got the buy, the witnesses, and the lab test. It's so simple it's amazing that it works. But after a few scores drug dealers become cocky. They think they're untouchable. They get careless. Next thing they know, somebody is reading them their Miranda rights.

I rubbed my eyes and tried to think. A pretty boy like Alex would have a rough time at the prison at Cedar Junction. To some inmates, it would be like having Madonna for a roommate. Alex's parents would be devastated. The scandal would spread and stain everybody in the family. My mother would blame me. I could see her sadly shaking her head saying, *You have failed us, Aristotle.*

There was nothing I could do now. Anyway, nothing I could *think* of doing. I headed north to Route 6A in Barnstable, then followed a side road to the bay. I stopped outside an old clapboard carriage house. The lights were on in the second-floor apartment. I sat in my truck for a moment and looked at my watch. Still time before I met Mac. I got out of the pickup, went up the stairs to the second floor, and rang the bell.

Sally came to the door. She was dressed in shorts

and a T-shirt. Her hair was loose around her shoulders and shiny and soft in the pale light.

"Soc. What a nice surprise. Come on in."

"I can only stay a few minutes. I was on my way home from Hyannis. Throw me out if you want to. . . ."

"I wouldn't think of it. I was just having a lemonade. Want a glass?"

"The bigger the better." At a work table, the screen of her MacIntosh computer glowed. "Doing some homework?"

"The usual dolphin behavioral stuff. I'm still keeping a daily journal. Maybe I'll turn it into a book some day."

I settled into the sofa. "I bet it will be a good one."

"Thank you," she said, coming back into the room with a tall tinkling glass. She sat next to me. "You look worried."

"It's that obvious?"

She nodded. "Anything you want to tell me?"

"Family business."

"Your mom got you doing another job?" Sally had met my mother.

"This could be a tough one. I'll fill you in later. How is your life going?"

"Pretty much the same since the last time I saw you."

"I enjoyed our date."

"So did I. Sorry I left you so abruptly that morning."

"I'm the one who should apologize for showing up out of the blue, then disappearing."

"You're constantly apologizing. I wish you'd stop."

"I'm sorry. Whoops."

"I think I've told you that working with dolphins makes you highly sensitive to nonverbal communication. What is it you really want to say, Soc?"

I thought about it. "I think you're pretty special, Sally."

"I hear a *but* in there."

"Things were going pretty well between us for a while, weren't they?"

"Yes, I think they were. So what's wrong with that?"

"It's an old Greek characteristic. When things are good, it's time to start worrying they'll go bad."

"I don't understand, Soc."

"I'm not ready for closeness, Sally. Maybe I never will be. I don't want to hurt you."

"You already have." She said it more in sadness than in anger.

"I'm sorry."

"You're doing it again."

We both laughed.

"I had a pretty good idea what was going on in your mind," she said. "I wanted to give you space to work it out."

"I appreciate that."

"You know more than anyone that life isn't without risks. You're still fighting losing battles in your mind. Look, don't worry about it. Relax. We can be friends. We can go out and have a good time. We can talk. I'd like it if you weren't so much of a stranger. What will happen will happen."

I leaned over and kissed her lips. She closed her eyes and smiled. I kissed her neck. "You're a very wise lady," I said.

I could still taste her a few minutes later as I headed out for my appointment with Mac.

C h a p t e r   1 7

Paws pattered softly on the unlit Crowell's Landing dock and a warm wet nose snuffed at my hand.

"Blackstone," roared a gruff voice from the darkness, "*get* your ass back here. Is that you, Soc?"

Mac doesn't talk so much as he *emits*. His whole body—not just his diaphragm and vocal cords—mobilizes to produce a sound that is part growl, part bark, part foghorn.

"I'm looking for McConnell's midnight boat tours."

Mac guffawed. It was a sound like a grizzly bear coughing. At the far end of the pier a bulky shadow loomed black against the night. A flashlight beam stabbed the darkness.

"You're in luck. We still have room in first class."

The light shifted to the end of the pier, outlining a sturdy fiberglass skiff, Mac's pride and joy.

Mac's Labrador retriever clambered into the boat after me. The skiff sank another foot under Mac's weight, but it didn't swamp. Mac had spent his whole life around boats. On land, he moved with all the grace of an army tank. But in a boat, he had an economy of motion and sense of balance that made me feel clumsy.

He punched the starter of the seventy-five-horsepower Johnson outboard and lit a butt while the motor warmed up. Then we cast off the dock lines and cruised across the quiet waters of the cove.

Once we reached Quanset Harbor, Mac pulled back on the throttle. The skiff lifted, and we skimmed across the harbor.

I sat in the bow, Blackstone took the middle. Mac stood in front of the console with his legs wide and his huge rubber boots braced. Orange embers streamed off the cigarette in his mouth like the tail of a comet. He moved the wheel with practiced and barely perceptible motions, picking out the markers more by feel than sight, scudding past the big summer houses on the shore. Stars glittered like gems sewn into the brocade of the night sky.

The channel passed between the great marsh on our left and a headland to the right. Mac cut back on the throttle. Moving at a couple of knots, the skiff approached the outer beach. The air became cool and damp from the mist kicked up by the silver-gray line of breakers marking the inlet.

"We're almost at the cut," Mac warned. "Could get

a little bumpy, so I'd advise you to hang on. Mae Wests are in that chest in the cuddy."

I pulled two life vests from the fiberglass box in the forward storage space, gave one to Mac, and slipped my arms into the other. Mac did the same. The straps on Mac's vest were too short to reach across his expansive belly. He didn't seem to care. He probably knew no life jacket made had enough flotation material to keep him above water anyway.

The cut can be as tranquil as a Buddhist monk in prayer or angry as a boil. Mostly it is just plain cranky and can flip a boat like a pancake on the griddle. Mac cruised back and forth, then moved the skiff forward gradually, taking his time probing for weak spots in the six-foot wall of oncoming seas.

"Blackstone's my pointer dog," Mac shouted. "I just follow his nose."

The Lab snuffled the air, moving its head back and forth like a compass needle near a magnet. Mac saw what he wanted and hit the throttle. The boat zipped forward like an orange pit squeezed between finger and thumb, climbed a wave, coasted down the other side, bounced over a short stretch of washboard bumps, then broke out past the rolling seas into open water.

"Hell," Mac shouted exultantly, "that wasn't so bad, was it?"

"Can I open my eyes now?"

He goosed the motor and his reply was lost in its whine.

We headed due east into the ocean to get clear of the pull of the surf. Then Mac spun the boat in a right-angle turn and ran south, parallel to the shore. The amber circles from the sodium lights at the Quanset Beach parking lot were visible. We continued south until the beach was dark again. After a few minutes, he slowed the boat and cut the motor back to an idle. The skiff rocked in the waves.

"I'll bet you wouldn't mind telling me what we're looking for."

"You'll see soon enough, if I calculated right. How about having a pop while we wait? There's some beer in that cooler."

He lit a battery-operated camp light so I could see what I was doing. I opened the green plastic thermos cooler, pulled out a couple of cans of Old Milwaukee, and tossed one to Mac.

"Don't you have any Sam Adams? I'd even settle for a Bud."

"Naw. Blackstone likes Ol' Mil'." He poured half the beer into a plastic bucket. Blackstone plunged his broad head in and slurped with noisy gusto. When he was through he looked at me expectantly. His muzzle was white with foam and his teeth were bared ferociously.

"Why does Blackstone look like he wants to eat me?"

"Hell, he can't help it. Got hit by a car when he was a pup and his jaw never set right, so he smiles all the time, especially when he's had too much to drink."

Under that unwavering canine grin, I poured some beer into Blackstone's bucket. Then I sat back and took a sip. Just two guys and a smiling Labrador retriever sippin' beer on the great big Atlantic Ocean.

The air was heavy and smelled of fish and kelp. Long shallow seas rolled under us. A spectral fog hunkered offshore like a shroud. Remembering what Mac had said about Blackstone getting upset just before something had eaten the bait off the jig lines, I kept an eye on the dog.

"This is sort of Zen fishing. A boat, a couple of fishermen, but no lines in the water, no baited hooks. Like the sound of one hand clapping."

"Shit, Soc, that's nothing new. I've been out here plenty of times when it's only been a mind exercise." He burped and wiped his beard with the back of his hand. "So tell me, how'd you ever get into fishing, city boy like you?"

"I could say that I was inspired by reading *Captains Courageous,* but I'd be lying. It was basically a case of burnout. I had a lot of things eating away at my brain. I thought that if I worked my ass off in the fresh air I wouldn't be able to think about something else. I met Sam and I found out I was right. Now I just think how damned hard fishing is."

"Know what you mean." He paused, studying the beach. "My old man was a skiff fisherman. I scalloped with him, went after stripers, raked for quahogs, whatever it took to make a buck. He wanted better for me. Made sure I went to college. He couldn't have been happier when I went to law school. I'm glad he died before I quit law and went back to fishing."

"Why did you leave the law?"

"Hell, Soc. You used to be a cop. You spent time in the courts. You know how tough it is to get a straight answer from anyone, and lawyers are the worst. The law's the law, or it should be, black and white, printed in all those books. But it seemed most of the lawyers I came across were trying to figure out how to get around the law or bend it. I like things clear-cut, the way they are out here. Either you catch a fish or you don't."

Before I had the chance to reply, Mac shooshed me.

"Look toward the beach," he whispered urgently.

I had been sitting with my back to the beach. I turned and saw only shades of darkness.

"What am I looking for?"

"Just hold on. Keep an eye on that area."

Minutes passed. Still nothing. Then a dazzling starburst of cold blue light blossomed on the beach.

"Did you see that?" Mac yelled.

A retinal ghost floated in my vision. "Yeah. What the hell was it?"

"Damned if I know. That's what I saw last night. I was setting off here jigging. Had a few lines in the water. When bam! That thing went off. Like a ray gun. It happened a bunch of times, then nothing. What do you make of it?"

"Looks like one of those laser beams they use for special shows."

"Yeah, that's what I thought. But who'd be shooting a laser off on the beach at night? And what for?"

"I've got another one for you." I pointed behind him. "Who's flashing that light on the water?"

An aureole of blue glowed through the gauzy curtain of fog. Veiled by the mist, and with no reference points to use on open water, it was hard to estimate how far away it was.

"Dunno," he said, "but we're going to find out."

The motor kicked into action, the bow lifted, and the skiff flew out into the fog toward the open ocean. Mac held a steady course. For several minutes there was no flash. Then again. It was the size of a nickel now.

"Ease off and see if we can hear anything," I shouted.

Mac cut the throttle to an idle. From the direction we were heading came the throaty roar of a powerful engine. The other boat headed south with no lights. The noise faded.

"Sounds like a big inboard. We'll never catch him with this putt-putt. What do you want to do?"

"I've got an idea. Let's head back to shore."

Mac swung the skiff around and gunned the motor. We were back at the cut within minutes, and made it through with only a few years scared off my life. We tied up at the dock, secured the boat, got into Mac's four-wheel-drive Ford pickup, and headed toward Quanset Beach.

Fifteen minutes later we pulled up to the Quanset Beach tollbooth. At night the town shuts down the beach buggy station and ORV's check in and out at the tollbooth. The guy on the graveyard shift was watching a rerun of *I Dream of Jeannie* on a small black-and-white TV set. Mac gave him the oversand permit number for his truck and the attendant logged us in.

"Been much traffic on the beach?" I asked.

"Nothing since I came on at midnight." He

glanced at the log. "Not a hell of a lot of action. Couple of guys fishing."

"Just thought we'd cruise down, see how they're doing," Mac said.

"Have a good one," the attendant said, turning his attention back to Barbara Eden. We headed across the deserted parking lot to the beach access road, past the daytime beach buggy check-in station, and drove onto the sand road behind the dunes. Blackstone sat between us.

"You think those lights were surf fishermen?" Mac asked.

"It's possible, but not probable. That was no headlight or flashlight we saw. It was just too bright."

He grunted. "So what was it?"

"That's what I'm hoping we're about to find out."

"Christ, Soc, things are too damn crazy around here," Mac grumbled. "Maybe there's something to that pirate curse. People getting bit to death, corpses washing ashore, me seeing a blob even when I'm sober. Now this. Goddammit, Quanset Beach used to be a nice quiet place except for a booze party now and then."

We turned onto the beach track that goes to the ocean. I asked Mac to douse his headlights. He hit the switch and let his tires follow the ruts. Once on the outer beach, he flipped the lights back on. Only empty sand and tire tracks stretched off into the darkness beyond the range of the beams.

He downshifted and crawled ahead at a few miles per hour. More nothing. Not even greenhead flies to keep us company. I got out and walked along the track, playing a flashlight over the sand. Mac and Blackstone slowly followed. I came upon a set of footprints, then another. They led from the dunes, crossed the track, and went toward the water. There was a line in the sand as if somebody had dragged a stick. The prints stopped and got messy a few yards short of the water. At rough center were three circular holes in the sand.

I backtracked to Mac's truck. Leaving Blackstone on guard duty, we followed the footprints through a cut in the dunes, hooding the flash, then across the beach buggy road. The prints and the furrow led to a white wooden footbridge that spanned a narrow tidal stream.

Mac grabbed my arm. "Looky there, Soc."

A bobbing yellow bull's-eye seemed to rise into the air about two hundred feet ahead. I pictured the terrain in my mind. A steep wooden staircase climbed a hill to the contemporary-style house at the top of the bluff. The Dwight place.

The light disappeared. Mac and I headed back to the truck. He leaned against the front fender and lit up a butt.

"Whaddaya think?" he said at last.

I told him about the British film crew living in the Dwight house.

"Think they made those flashes with their camera stuff? Could be the will-o'-the-wisp we chased was nothing but a strobe going off."

"Could be. But how does that explain the lights out there?" I pointed at the ocean. "More photographers?"

"Got me. What next?"

I listened to the crumple and hiss of the waves as if

there were voices in the surf that could give me an answer. After a minute, I said: "Let's go get a drink."

The bartender at the 'Hole saw Mac and me headed for oblivion and shut us off. He poured black coffee down our throats, gave us plates of chicken fingers to soak up the booze, and when he thought we were fit to drive, kicked us out. Mac and I stood in the parking lot letting our lungs adjust to fresh air.

"When are you going fishing again?" I asked.

"Probably tomorrow. I'll have to work a month to pay the bar bill for tonight."

"*Two* months. Do me a favor. Let me know if you see those lights again. Or anything out of the ordinary."

Mac belched. "Shit, you'll be the first to know. In fact, you'll be the *only* one to know."

"Mac—just some advice. Don't go chasing anything on your own. Whatever was out there didn't want us to get too close."

"Hell, you don't have to worry about *that*. First sign of anything crazy, I head for the hills." He burped again and hitched his pants over his belly.

We shook hands and, pledged to silence, went our separate ways.

Chapter 18

The next morning my head felt as if somebody had squeezed it into a bottle of rubbing alcohol. Spry little men played handball on the inside of my temples. My tongue tasted as if it had been coated with shoe-blacking. Just another tequila sunrise.

I crawled stiffly out of bed, staggered into the kitchen, and boiled up a mug of Stop & Shop instant coffee. Kojak followed me from the bedroom sleepy-eyed. He looked as if he had a bad hangover. I've heard people can come to resemble their pets, but I didn't think it worked the other way. I gave him some milk and he perked up.

After another cup, I began to formulate a plan for the day. The sea adventure with Mac last night was an interesting, and puzzling, episode, but answers would have to wait. I had told Tillie Talbot I would try to help her. I showered, shaved, put on jeans, T-shirt, sneakers, and ball cap and looked in the mirror at the dark smears under my pink eyes. It had been my idea to do shots of Cuervo. Smart guy, Socarides. I covered up the reminders of my dissipation with a pair of Ray-Bans and ventured outside.

In town, I bought a bouquet of the yellow and white mums that were on sale at Miss Dooley's florist shop. Minutes later, I parked in front of Town Hall and went into the assessors' office. Martha Snow was sitting at an IBM word processor.

"Good morning," I said. "Special delivery for Ms. Snow?"

Martha has a square, plump face and unflattering thick glasses. But her smile would register on a light meter.

"My goodness, you *didn't* leave town."

I stepped into the office. "Who says I did?"

"I just assumed you had because I hadn't seen you in the usual places like the laundromat or the ice cream shop."

"I keep a low profile when the summer folk are abroad in the land. Got a vase for these posies?"

She took the flowers and went into the bathroom. She emerged a minute later with the mums stuck in a bottle-green glass vase.

"They're beautiful," she said, and came over to the counter. "Thank you very much. But I'll bet you didn't drop by just to deliver flowers."

"You win. I'm interested in Fred Costello."

Her small eyes widened behind the Coke bottle glass. "Fast Freddy?"

"One and the same. I was wondering what property he owns in town. Also interested in the names of his partners."

Martha Snow is the assistant assessor, but she runs the office. All land transactions cross her desk and she has a near photographic memory. Martha's a walking encyclopedia of every square inch of property in this town. She went over to a wooden box on her desk, brought it back to the counter, and opened it. Inside were dozens of five-by-seven index cards.

"Everything is logged onto the computer, but this is *my* system. I keep a tickle file of my own on property people ask about a lot."

"Who else has been asking about Freddy?"

"No one recently. But the state police or federal government people used to come by a few times a month to check out his holdings." She withdrew a handful of cards. "These are all companies Fred is involved in directly or indirectly. You can sit at my desk. I've got to do some filing."

I spread the cards out on the green blotter. Eighteen properties were listed. They were owned by three companies set up as trusts, with Freddie as the trustee.

"Fred's the only one named here," I told Martha. "Do you have any stuff on the corporate officers?"

"Nope. That's all the information we have in this office. You might be able to get more from the secretary of state."

I jotted the names of the properties and trusts in a

notepad. When I had finished that, I went through the oversized assessors' books on the counter. With Martha's help, I tracked down each piece of property so I could see it on the assessors' maps. Most were subdivisions. A couple of house lots were listed within the town limits, as well as some commercial stuff like mini-malls, office buildings, and a restaurant.

I found the map of Tillie's camp and checked the surrounding properties to see if Freddie or his corporate trusts controlled land nearby. No dice. The adjacent land was owned by the town or by the Commonwealth of Massachusetts. Some of it was unbuildable wetlands that had been placed in conservation trusts.

I stared into space, thinking. Martha came over.

"Any surprises in there?"

"I didn't realize Freddy or his trusts owned so much. Nothing on any possible partners. Any scuttlebutt around Town Hall?"

"Oh, there's lots of that."

"Would Mr. Olney's name be bandied about?"

"The lieutenant governor? Oh sure, that's old stuff, Soc."

"What's new stuff, then?"

Grinning, she said, "One of our selectman is in bed with Mr. Costello. I can't tell you his name, but he's got white hair and a big red nose."

"Interesting, but not surprising. Anybody else?"

"God, Soc, isn't that enough?"

"Another question. Any gossip on Tillie Talbot's property? Anything beyond the usual real estate shop talk?"

"It's been pretty quiet. Every real estate person in town was drooling at the mouth over it. I guess interest has dropped off because of the market, but it'll start again. It's a beautiful piece. Don't tell me Tillie is actually thinking of selling?"

"Not as long as she can hold onto it."

Martha sighed. "I'm glad to hear that. It would be a shame to see that land get split up for houses. I know the town conservation commission would love to acquire it for open space."

"Why don't they?"

"The town doesn't have the money. The chairman of selectmen says the Town Meeting voters would blow any land acquisition request out of the water. Unfortunately, he's probably right. This town has a tight pocketbook right now."

I shut the assessors' book and pointed to a phone. "Can I use that? It's a Boston call."

"Go ahead. You're a taxpayer in good standing. It's a WATS line. Use the one in my office."

I went into the cubicle and dialed a number in Boston.

"Beacon Research. Norma speaking."

"Hi, Norma, it's your favorite Greek gumshoe. How are you and Max?"

"Soc! How nice to hear from you. Max and I are fine, except that we're both on Slimfast diets and it's sheer agony. Business is booming, though. Lots of government work. Mostly savings and loan associations, trying to track down assets. You wouldn't believe some of these people, Soc. They've stashed away *millions*."

"Norma, I know you're busy, but could you do a rush job for me? No heavy lifting. I need a trace on some corporations. I'm looking for names, particularly connections to well-placed politicians, past or present."

Norma was a computer whiz and her husband Max was a CPA. What they call a "forensic accountant" these days. I met them when I was doing white-collar crime in my Boston PD days. They were free-lance insurance investigators. The old cop techniques like pounding on doors and flashing a badge rarely work when you're following a paper trail. They *never* work when computers are involved. Beacon Research has flourished, thanks to an avalanche of bank failures, bankruptcies, and financial scandals.

I rattled off the list of the Costello-affiliated trusts, Costellos' address, the make of his car, and his license plate number. Then I told her what I knew about Olney.

"This shouldn't be too hard, Soc. Give me an hour and I can tell you a person's salary, the money in his bank account, his credit card bills, where he shops, what he eats, whether it's been giving him an ulcer, and what kind of medicine the doctor's prescribed. I'll try to get something out to you before I faint from starvation."

"For Godsakes Norma, how long have you and Max been dieting?"

"About an hour and forty-one minutes by my clock. I know that doesn't sound like very much, but it's been a hellish eternity. Ummm. Is that the smell of fried Cape Cod clams coming through the telephone line? And baked stuffed lobster. And onion rings. And . . ."

"Bye, Norma. Talk to you tomorrow."

". . . quahog chowder. And . . ."

I hung up. Just listening to Norma could add inches to your waistline. I went out into the assessors' office.

"Thanks for the help, Martha."

"Anytime, Soc." She sighed heavily. "Dear me. I don't know what's happening to this town."

"Don't worry too much about it. You'll find characters like Fast Freddy and his friends any place you go."

"Oh, I didn't mean that. Barbara from the tax collector's office came in while you were on the phone. She said she heard from her husband who's on the police department that more bodies have come ashore at Quanset Beach."

Chapter 19

Rollins saw my truck fly into the Quanset Beach parking lot. He detached himself from the gaggle of people milling around in front of the administration building and trotted over, camera and notebook in hand.

"You heard?"

"I heard," I replied.

Gary and Charlie Nevers were headed toward the red beach-patrol truck. Gary looked grim. Charlie looked plain unhappy. Seeing us, Gary gestured to the back of the truck. We climbed aboard, and the truck jogged onto the now-familiar sand road. There was a rescue squad ambulance and a police cruiser near the beach buggy check-in station. Gary drove by without stopping.

About an eighth of a mile south of where the first body was discovered, we pulled up next to a blue park-department pickup. Four men stood around looking at something on the sand. One was Eddy, the park commissioner. The others were two EMT's and a cop.

Eddy eyed me with curiosity then glanced balefully at Rollins.

"Well, well, the press is here. Guess you'll want a few pictures of these folks."

He pulled back the unzipped covers of the body bags. It was a cruel move, motivated by a combination of frustration and natural meanness. The overpowering smell of the sea and decay washed out. Eddy's head jerked as if slapped by an invisible hand, and he took a step back. Charlie Nevers's face went ashen. This was an encore for him and he didn't like it any better than the first time.

In death, the bodies were practically twins, laughing at the world with identical gaping mouths and swollen black tongues. One body had only shreds of clothing, the other still wore part of a shirt. The shirt was frayed and ripped, but the left sleeve had somehow remained intact, protecting the arm so that the skin was paler in its greenish marbling than the exposed parts. There was a faint mark on the forearm. I looked closer. It was a stylized flying fish. Below it was a word. *THIRA*.

Eddy tried to reassert his authority. His voice had gravel in it, as if his salivary glands were working overtime.

"Okay, that's enough looking. Let's get these guys to the M.E."

He let the EMT's zip the bags. Eddy didn't want overripe hitchhikers smelling up his truck, so we loaded them in the red pickup. Rollins and Charlie rode in front. I said I didn't mind riding in back.

Back at the parking lot, Rollins got on his Kawasaki. As he roared off, he shouted over his shoulder to keep in touch.

I needed to clear my lungs of the smell of death. At the 'Hole, I sucked in a deep breath of yeasty air, stale cigarette smoke, and Pine Sol disinfectant. On summer days the bar is deserted except for a few hard-core toss-pots who wouldn't know the sun was out if it fell on them. I took a stool far away from a resident lush who had stopped by for a matinee. I had five minutes before he slid down to my end and started talking to me about drywall. The Bud draft tasted good. I ordered another.

THIRA.

I knew of only one place by that name. It wasn't much to go on, but it was something. A nugget of information. A seed. How to go about planting it? The bodies were linked to the shipwreck Flagg wanted me to dive on. I was sure of it. Where the hell was that damn spook? He had given me a phone number to call if I needed him. I went to a pay phone and dialed. I got an answering service. I said I wanted to speak to Flagg. The woman on the phone said she would relay my message and have him call me. I gave her the number of the 'Hole.

On the other side of the paper with Flagg's information was the code number from the telephone answering machine at Alex's house. I stared at it a few seconds then dialed Alex's phone. A recorded voice came on. It was Alex's friend, T.J. Talking in his polished, prep school, nice-boy manner, he asked me to leave a message. I punched out the retrieval code. There were a few boops and beeps, then the machine played back three calls. One was a hang-up. The other was a woman calling for T.J. The third was the most interesting.

A rough male voice simply said, "Tomorrow night. It's a go. Same as before."

I hung up and pondered the message. Taking a not-very-wild guess, I figured the guy who met Alex and his friends outside the sports bar the other night was arranging a score. For a brief moment, I considered brother George's advice. Let Alex twist in the wind. But the feeling of family responsibility sat on my chest like a concrete block. My thoughts flicked back to the *Gazette.* Maybe there *was* a pirate curse. Rollins's suspicions that the story was a phony raised a lot of questions. Particularly about the role of his boss, Wes Thacher.

The story came from Huggins. Town historians are a funny breed. I've seen them almost come to blows over some minor historic footnote. Did Chastity or Patience marry the Reverend Enoch Snow back in seventeen ought-six? Or was that ought-seven? Town historian is a nonofficial position. All you have to do is outlive the other self-appointed historians who might contradict you and the newspapers start adding the title to your name.

I dialed the number of a friendly real estate broker. I asked him if he knew of any antique Cape Cod houses on the market. He had one in the Multiple Listing Service. The old Basset place on Cranberry Lane was a nice half-Cape built around 1790. Did I know somebody who might be interested? I said I'd let him know.

Huggins lived in the east side of town off the Quanset Beach road in a low-slung Cape Cod cottage that looked as if the carpenters had pounded in the last nails and painted the white trim only hours before I drove up. The hand-carved quarterboard over the lintel had the date 1787 on it.

I went up the flagstone walk and rang the bell. Big Ben chimes echoed inside. The door was answered by a Hobbit. He had pointed ears and a fringe of red hair around his bald freckled head. His white polo shirt bulged out over a small potbelly and baggy tan shorts. He inspected me through square Ben Franklin bifocals.

"Mr. Huggins?" I asked. He nodded. I gave him my name and said, "I'm thinking about buying an old house on Cranberry Lane. The real estate office says the place was built in the seventeen hundreds. I was wondering if it was true. A few people suggested that if anyone in town knew, it would be you."

He preened. "Cranberry Lane? You must mean the Basset place."

"That's right."

"How old they say it was?"

"Seventeen ninety."

He chortled. "Way off the mark. C'mon in, I'll give you the real date."

The door opened into a tiny hallway with a near vertical set of stairs rising to the second floor. We went into the room on the right, traditionally the parlor in a Cape Cod house, now a study. The room had wide floorboards and tulip borders hand-stenciled on the walls. Over the shallow fireplace was a large sepia photograph of the treeless Cape Cod of a hundred years ago. Most of the room was taken up by bookshelves. More books were piled on the floor and on an old oak desk. The odor of old paper was pervasive.

Huggins got behind his desk and indicated a chair. I sat. He plucked a gilt-edged volume from a pile, and opened the book to a photograph of a house with two windows to the right of the front door.

"Here's a half-Cape just like the Basset house."

"That looks like it all right."

Huggins grunted with satisfaction. "This one's over in Brewster. See, there's a space between the top of the windows and the edge of the roof. It's got a skinny chimney. That means it was probably built after 1830. That's when the traditional style broke and people started fooling around with different designs. Up to then there was only one design for a Cape Cod house." He flipped to another page. "Here's an older house. Windows directly under the eaves. Big fat chimney anchoring the house solidly to the ground." He shut the book. "My guess is the Basset house was built in 1832."

"Amazing," I gushed. "You can tell all that from the design?"

His small mouth widened in a smug grin. "Damned right I can. But in this case, I know I'm right because it says so in the town history. Third book from the right up there on the top shelf. I know it by heart."

"So the real estate office was taking liberties with the facts?"

"Yes and no. I've been in the Basset house. The old post-and-beam timbers in the attic are older than the walls and roof. There was a place there before, maybe built in the seventeen hundreds, that was torn down. Some of the lumber was used to build the newer house."

"I never realized you can play with historical accuracy that way. . . ."

"You can't," he said firmly. "You can fool around with dates, but a historical fact is a fact. History is the most precise of endeavors. When something happened, it *happened,* you can't change that. People can get names wrong or dates wrong, but that doesn't change the facts."

"So you're saying that human beings are the recorders of history, and human beings are fallible."

"Unfortunately, yes. If somebody gets the fact wrong first time around, it comes down through the centuries as gospel. The only way to be sure is to verify with other sources."

"Is that what you did with the story of the pirate curse?"

The corners of his mouth drooped. He eyed me warily. "What do you mean?"

"I saw your name in the *Gazette.* I wondered if you had to do a lot of digging to verify the story in that case?"

Huggins studied me for a moment, then decided it was a fair question. He pulled a folder out of a desk drawer, opened it, and slid over a packet of papers stapled at one corner. They were photocopies of what looked like old printing.

"You remember Cotton Mather?"

"He liked to burn witches up in Salem."

Huggins snorted. "Wrong. Hanged them and pressed them to death, but never burned them. He apologized later."

"That was swell of him."

"Mather was an old hypocrite, no argument there. He went from witches to pirates. Decided they needed their souls saved. That stuff you're looking at is a copy of a tract Mather had printed. He interviewed the Quanset pirates in their cells, hounded them all the way to the gallows with his damn preaching, and described their execution in this pamphlet as a warning to all who might follow in their path. Probably picked up some pin money for it. The transcripts of the trials are there, too. The government appointed an attorney for the pirates. Pretty sharp guy, I'd venture. He tried to get the case thrown out of the Admiralty court. Claimed that since the English sovereign who instituted the piracy laws was dead, the court no longer had jurisdiction. The court didn't agree. They put the pirates on trial, found them guilty, and sentenced them to hang."

"Is that the record shown with the newspaper article?"

He nodded.

"So Jack Graff's curse was contained in those documents?"

Huggins tugged nervously at his right ear lobe. "Not exactly. These are the supplementary sources. They show the pirates were captured, tried, and so on."

"Then the curse was in another document?"

"In a manner of speaking."

I shook my head. When he realized I wasn't going anywhere until he gave me an answer, Huggins said, "The original document was destroyed. What I had were typewritten transcripts copied from a handwritten account of the original document. Basically, it's oral history."

"How can you be sure that it's authentic, without the original document?"

His eyes hardened and his small mouth clamped shut in a stubborn pucker. But it was just an instant before the laugh crinkles came back and the wry smile reappeared. "You sure ask a lot of questions, young man."

Huggins clearly didn't want to talk about pirates any more.

I gave him my most innocent smile. "Sorry to be so inquisitive. It's just so darned fascinating."

He relaxed. "That's the truth. Anything more I can tell you about the Basset house?"

"No," I said, rising. "Thanks, you've been very helpful. I'll take another look at it. I've always wanted to own an old Cape. It really doesn't make any difference if it's seventeenth or eighteenth century as long as I like it."

"That's the spirit," he said, getting from behind his desk. "We need more people who think like you, who appreciate Cape Cod for its sense of history." He was ushering me to the door as he talked. I thanked him again and said good-bye.

I stopped at a seafood shack and had a clam roll,

thinking about Huggins. First he said how important it is to be absolutely accurate in recounting history. Then he admitted the pirate story was based on a typewritten transcript, something anyone with an Underwood and an imagination could have written. He was obviously a guy who savored names and dates the way some men are addicted to food and booze. It didn't figure.

I washed down the last of the clams with Coke and found a pay phone. Alex was home. I said I wanted to come by for a visit. He said no problem. He didn't sound too enthusiastic about it. But as Rhett said to Scarlett, frankly, I didn't give a damn.

The blond kid who answered the door at Alex's house had a face I had seen before. And it wasn't smiling.

Alex edged in beside his buddy. "Soc. C'mon in. This is Steve, a friend of mine."

I stuck out my hand. Steve took it as if I had just handed him a fillet of raw fish and let go immediately. Then he disappeared inside.

I stayed on the doorstep. "Let's take a walk around the neighborhood. I need the exercise."

Alex shrugged. "Sure, Soc."

We walked down the drive to the street. I ran my hand over the glossy fender of a red Corvette. "These Steve's wheels?"

"Yeah. It's a beauty, isn't it?"

"How'd you meet Steve, T.J., and the other guys?"

"School. T.J.'s dad is in Ford and Toyota dealerships. Steve's father was lieutenant governor." Of course, Olney's kid, the sullen James Dean look-alike I'd met at Costello's party.

"What about Chili and Tanya? They don't look like the prep school type."

"They're from Jamaica Plain."

I remembered Jamaica Plain from my cop days. JP was an old residential neighborhood that was going rotten. Now parts of it were like Punk City.

"You're in pretty upscale company," I said.

Alex didn't catch the sardonic undertone. He beamed. "Yeah, they're good people."

I let that slide. "Speaking of good people, have you heard from your folks?"

A cloud crossed his face. "Not recently."

"What's the deal with you and them?"

"Huh?"

"I'd guess you were having problems. I wondered why."

"*They're* the ones with the problems. You know them, high achievers. They think everyone is a brain like them."

"They've done a lot for you," I said. It was the wrong thing to say.

Alex stopped short. "Your parents gave *you* everything, too. I used to hear my mother talk about how you were a big disappointment to them."

"Then you know where I'm coming from."

His eyes narrowed. I could feel the heat coming off his angry face. "I don't see you in any big hurry to move to Lowell and work in the bakery."

"You're absolutely right, Alex, I have no intention of moving back with the family."

"Okay, so you've done your own thing. Now let me do mine."

I grabbed him by the arm. I may have squeezed too hard because he looked scared. Alex was irritating me and I didn't care if he knew it. "I've done some dumb things that hurt my family, but nothing that would get me thrown in jail."

His eyes grew wider. "I don't know what you're talking about."

"You know damned well what I mean."

He jerked his arm away and started back to the house. "I don't have to listen to you. You're not my fucking boss."

"Alex," I yelled after him, "you're in way over your head."

He turned around and flipped me the bird. Little bastard. I almost went for him. Maybe I *should* let him sink. I only held the thought for a second. For all their faults, his parents were nice people who didn't deserve the shame and trouble of having their kid up on heavy drug charges. I wouldn't be able to face my mother in a million years if I let Alex slide into the pit without a fight.

But I didn't have a clue how to reach him, and the more I tried, the worse it got.

Chapter 20

The young wood gods and goddesses who in-
habitedthe Quanset Beach Sailing Camp had gone to
earth.The camp was virtually deserted except for Leon,
the cook. He was sweeping the mess hall at the main
lodge.

"Where is everybody?" I asked.

"Mrs. T's in town." He put the broom aside.
"Batch are down-Cape on a field trip. Rest of the camp's
out for an afternoon sail. They should be coming in
pretty soon. It's almost supper time. God, you should see
the way these kids eat. They inhale the stuff off their
plates."

"Obviously your good cooking."

He grinned and wiped his hands on his apron. "It's
better than what you get in half the restaurants around

here, that's for sure. I should know. I've worked in enough of them."

He waddled back into the kitchen. I left the lodge and followed a path to the bluff Tillie had taken me to on my first visit. I settled into a rough-hewn bench near the narrow wooden stairway that ran down the side of the cliff. My eyes did a panoramic sweep, settling on the contemporary architecture of the Dwight house about a half mile distant on an adjoining bluff.

Flagg gave me some advice a long time ago.

The trouble with you white men is you try to think things out instead of feeling them.

Sometimes you just got to sit back, let your mind catch a passing hawk, let it float on the wind, round and round. That bird, he can see and hear things no one else can . . . mouse rustling in the sawgrass two hundred feet away. . . .

A marsh hawk was circling over the river. I projected myself into its head, looking down at the earth through its sharp eyes. I was a dark, doomful shadow gliding above the velvety grass like a death spirit. Out over the cove and the beach, hovering, then balancing on an updraft, my wings trembling, a hunger for blood gnawing at my stomach. I cruised over the Dwight house, moving closer to its cantilevered levels and shed roofs. Below me were two figures. . . .

Closer, a voice was saying, *fold your wings—*

"Soc, are you all right?"

I jumped a foot off the bench. Tillie Talbot stood on the path looking at me.

"I saw you sitting here. You seemed so still—is something wrong?"

"No, nothing wrong. It's easy to get lost in thought, the view is so beautiful."

She glanced out over the cove. "It is, isn't it? If I came here a thousand times more, I'd still be astounded. It changes from hour to hour. The angle of the light, the tides and currents . . . Sometimes I think it must be the loveliest place on earth." She grinned at her hyperbole. "But I'm prejudiced, aren't I? I just got back from doing some errands in town. The weather was so nice today we sent half the camp out sailing."

She lifted the binoculars around her neck to her eyes. "Hmmm. Looks like the regatta is heading home. They should be back shortly. Well, my friend, tell me, have you made any headway with this impossible job I've asked you to do?"

"Some. It's a little like getting the knots out of a line that's been improperly tied. Have a seat and I'll tell you what I've got."

She settled onto the bench beside me and I told her about my visit with Costello, his party, my stop at Town Hall, the trace I put through Beacon Research.

Tillie listened quietly, absorbing every detail, then cut right to the nub. "If I understand what you're saying, Mr. Costello has business dealings with the lieutenant governor and the chairman of selectmen. That could explain all the harrassment I've been getting."

"It could, but it's only surmise at this point. I want to know who else might be interested in this land. And why now, when the real estate market is so soft."

"Well, if they don't want it for houses, they must want it for something else."

It was a simple conclusion, so simple I wondered

why I hadn't thought of it. "You're absolutely right. But what?"

She looked through her binocs again. "I'm afraid I'll have to leave you to your own devices. The shrimp boats are a-coming and cook has promised them burgers and fries. You have an open invitation to join us."

"Tell you what: I'll take you up on your offer when this case is over."

"Then it will be soon, I hope, Soc."

"Soon, Tillie."

"Those are the boats my husband designed. Aren't they pretty?"

She handed me the binoculars. I focused on the sailing fleet. There were ten of them, two kids in each boat. They moved across the cove like blasé swans, the afternoon sun reflecting off their sails.

The quickest course to the pier was a straight line, but they couldn't sail directly into the light southwest breeze, so they were tacking back and forth across it. They had the choice of making several short legs or a couple of long ones. They must have been tired from sailing, because they took the long one, following a heading that took them just south of the cut in the beach. A few hundred feet from the back side of the beach, the ten boats came about nicely, and pointed their bows across the cove on a line that should take them right to the dock.

I started to lower the glasses. Something caught my eye. A flicker of white, just behind the boats, moving over the water from the direction of the inlet. I raised the lenses again and adjusted the focus knob.

Birds.

A thick flock of them. Seabirds. Terns, maybe. Or gulls. It was hard to tell. Dozens, wheeling and dipping, skimming to within inches of the water.

Pictures flashed through my mind. Gary cutting through the waves toward a pale face bobbing in the dark sea, while around them whirled a feathery tornado.

Jeezus!

My feet were a step ahead of my brain. I sprinted for the stairway. Behind me, Tillie Talbot called, "Soc, what's wrong?" I didn't stop to answer. I half fell down the steep set of stairs, hit the beach, ran across the soft sand, and pounded along the boards to the end of the dock.

The sailing fleet was about a hundred yards away. The kids were racing to be the first to tie up and get to the mess hall. Their smiles were bright against their tanned faces. They saw me and waved.

They were headed toward a small fleet of skiffs moored fifty feet or so from the dock. Snagging a sailboat mooring requires good timing. You maintain just enough speed to come up on the mooring float, point the boat into the wind to slow you down, then lean over, grab the line, and cleat the loop. Done properly, it's a beautiful maneuver. Miss the mooring, and you have to keep going and make another pass.

The kids weren't doing too badly. Some fetched their moorings on the first try. Others missed, but trimmed sail to catch the wind and glide back into the cove.

One boy miscalculated the distance and speed. He reached out for his mooring. He got his fingers around the line, but the boat was moving too fast. He should have let go and made another pass. But he held onto the line. Always a mistake. The space between boat and mooring widened. He found himself stretched between the sailboat and the marker.

The inevitable happened. He splashed face-first into the water. He was wearing his flotation vest, and bobbed up laughing a second later. The young girl at the boat's tiller neatly hauled in the mainsheet to catch the wind. The sailboat swung out into the cove. The boy breast-stroked his way toward the pier.

I slid into a fiberglass pram tied up at the pier, stuck the oars in the oarlocks, uncleated the line, and pulled mightily. I was going against the current. After a couple of yards, the oars slipped out of the locks and I drifted back. I was rowing too wildly. I cursed, got the oars back in place, and started rowing again. Still strongly, but with more control. I steered around some anchored prams. Each time I had to regain lost headway. The boy was pushed along by the current and the distance between us narrowed to about thirty feet. I kept glancing over my shoulder to keep him in sight.

The birds moved away. I breathed a sigh of relief. It was short-lived. The flock swung around in an arc that took them right behind the swimming youngster.

Underneath the darting and swooping birds, the water bubbled and roiled.

There was a rank fishy smell in the air.

I recognized the boy's face. It was the Mickey Rooney look-alike, the camper I taught to tie a bowline.

I rowed frantically.

We drew closer.

The patch of boiling water was now a few feet behind him. The birds made a deafening racket.

Yards separated us. I pulled hard on the oars to maintain momentum, shipped them briskly, then reached over. I grabbed his life jacket, pulled him closer. Then tried to get my hands under his armpits.

He wasn't heavy, but the pram rocked dangerously with the sudden shift in weight. I sat back so we wouldn't capsize. The boy slipped out of my grasp.

I tried again. My fingers dug into the spongy fabric of the life jacket.

I pulled him toward me, lifted him clear of the water, hauled him into the pram, and held him tightly to my chest.

Birds swirled around us in a feathery squall. The water churned and boiled. Something was driving baitfish to the surface and the birds were going crazy with excitement.

I shouted madly, as if I could drive them away by sheer lung-power.

They dove all around us. We were at the bottom of a white feathery funnel. The birds shrieked madly. The noise echoed inside my skull.

The water went flat.

The birds moved off.

Their diminishing cries mingled with the shouts of children. Hulls thudded against each other in the bedlam caused by the sailboats all trying to swing into the wind and tie up.

The boy in the pram grinned and stuck a dripping length of line with a knot tied in it under my nose.

"Look," he announced. "I tied it with my eyes closed. It's the best bowline ever."

My heart clanged madly in my chest. I gulped hungry lungfuls of air.

I took the line. My fingers were trembling. It was a lousy knot. It wasn't even a bowline. Somehow he had tied a half-hitch, and hadn't done a bad job of it.

"Isn't it totally awesome?" he said proudly.

I patted his damp hair. "So it is, buddy," I said. "So it is."

Ten minutes later Tillie Talbot sat in her office and listened calmly as I explained about the birds flocking before the Quanset Beach attacks and pleaded with her to keep the campers away from the water. She refilled my iced tea glass and gazed at me with a grave expression in her gray eyes. "It's not unusual for seabirds to flock around boats, Soc. They can't always discriminate between a fishing boat that leaves them scraps and a group of children out for a sail."

I took a sip of tea and let the cool liquid trickle down my throat. "You're right, Tillie. I've seen it happen a hundred times before. But I had a bad feeling about this. I still do."

Tillie spread her hands. "I can sympathize with that, but what you're asking me to do, stop the sailing program, is tantamount to closing my camp. Water activities are the foundation of this camp. Without them, we might just as well be in the desert. It would do more harm than all of the inspections put together."

"How about this? Keep the kids upriver as much as

possible, away from where the inlet opens to the ocean. Have your counselors watch for birds flocking when there's no apparent reason."

"I think I can do that." She looked over at the pictures of her husband hanging on the wall. A sad smile crossed her face. "Remember what I told you before, Soc. Beware of deathbed promises."

Kojak was overjoyed to see me. He danced around my ankles until I fed him, then promptly forgot me. I grabbed a Bud out of the fridge and I sat on the deck watching a blue heron as tall as a child root in the cord grass about fifty yards away. My pulse was still pounding from the sailing camp incident.

I didn't have a chance to think about it. The phone was ringing inside the boathouse.

It was Flagg. "Heard you've been looking for me," he said.

"I was wondering what was happening with that job we talked about."

"Sorry about that. There have been some promising developments. I can come by to talk to you about them. You going to be home later tonight, around eleven maybe?"

"I'll make a point of it."

"Good. See you then."

Until a few days ago, Quanset Beach was a quiet little place where people went for relaxation, sun and sea. Then came the attacks, the mysterious lights, and the bodies. My gut told me they were all related. Flagg would have to make the connections.

Eleven o'clock. That gave me time to snoop around on my own.

I went inside, called Gary, and asked if I could borrow his Jeep tonight. No problem. He'd leave the keys under the front right wheel and take a town truck home.

I had plenty of time. I sat at the kitchen table with a notebook. I wrote out the word tattoed on the most recent floater's arm. *THIRA.* I looked at it and thought about Santorini, a black-lava Aegean island that looks like the devil's playground. Thira, or Thera as it's sometimes spelled, is the island's capital. It's a whitewashed town perched high on a cliff above the caldera left when a volcano blew its stack five thousand years ago. A few years ago I stopped there on a trip through Greece. The wine was good.

I picked up the phone and dialed overseas information. A few minutes later, I was talking to a sonorous voice at the American consulate in Athens. I identified myself as Sergeant Neal with the Boston PD, explained it was an emergency and I was trying to reach the police station on Santorini. Could I get the number? No problem. Call back in twenty minutes.

It was a long shot, but Santorini was a small place.

Twenty minutes later to the second, I called the consulate again and got the number.

I dialed what seemed like a couple of hundred digits.

"Ebros," a man said. *"Astinomiko,"* which is Greek for police.

"Kalispera." Good afternoon. I repeated the Sergeant Neal story, told him a sailor's body had come ashore, and

said I had reason to believe the dead man might be from Thira. My Greek was rusty, but I got the point across.

The cop's name was Sergeant Demos. "I speak a little English. You know my cousin in Queens?" he demanded. "He drives a taxi."

"Is his name George?" Half the men in Greece are named George.

"Yes, yes, do you know him?"

"I think I bumped into him the other day. Nice fellow." Sergeant Demos and I were buddy-buddy after that.

"What was the sailor's name?" the sergeant said. The chief was out, which clearly delighted him, because he could boast around town that he handled a big police case from America.

"That's the problem. I don't know. He had no identification. Only the word Thira tattooed on his arm."

"Please wait." Minutes passed. Voices mumbled in the background. Demos came back on. "We have," he said carefully, "no information on no missing sailor."

I translated that and thanked him. It wasn't the answer I wanted to hear, but I made one last try. "Is there anyone else on your island who might have information about such a man?"

More mumbled voices. "Yes, wait. Ring Father Peter. He maybe knows something."

I thanked him, promised to drop by the next time I was in town, said I'd say hello to his cousin George, and dialed the number he'd given me. The international lines were busy. I got through after about fifteen minutes. A woman answered the phone. Father Peter's housekeeper. My Greek skills got another workout. A mellow-voiced man came on. I asked if he spoke English. He said he did.

"Good, my Greek is a little rough."

"Not at all. You have a very nice accent."

"So do you. Sounds American."

"It should. I had a parish outside of Cleveland for a few years. I came back to Santorini after my wife died." Unlike Roman Catholic priests, Greek Orthodox Fathers are allowed to marry.

"So you're a native of the island."

"Born and bred."

I told Father Peter the story I gave Sergeant Demos. When I was done, he murmured, "Ah, poor Helen."

"Pardon me, Father?"

"Helen Zervas. One of my parishioners. A lovely lady. Her husband George is a ship captain. He should have been home by now. She hasn't heard from him in days. He was quite faithful about phoning. She's terribly worried. He has two children and always tried to keep in touch, no matter where he was. She has no faith in the police and came to me."

"Do you know the name of the ship he last worked on?"

"That's the problem, you see. Captain Zervas worked on many ships. It's my understanding that most of his runs were relatively short. The last his wife knew was that he was in the States."

"Did she mention a port of call?"

"He telephoned her from New Orleans and said he'd contact her within several days to talk about when he'd be home. That's all I know."

"Thank you, Father. You've been very helpful. One

other thing. Did Captain Zervas have a tattoo on his arm?"

"Why, I don't know. Hold on please, I'll speak to my housekeeper. She's lived on the island all her life and knows everything about everyone."

A minute later Father Peter was back on the phone.

"This tattoo. Is it a fish and the word Thira?"

"Yes, Father."

"Then I'm afraid I'm going to have very bad news for Helen," he said sadly. "My housekeeper remembers seeing this tattoo on Captain Zervas's arm. This is going to be so hard on Helen and the children. Her husband was a fine man."

"I'm very sorry about this, Father."

"Thank you, my son."

I suggested that the priest have the Greek consulate in Boston get in touch with the Coast Guard. I hung up and looked at the word *New Orleans* circled on my notepad. Then I called Louisiana information. I asked for the office of the New Orleans harbor pilot. Every big ship leaving a major harbor must have a pilot on board.

A few minutes later I was talking to a man named Dubois.

I told him a variation of my early story, that I was trying to track down a ship's officer in an emergency, and I gave him Zervas's name.

"Hell, yeah, I remember him," he drawled. "Nice fella, seemed to know his business. I wondered what he was doing on an old rust-bucket like that. Nothin' you'd ever want to set foot on. I couldn't wait to get off her."

"What was the ship's name?"

"*Pandora.* Tramp steamer, must be fifty years old, and looks every minute of it. South American crew. Bound for Boston couple of weeks ago with a load of fertilizer."

Boston. That would take her off Cape Cod. It fit. I thanked him and called MassPort. No ship named *Pandora* had arrived in Boston Harbor.

My ear was sore from so much time spent on the phone. I looked down at my notepad. Captain George Zervas of the good ship *Pandora* had left New Orleans for Boston and never arrived.

The ship could have changed course. Or it could have sunk. When a ship sinks, people usually *know* about it. Or somebody picks up a distress signal. A ship doesn't just vanish into thin air. The vessel's owner, the people shipping the cargo, *some*body has got to be concerned enough to start asking questions.

Unless, of course, they didn't want anybody to know about it.

The combination of beer and brainwork made me sleepy. I went into the bedroom, pushed Kojak aside, and lay belly-down on the sheets. The breeze blowing through the window cooled my face. I was only going to rest for a few minutes. The sunlight faded. I dozed off. The doze became sleep. I dreamed of many things.

I awoke in a panic, completely disoriented. It was black outside my window. Had I slept through the night? Was it another day? I rolled over and looked at my alarm clock. It was nine o'clock.

Somebody had replaced my head with a cannonball and my mouth tasted sourly of beer. I climbed groggily out of bed, showered my sweaty body, and pulled on fresh clothes. I rinsed my mouth with Kool-Aid and went out to the truck.

The night air brushed the cobwebs out of my eyes. I drove to Quanset Beach. Gary had left his Jeep in the parking lot as promised. Minutes later I was bouncing down the beach road. I pulled over at a wide place and switched the lights off. Then I waited. There was no reflected glow from other buggies in the starlit sky.

I grabbed a flashlight from the glove compartment, and started walking. The track loomed silver-gray against the beach grass on either side, and I could follow it without a light. The dunes have been chewed away by wind and waves, and a concave banking, varying from five to eight feet high, ran along the length of the beach. I headed south, keeping within a few feet of the sandy wall on my right.

The banking ended at the break in the dunes where Mac and I had followed footprints. I sat on a driftwood log that looked like a sleeping alligator and listened to the low roar of the sea.

The glowing dial of my Swatch showed fifteen minutes had passed. Then a half hour. Then an hour and fifteen. Down the beach the headlights from a fisherman's beach buggy flickered. Other than that, dullsville. I decided to stick it out for two hours.

I didn't have to. Someone was talking, seemingly an arm's length away.

I rolled off the log and threw myself face-down in the cold sand. I recognized Nigel's cultured English accent. The other voice was more guttural.

Two figures emerged from the dunes and moved toward the ocean. I scrambled to my feet and followed them to mid-beach. I slid down on my belly again.

A light clicked on and went off. There was more talk, lost in the growl of the surf. Then a blue flash dazzled the night. After a few minutes it blazed again. A cold eye winked in answer from the sea.

I crawled back up the beach. Far enough away to feel safe, I bent over in a crouch until I reached the opening in the dunes. I headed toward the footbridge, planning to hide in the marsh grass. Maybe I could pick up a fragment of conversation.

I was almost to the bridge. A halogen flower bloomed in the darkness about ten feet in front of me.

"What are *you* doing here?"

Nigel's assistant, Solange. I blinked the spots out of my eyes. "Last I heard this was a public beach."

There were soft footfalls in the sand. She stood close enough that I could smell the shampoo in her hair. Rose petal.

"You shouldn't be here," she said.

"Why not? It's a perfect night for a stroll under the stars."

"You must go," she whispered. "If they find you here, they'll kill you."

That caught my attention. "Who will kill me?"

"They'll be back any minute."

"Nigel and Jack? Why would they want to kill me?"

"We can't talk now. He'll think we met on purpose. They'll kill us both. Please go." Her voice was panic on the verge of hysteria. "You must leave before they come back." A warm hand reached out and touched my arm.

I used her fear as a lever. "Only if I can talk to you again," I insisted stubbornly, not moving.

"All right," she said impatiently. "Where?"

I remembered my meeting with Flagg. "There's a place called Fort Hill. It's not far from here. Tell me when you can be there."

A dead pause. I thought she was changing her mind. "Tomorrow morning at nine. If I don't come, I'll try to be there the next day. Now go. *Please.*"

"I'll see you tomorrow."

She turned and vanished into blackness.

Something skittered in the beach grass. It was probably only a rabbit, but I didn't hang around to find out. The beach had become an unfriendly place. I started along the buggy track, walking briskly at first, then trotting as my feet hit harder sand. When I got to the Jeep I was sweating.

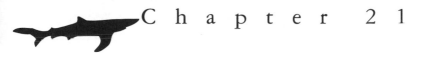C h a p t e r 2 1

"Don't you ever feed your cat?"

Flagg was sitting at my green Formica-and-aluminum kitchen table. One big hand was wrapped around a plastic tumbler of lime Kool-Aid, the other buried in a bag of Cape Cod potato chips. Health food. I poured myself a glass of Kool-Aid and dragged a chair up to the table.

"Yeah, I feed him. I just dumped some food into him a couple of hours ago, in fact."

"You wouldn't know it from the way he attacked me. I gave him a pile of that dry stuff. He was still hungry so I gave him the canned mush. Cat's got a straight gut."

"It's purely psychological. He was the runt of the litter and spent his formative years in an orphanage, so he still worries about where his next meal is coming from."

Maine coon cats are slightly smaller than horses to begin with and Kojak had added girth to his width. Flagg shook his head in wonderment. "Hate to bump into one that *wasn't* a runt." He looked around. "Nice digs. Real homey."

"Welcome to what our Chamber of Commerce was thinking of when it invented the term 'rural seaside charm.' "

"Doesn't look much different than the shack I grew up in on the Vineyard. Only difference is we didn't have a TV and there were religious pictures all over the place. My mother was a Jesus freak before there was such a thing. Now I've got a condo outside of D.C., but I travel a lot and don't use it much."

"You must be cutting back on the hush-hush cloak-and-dagger stuff now that the KGB has been turned into a fraternal organization."

"Not all the bad boys had Russian accents, Soc." He grabbed a handful of potato chips and chewed on them. "How long you had these chips?"

"If they were any older they'd qualify for Social Security."

"Thought so. Good thing I like them aged." He grabbed another handful.

Kojak burped and waddled off to my bedroom. He was so full he could hardly walk.

Flagg looked out into the night through the kitchen door where buzzing suicide squadrons of light-crazed June bugs slammed themselves against the screen.

"There's a ship," he said.

"What kind of ship?"

"A freighter, went down off Cape Cod in a storm not long ago."

"Her name wouldn't be the *Pandora,* would it? With a skipper named George Zervas?"

Flagg's black eyes stared at me like twin beads of malachite. Then his thin lips stretched in a wide grin and he broke into deep, easy laughter.

"So much for national security," he said. "Mind telling me how you know?"

I told him about my calls to Greece, New Orleans, and Boston.

"Not bad as far as it goes," he said.

"How come there was nothing in the papers about a missing ship?"

"The owners had good reasons not to report her missing. We knew she went down off here, but we didn't know exactly where. Our plane used remote sensing. Got a fix on her position today. She's about a half mile off shore. Not too far from Quanset Beach, in seventy to one hundred feet of water. Now we need someone to dive on her."

"The *Pandora* was supposedly hauling chemical fertilizer. You going to do a little gardening, Flagg?"

He shook his head. "I've gone as far as I can go, Soc. Unless you're part of the team."

"Why not bring in navy SEALs? Or send down a remote operated vehicle?"

"Navy divers would mean paperwork. Human eyes can pick up on stuff an ROV might miss. Look, Soc, I don't want you doing this because we're friends. That wouldn't be fair. It could be dangerous."

"Thanks for the warning. When do we start?"

"How about tomorrow?"

"Sounds like a rush job."

He nodded. "Can we use your fishing boat as a cover? Call it a government charter."

"I'll talk to Sam about using the boat. I can pick up some air tanks on the way. I've got an errand in the morning. Can you meet me at the fish pier around ten A.M.?"

"I'll be there." He took one last handful of chips. Kojak came out of the bedroom to rub against his legs. Flagg looked at the cat and shook his head in amazement.

Seconds later he was gone. I heard the sound of a car. Then there was only silence except for the suicidal insects throwing themselves against the screen door. I could have convinced myself Flagg's visit was a dream if his empty Kool-Aid glass weren't on the table.

I dug my dive gear out of the closet, checked the regulator and hoses, then loaded the equipment in a duffel bag and piled it near the front door. I thought about going into town for a six-pack, but decided against it. Flagg sucks up danger the way I suck down booze; we both know we can get hurt, but we like the high. If he says a mission is hazardous, you can multiply that by a factor of ten. I wasn't embarrassed to admit he had scared me. When the sun rose the next morning, I wanted to have a clear head.

Chapter 22

Solange stood me up. I waited at Fort Hill until nine-thirty, then drove to the fish pier.

Flagg stood watching a couple of whiskery fishermen unravel their gill nets. He wore jeans, a black T-shirt under a denim jacket, and high-top moccasins. In his hand was an attaché case. I waved him aboard the *Millie D.* and tossed him a pair of knee-high black rubber fisherman's boots.

"These'll keep your tootsies dry in case we run into some slop."

"We shouldn't. Weather report's the same as yesterday. Hotter'n hell."

He put the boots on anyway. They were a little tight, and he made a face as he pulled them onto his feet.

I started the engine, and while it warmed up,

checked the boat, which didn't take long. Sam would run the *Millie D.* through a car wash if he could. The boat was in what sailors call shipshape in Bristol fashion. I had called Sam earlier that morning to say I was taking the boat out. He had been ordered to stay home and take it easy until his tests were in, and he didn't like being confined. He grumbled that it was probably a good idea to go back to work, but I could tell from the unhappy tone of his voice he missed fishing.

We cast the lines off, pointed the bow into the harbor, and within minutes, the *Millie D.* was plowing between the channel marker buoys. The passage through the barrier beach used to be at the southernmost end of the harbor over a series of ever-shifting sandbars. Those bars probably brought more fishermen to religion than all the preachers in town. Several years ago, the Atlantic breached the outer beach at a new place and quickly widened the gap so that it was about a half mile wide. Now the route to the fishing grounds is more direct, but the harbor shoaling has worsened. It was a case of Nature giving and taking away.

We steamed into the Atlantic and I set a course north as Flagg directed. The morning air was fresh and sweet. The ocean was glassy calm under a fiery sun. With no seas to buck, we made excellent time. Behind the trawler trailed two wakes, one in the green ocean, the other made up of hovering herring gulls.

I took the wheel and Flagg pored over a NOAA marine chart of Cape Cod. From time to time, he'd glance up and scan the water as if he were looking for road lines.

"There was something I meant to mention last night at the boathouse," I said.

Flagg grunted with disinterest, his nose pointed like a compass needle at the squiggles and swirls on the chart.

"I was off the outer beach in a boat earlier this week and saw some weird lights."

That got his attention. He raised his head and his eyes bored into mine. "What kind of lights?"

"Blue-green ones. Bright as the sun up there. Flashing on the beach. There seemed to be lights answering them out at sea, in the general direction we're heading."

Flagg shoved the chart aside, suddenly very interested. "Tell me about them," he demanded.

I described my boat ride with Mac and our fruitless attempt to track down the source of the blue lights. Flagg listened impassively until I told him my theory that the film crew had something to do with the lights.

"What film crew?"

"British guy with a pretty dark-skinned woman and a muscle-bound assistant."

Flagg rubbed his chin. "This English guy, was he a blondish redhaired dude with a beard? Real smooth talker?"

"That's Nigel Eden to a T. Who are they?"

"They're trouble," he rumbled. "*Real* trouble."

"Are you saying they're *not* a film crew?"

"I'm not saying anything, except stay the hell away from them."

I tried again. "What about the lights, then? They looked like lasers."

237

"You got it. Probably being used as position find-ers."

A mental link fell into place. "There's a connection between the film crew and this ship we're going after."

"I won't say you're wrong, Soc. I wish I could tell you more, but I can't." He bent back over the chart.

Damned tight-lipped spook. We didn't talk again for twenty minutes. Flagg checked the compass, loran, and depth finder one more time. "Better slow us down. We're getting real close."

I cut power and the bow settled into the water. I gave the engine just enough throttle to maintain head-way, following Flagg's directions until he announced: "We're over her."

Quanset Beach stretched north and south like a gold satin ribbon. I pointed out the Dwight house, high on its bluff. Flagg watched it through binoculars for a few mo-ments, then shook his head and handed the glasses to me. I didn't see anything stirring either, but that didn't mean Nigel and crew weren't up and around.

"They could be checking us out, too," I said. "Let's get the trawl lines in."

Flagg helped me set a couple of lines of trawl. I threw the anchor over and watched the bull's-eye ripples as it disappeared into the ocean. It was hard to believe a freighter lay beneath this placid sun-speckled water. But the sea held many secrets, and it hid them well. I ar-ranged my dive equipment on the deck and turned to Flagg.

"Gear's set to go," I said. "What are my marching orders?"

A black cloud sat on Flagg's wide brow. "First we need to verify that this *is* the *Pandora*. Check out her name, numbers, anything you can find. Try to remember as much detail as you can, especially any features that would help with an ID."

"Sounds like a piece of cake so far, Flagg."

"That's the easy part. Next, see how she's lying, whether she's resting on her keel, or on the side. We want to know if she broke apart or if there's any sign she got *blown* up. You know what to look for. See if there's any damage to the superstructure or the hull. Another thing we're really interested in is any sign someone's tried to salvage her."

"Okay, buddy," I said, "let's do it." I was acting cocky to cover my own nervousness.

Flagg gripped my arm. "Here's the most important part. Under no circumstances are you to get closer than fifty feet to that ship. Understand? No closer than fifty feet. Just do your thing real quick and come up."

"You make it sound as if the *Pandora*'s radioactive, Flagg."

"I wish it *were* hot," he answered grimly. "At least we'd have a good idea what we're dealing with. Treat her like she is loaded with plutonium. Don't forget. You don't have to get close. If you can't make her, we can always send down an ROV."

His fingers were biting into my arm. "Now can I get suited up?"

He released me. "Yeah." He started to add something, but changed his mind.

Flagg was a strange duck. He had little respect for the government *apparat* he worked for. He lumped all federal employees into a faceless bureaucratic machine that traced its lineage to General Custer. But he had an unswerving sense of loyalty to individuals. His boss had told him to keep his mouth shut. And that's what he would do.

I stepped into a red-and-black Viking drysuit like a kid getting into his one-piece PJ's. Flagg helped me zip up. When I was sewn up like a kielbasa sausage, he handed me the weight belt. Next came the buoyancy compensator, an inflatable vest that holds the air tank. I pulled on my hood, mask and fins, and tested the inflate and exhaust valves and the regulator. Finally, I strapped a knife to my thigh and waddled over to the gunwale. I swung my legs over the side and balanced on the rail. Flagg handed me a black plastic three-cell torch and I slipped the loop over my wrist. I bit down on the regulator mouthpiece, held onto my face mask so it wouldn't get knocked off, and jumped feet first into the Atlantic Ocean.

I sank about ten feet in a green sparkle of bubbles, then the air in the B.C. overcame my weight and I shot upward. My head popped out of the water like the plastic cork on a bottle of cheap champagne. I breast-stroked closer to the anchor line. Flagg leaned over the rail.

"Remember," he called, as I bobbed in the easy swells. "No closer than fifty feet."

I gave him the high sign, opened the exhaust valve on my B.C., and sank beneath the sun-speckled waves. I grabbed the anchor line, and dropped a fathom or two while I tested my regulator. Then I pinched my nose to equalize the pressure on my ears, rolled over facing toward the bottom, and with rhythmical kicks of my fins began the descent.

The current was only a couple of knots. That was good, because the more energy you expend underwater, the quicker your air is exhausted. I glanced at my watch. I had about twenty-five minutes of air.

Down I went, one hand on the line, the other trailing by my side. The ocean enfolded me and pressed against the thin rubber skin of my drysuit. I kept checking my depth gauge. At fifty feet I stopped.

Holding onto the anchor line, I pivoted a full turn to get my bearings. My heart did a cartwheel. A huge shadow loomed darkly about a hundred meters to the east. Swimming about twenty feet above the sandy ocean bottom, I moved in closer and switched on my light. The beam cut through brown motes of monkey fur seaweed and splashed against the massive black hull of a ship. I swam toward it.

Flagg's warning echoed in my brain.

No closer than fifty feet. I made a mental note of the registration number on the hull, then angled off and glided parallel to the ship. The wreck had become a haven for marine life. My beam caught the silvered reflection of schools of fish nosing around in search of fast food. Halfway along the hull, the ship ended abruptly. It looked as if a giant cleaver had come down around midships, separating one half from the other, leaving a big puddle of liquid darkness in the middle. The break was clean, as if the big old vessel had split along a seam. Both sections lay on their port side. I swam the length of the ship, then hovered like a hummingbird.

I played the light along the rounded stern. White letters stood out against the black paint.

PANDORA. Underneath were the words: Panama City.

I had about twenty minutes of air left. I looked at my compass, preparing to swim back to the anchor line. I leveled out and kicked briskly with my fins, taking pleasure in the sensation of flying. The black hulk of the dead ship went by on my right. I was almost back at the bow when it happened.

Jeezus!

Something slammed me hard between the shoulder blades. The buoyancy compensator and my air tank absorbed the shock, but the force of the blow spun me onto my side. With the unexpected weight change, my center of gravity shifted. I wobbled crazily off-course like a bomber hit by flak.

Fighting for balance, I jerked my head around to see what the hell was going on. All I saw through the lens of my face mask were the clouds of bubbles produced by my frantic exhalations.

Then came quick movement, silver-green and undefinable, at the very edge of my peripheral vision. What the hell? I had a crazy vision of a peacock's fan with dozens of staring eyes, then it was gone.

My mind went in a hundred directions at once.

Adrenaline pumped through my veins. I flailed the water.

A second later, something grabbed my right fin.

Primal memories raced through my mind.

Something was trying to eat me.

My legs pumped like pistons. No finesse now. Just sheer terror. The fin started to slide off my foot, then it pulled free of what was holding it. I lunged forward, looking for shelter. Somewhere. *Any*where.

My heart hammered wildly; my breath expelled in loud burbling explosions.

Dead ahead was the cave formed by the hull sections of the broken ship. I plunged blindly into the darkness.

Chapter 23

I was thirty feet into the broken hull before it dawned on me that the darkness could be hiding jagged razor-sharp steel projections. I stopped and looked back toward open water. Nothing moved in the soupy green. I flicked on the torch dangling from my wrist and pointed into the interior of the fractured ship. The yellow beam washed against the gloom and faded after a couple of dozen feet. The big hull soared out of sight on either side of me. I swam cautiously forward, fighting growing claustrophobia. The flash began to pick out debris on the ocean floor. Pipes, engine parts, and cans of food littered the sand. Then the beam reflected dully off black metal. I swam down to a barrel, stenciled with the words *Chemical Fertilizer.* Dozens just like it littered the bottom.

Flagg's warning rang in my ears. *Great going. Flagg*

tells you it's dangerous to get closer than fifty feet to the Pandora, *so of course you end up* inside *the damn ship!* I checked my pressure gauge. My air supply was getting low. Well, I could stay and die, or move and die. I decided to move.

I made one last sweep of my light, then turned and headed back the way I'd come. Then stopped.

I've had dizzy spells in the water before. You can't subject yourself to unnatural pressures and canned air at depth without having your head spin once in a while. But this was different. My heart fluttered like a trapped bird. I was gripped by a numbing anxiety, like the paralysis a gazelle must feel when it's being stalked by a lion. I blinked and squinted through the Plexiglas of the face mask. Shook my head. Even pinched myself. Looked again. The hairs on the back of my neck stood up and saluted. Was that movement I saw in the murk? What the hell *was* going on here?

I swept the beam back and forth.

Nothing.

Still, I felt the presence of Something incredibly evil, sensed it deep in my bones. Crazy pictures raced through my mind. Terrifying flashbacks. I was eight years old again and I had just crashed through the rotted floor of a "haunted house" I was exploring. I landed in the cellar with my feet trapped in debris and couldn't move. I could hear my friends calling above. I was too scared to reply. The stink of musk and animal excrement was in my nostrils. Red eyes burned in the darkness. I could hear the scurrying of claws and the sound of high-pitched squeaks. Small furry bodies scampered across my hands. My friends pulled me out. They thought it was a big joke. I remembered reading about people whose hair turned white after being scared half to death. For weeks I checked my hair every day in the mirror. And I slept with my light on.

Now it was happening again. The dark cellar. The feet glued to the floor. The glowing red eyes. I grabbed my brain by the scruff of the neck and gave it a pep talk. *You are* not *in a cellar. You are at the bottom of the Atlantic Ocean. Your air supply is running out. If you don't move immediately, you will die.*

I backed away from the interior of the ship. I stopped before I swam into the clear and looked around. Nothing threatened that I could see. I took a deep breath, let it out, then launched my body from the shadowy innards of the *Pandora.* I reached automatically for the bouyancy compensator inflation valve. Air from the tank hissed into the vest. I ascended toward the shimmering surface like a heat-seeking rocket.

My head broke through the water. Droplets of water obscured my face mask. I began to swim. Something was still after me. I was sure of it. I tried to escape. A voice was calling as if from a great distance.

"Soc!"

I flailed the water in terror. Encumbered by my dive gear I took in mouthfuls of choking seawater.

"Soc!" Louder now.

Something grabbed me by the shoulder.

I screamed.

Chapter 24

Strange dreams were running through my head. Suns and moons and stars floated against a tortoiseshell sky. A chorus of wan voices called, like children lost in a cave. One moon grew larger than the rest and moved in closer. I blinked the water out of my eyes. The moon became Flagg's face, the children's cries the harsh squalling of gulls.

"Soc, hey, man, you okay?"

Flagg's wide face was inches away. His brow was wrinkled with worry. I lay on my back on the *Millie D*'s steel deck, gasping. I looked around, reassured by the familiar sight of the *Millie D*'s plastic tubs and coiled trawl line.

I spit seawater out of my mouth. "Phooey. Yeah, I'm all right. Tastes like I've been eating goldfish food."

"Try some of this." He adjusted the life jackets that propped my head off the deck and put a glass to my lips. Sweet fire trickled down my throat.

I coughed and took another sip. "Where'd you find brandy on this boat? Sam's a good Methodist."

"I carry a flash in my pack for medicinal purposes."

I took more brandy. "What the hell happened?"

"You tell *me*. I was watching the clock. You were down a long time and I started to get worried. I was trying to figure out what to do when I heard you yelling from astern. You were thrashing around, screaming whacko things I couldn't understand. I dove in, got a line around your waist, hoisted you aboard. That was five minutes ago. You've been babbling off and on since then."

My mind felt as if it were tumbling down a fast-flowing brook. I grabbed onto a mental boulder and held on, forcing my thoughts back to the dive. It seemed as if hours had passed since I jumped into the sea and slid down the anchor line. I coughed out the last of the sea water lodged in my throat.

"I found the ship, Flagg. I found the *Pandora*."

Flagg waited.

"She's lying on her side, broken in two sections."

I was swimming again alongside the dark hulk. I remembered the big white letters, stopping to get my bearings, then the sharp blow from behind. I struggled to sit up.

"Something hit me."

"What are you talking about, man?"

"I found the ship and was getting ready to come back up to the *Millie D*. Something slammed into my back. I never saw what it was. Not clearly, anyhow. Only that it was shiny." A thought stumbled into my head like a drunk in the wrong hotel room. The eyes. I had seen eyes. This was too crazy. "Whatever it was grabbed at my fin. I panicked. That's when I swam into the ship."

Flagg's dusky features went pale. "You went *inside* the *Pandora?*"

"Where the hull had cracked open, there was space big enough to drive my pickup through. I got scared. I was looking for a place to hide."

"What happened next, Soc?" His voice was a rasp.

"I waited, hoping that whatever was after me would lose interest and go away. After a few minutes, I thought it might be safe to leave, and I was getting low on air. But I had a weird feeling, as if I weren't alone. I got dizzy. Then I had a strange flashback to when I was a kid. Something down there that wanted me. I had to get out fast." I started to shiver. Flagg poured another shot of brandy. "Flagg, is that ship haunted or am I going crazy?"

Flagg got up and walked over to the rail. He gazed at the ocean, then came back. His face looked as if it had been carved out of oak.

"You're not going crazy, Soc. The rest of the world is, maybe."

I pulled myself erect. My hands were trembling, but I reached out and grabbed Flagg's T-shirt.

"Flagg, I almost got killed down there. I don't care *what* your orders are. You've got to tell me why I shouldn't commit myself at the nearest funny farm. You owe me that."

He looked at me, then nodded. "Yeah," he said.

"Guess I do. I'll go make some coffee. You get into dry clothes. When you're ready we'll talk about it."

"The *Pandora*'s an old World War Two cargo ship. Saw some action, even got hit once. She's registered in Liberia now. Her home base is in Panama, but she's got no regular port; she just goes where the work is. Her last port of call was New Orleans. She took on cargo there and sailed up the East Coast bound for Boston. Got caught in a storm off here and sank."

"Same thing nearly happened a few years ago with a Maltese freighter called the *Eldia*," I said. "A northeaster pushed her right up on the beach not far from here."

"I remember that. The *Pandora* was no ordinary ship, though, on account of her cargo."

"The cans I saw had chemical fertilizer printed on them."

"That was just a cover. Got to give you a history lesson first." He chewed his lower lip. "Back in 'eighty-five, the government decided to get rid of some obsolete chemical weapons at eight storage sites around the U.S. The feds wanted a stockpile of new-generation nerve gas to keep on hand until a treaty was worked out. Trouble is, you can't just put poison in a Hefty garbage bag and leave it at the dump. When they went to incinerate the old gas, the people living near the burn sites objected, so they put the stuff in storage. You know how people get after they've been standing watch over something they don't think anyone's interested in."

"Bored and sloppy?"

250

"Uh-huh. That's what happened. At this place in Utah. A pile of the stuff was stolen. Independent contractors took it. That's what made it so hard to get a lead on them. The feds finally tracked the load south to the Gulf coast."

"And the stolen chemicals were loaded on the *Pandora.*"

"That's right. By the time the good guys figured that out, the ship was at sea."

"Just exactly what is this 'stuff'?"

"A special kind of nerve gas. Called K-Twenty-two."

"Sounds like a hair gel. What's that stand for?"

"The twenty-two is the batch that finally worked. The K stands for Krueger, dude in those nightmare movies where the guy goes around with the blades on his fingers hacking people up in their dreams."

"Cute. What did you mean by special?"

"Some scientist's bright idea. Hell, he says, anyone can make something that *kills* people. Gas in your stove will do that. So he came up with something that makes people start seeing things. Bad things. Spread it around a garrison, guards'll shoot each other. All you do is waltz in and take over whatever's there. Rockets. Subs." He smiled sourly. "What you'd call a turnkey operation."

"That's a new one on me, Flagg."

"Was for a lot of people. But the upstairs brass at the Pentagon said no fancy stuff. We just want your basic aerosol Raid. You know, like the ads say, kills 'em dead. They'd basically forgotten all about the stuff until it was ripped off."

My throat got Sahara dry. "Flagg, are you going to tell me the nerve gas went down with the ship?"

"Yep. My guess is we're sitting right over nearly a hundred barrels of K-Twenty-two."

"What the hell happened to me down there?"

"Don't know for sure, but I can guess. I think there's a leak in one or more barrels. You were exposed to the K-Twenty-two."

"How could that happen? I was breathing from my own air supply."

"Doesn't make any difference. It's absorbed through the skin."

"I don't understand. I didn't want to shoot anyone. I was scared stiff. I felt like a kid who thinks there's a snake-eyed monster in his closet waiting for the lights to go off so he can sneak out. I knew there was something watching. Hungry to get at me."

"Something like what?"

I paused, almost embarrassed. "Rats."

"Rats?"

I told him the story about the haunted house.

He didn't seem surprised. "That figures. K-Twenty-two taps into your basic fears. Critters. Bogeymen. Dripping fangs and sharp claws. We've all got monsters in our heads. This stuff brings back all the bad things you forgot since you were a kid, only big time. I'd probably see the headless horseman Grandma used to scare me good with back on the Vineyard."

"How come we're not hallucinating now?"

"The gas dissipates in water. The chemical is liquid under pressure. You were lucky. You didn't have much skin exposed, and you got out of there in a hurry. The guys I talked to said it'd be safe to go as close as fifty feet. Maybe they didn't tell me everything."

I pictured the barrels in the hold. "If there was a leak, the gas could have found its way into the *Pandora*'s ventilation system."

"One of our guys had the same theory."

"Could the crew have operated if that happened?"

"Could you operate when you thought big-ass rats were chasing you?"

"No, I just wanted to run like hell. Poor bastards. It's unbelievable."

"Believe it, Soc."

"How did you know the ship was off the Cape?"

"We'd been watching her on a satellite. We could have boarded anytime, but we wanted to nail the suckers in Boston. We lost contact in the storm, and thought she might have sunk. When the bodies came ashore, we got the spotter plane up."

"Those independent contractors you mentioned . . . Nigel and his friend?"

"Uh-huh. Nigel calls himself a soldier of fortune. Not the kind of dirtbags who run tough-guy ads in the mercenary magazines; this guy's the real thing. His specialty is exotic weapons."

"Who's Jack Morgan?"

"A career Army guy. Got thrown in the can and mustered out for corruption. He's had a grudge against the Army ever since. Morgan's a demo expert, stationed up in Utah. We figure he was the inside man."

"Evil draws men together," I mused.

"Huh?"

"Something Plato said."

"My grandmother used to tell me birds of a feather flock together."

"Same thing. This is a major operation. Nigel'd need more than an insider's help. He'd need big money. Who's bankrolling him?"

"Still working on that. The best bet is that it's a cartel. American Mafia, Colombians, and the Camorra, the Naples mob. Take your pick. They would have the money and the organization for an operation like this."

"Any idea what they plan to do with the K-Twenty-two?"

"Blackmail? They could hit on the brass who were supposed to burn the stuff and didn't. Robbery? They could take out the guards at an armory and walk off with all the tanks, choppers, and nukes they could tuck under their belts. Extortion? They could threaten a whole country. Or they could just sell it to the highest bidder."

"Sounds like a practical joker's dream. When do we make our move?"

"No 'we,' this time, kemo sabe. You could've been hurt or killed, and I feel responsible. You were entitled to know what almost killed you. That's as far as it goes. Let us take care of these guys."

I got up and went over to the rail, expecting to see noxious green vapor bubbling from the sea. The ocean seemed no different from any other time. I turned back to Flagg. "What about the *Pandora?*"

He snapped open his attaché case and pulled out a cellular phone. "There's a salvage ship on its way here. It was going to hang around until we got a positive ID, then come in and take the stuff out real quiet-like."

"When's this supposed to happen?"

"Depends. Maybe they can start the day after to-morrow."

"Three days? This is Cape Cod in July. Hundreds of people use these beaches. There's a camp full of kids not far from here. You've got fishermen, pleasure boaters go-ing right past this spot every day. Maybe even a few divers, too. What if that crap starts drifting ashore or gets into something people eat? Shouldn't there be some kind of public alert?" I was almost shouting with anger.

"Uh-uh, Soc. We got to keep it quiet. Don't want to cause a panic."

"*Panic?* You think people rushing around might hurt themselves more than leaky barrels of poison gas? What about the panic from bodies dropping in for a visit every time Mom and Pop take their kids for a beach picnic?"

"I mean a panic in the brass. This gets out, and it'll mean their balls. I'm not saying that's right. I'm just saying that's the way it is. I'd appreciate it if you kept your mouth shut until we can do something about this."

"Flagg, this whole thing stinks. It's absolutely criminal to keep this story under wraps—"

"I've got my duty, Soc."

I stuck my face in his. "Duty to whom? A bunch of faceless Washington bureaucrats who don't give a shit about you?"

He stared at me with his flat black eyes. His calm-ness infuriated me.

"What the hell's gone wrong with you, Flagg? I remember your stories about going to high school on the Vineyard, how you punched out the white kids who called you chief until they didn't call you that any more."

"What's that got to do with anything?"

"It's got *every*thing to do with it. You've sold out, Flagg. You're no better than the Indian scouts the cavalry used to hire for a few beads. The only difference is instead of beads they've given you a portable phone. They're still calling you chief, but now you're letting them get away with it." I turned away, too out of control to face him.

Flagg grabbed me by the shoulder and spun me around. I expected him to lay into me, probably *wanted* him to so I could hit him back, but he only said, "I thought we were friends, Soc."

"Aw, hell," I spat. "I've got to get these trawls in. Don't let me keep you from your phone call."

Flagg nodded. He went into the pilothouse where he could talk in private. I quickly gathered up my dive equipment. It was then I noticed my right swim fin. A corner of it was missing. I ran my finger along the ragged end and remembered the surfboard owned by the kid who had been attacked off Quanset Beach. I looked at my air tank. The metal was dented and scratched deeply in a dozen places, as if somebody had attacked it with a mace. When Flagg finished his calls I showed it to him.

"Ho-ly shit," he murmured.

"This have anything to do with what you're not telling me?"

He raised his eyebrows. "Nothing that I know of."
Flagg didn't lie.

We hauled in the trawls, which didn't take long
because I hadn't baited the hooks.

An hour later, the *Millie D.* bumped over the shoals
into the harbor. We tied up, secured the boat, and
headed back to our vehicles.

"I'm sorry for what I said. Indian scout and all
that."

"I don't blame you for being pissed after what I got
you into." He was being conciliatory, but I knew Flagg
too well. There'd been enough truth in my brainless ti-
rade to wound. His voice had a note of coolness.

"So I feel even more like a jerk now asking you for
some help with a job."

"We go back a long way, Soc. All you have to do is
ask. What kind of job is it?"

"A family matter," I said.

Chapter 25

High beams glared in my rearview mirror and blinked off. Flagg climbed out of his LTD and came over to the pickup. He was wearing Nike running shoes and a dark blue track suit. A toothpick dangled from his mouth. My truck was parked on a side street next to the sports bar. Traffic droned on Route 28 a couple of hundred yards away. Flagg swept the area with his hooded eyes.

"How's it look?" he said.

"There's a Ford van with smoked windows next to the discount sneaker outlet on the corner. I saw the same van before. I'm pretty sure it's the cops."

He nodded. "I made them when I did a recon a half hour ago. You missed the black Mustang behind the bar. Two guys just sitting there. Every time somebody goes by, they start reading the paper. Funny place to catch up on the news. Maybe they think it's a Christian Science Reading Room. When the narc gets here to make the buy, that'll give them three cars. Plenty enough to handle a bunch of shithead kids. Probably got more people on standby. I would have. So what's your plan?"

"Depends. The last time, Alex and his buddies parked behind the bar. A guy named Chili went inside and came out with the narc. They went over to the guy's BMW for a few minutes. Then they got back in their cars and took off in opposite directions on Route 28. The BMW hooked up with the guys in the van. My guess is Alex and pals let him sample the goods and they agreed on a price. The real score will go down tonight. When the undercover cop has his dope and Alex's friends have their money, the bust will happen real quick. I want Alex out of there before the cops do their thing."

He flicked the toothpick into the street. "Easy. While the deal goes down in the Beemer, I'll go over and persuade Cousin Alex to come with me. The fuzz make their move, but li'l Alex is long gone and they catch the bad guys."

I thought about it. "Those kids might just be stupid enough to be carrying."

He patted his heart. The bulge of a shoulder holster was barely visible. "Doesn't bother me."

"But Alex's parents won't like it if he comes home looking like Swiss cheese. Let's stay flexible for now. Keep an eye out for a silver Toyota 4Runner. When things start moving, we improvise."

"So that's your plan, that we *improvise* a plan?"

"Right."

Flagg shook his head. "You spent too much time in the Marine Corps."

"Okay, Mr. One-Hundred-First Airborne. You got a better idea? We going to *parachute* down on top of them?"

He studied the street. "I'll be in that straggly little patch of trees behind the joint. You keep an eye out. When you figure out what's happening, come over and we'll consult a Ouija board." He slipped a slim halogen torch from his pocket. "I'll flash one-twos for the BMW, one-two-threes for the Toyota."

He crossed the street and disappeared into the shadows behind the bar.

Flagg hadn't hesitated a second when I asked him to help me with Alex's problem. But I was kidding himself if I thought it was a payback for almost getting me killed on the *Pandora*. He was doing it because he *wanted* to.

The parking lot wrapped around the bar in the shape of a U, with part of it hidden by the building. Cars came and went. After about fifteen minutes, the light flashed one-two in the woods. One-two again. The BMW swung into the parking lot, then out of sight on the other side of the building.

Minutes later, Flagg's light flashed three times. The 4Runner cruised into the lot, circled once and parked to the rear of the building next to the woods.

I crossed the street, and joined Flagg in the scrub pine and oak. Rock music thudded from the bar. The clanking of pots and pans came through an open window. They were cooking pizza and it smelled good. We edged to within a few yards of the Toyota.

The Toyota's door opened and the dome light went on. T.J. was behind the wheel. Chili sat beside him. Alex was in back with T.J.'s anorexic girlfriend Tanya. Steve Olney, the lieutenant-governor's son, wasn't with them. Alex got out of the car and started across the parking lot. He had a plastic shopping bag in his hand.

"Goddamnit," I growled. "This is unbelievable. *Alex* is doing the deal."

Crouching low, we moved in between a line of parked cars. Alex got in the BMW. After a few minutes, the door opened and Alex started back. He was walking fast. At a corner of the bar, he was out of sight to the BMW and not quite in view of the 4Runner. Flagg made his move.

He darted out from between the cars, as swift and as quiet as a shadow, came up behind Alex, and wrapped his arm around his neck. Alex struggled, but Flagg lifted him off his feet effortlessly and dragged him over to me. I grabbed his kicking ankles. Together we carried him like a trussed deer through the woods and across the street to Flagg's car.

We stuffed him between us in the front seat. Alex's mouth dropped down to his belly button.

"Soc, what the hell—?"

"Shut up and watch."

He struggled to get out of the car. "Watch *what?*"

I grabbed his collar and swiveled him around.

"That." I pointed to the parking lot.

The van swung into view and blocked off the

Toyota. Then the Ford Mustang squealed around the corner. Blue lights flashed. Cops poured out of each vehicle. The guy from the BMW came running over. I counted eight uniforms.

Guns leveled, the cops surrounded the 4Runner. T.J. and Chili were yanked out and spread-eagled against their car. Cops frisked them down. The girl was standing off to the side, probably waiting for a matron to show up, but a uniform kept a close eye on her.

"What the hell's going on?" Alex demanded.

"Your buddies just got busted. The guy you sold dope to is an undercover cop."

He slumped down in his seat. "Jeezus," he said.

"What next?" Flagg asked.

"I'll give Cousin Alexander here a ride home."

"What's going to happen to T.J. and the guys?" Alex said.

"You'd better worry about your *own* ass, Alex. It's hanging out there in the breeze. Hand over the cash. I'll get it back to the cops."

"*Wait*aminute. I can't do that. What am I going to tell my friends?"

I drew in a long breath and let it out. Child-rearing was definitely not my bag.

"You're not going to tell them shit. You're going to get your things out of the cottage and your tail off Cape Cod. You're going to pray that the cops don't connect you with this deal. Give me the money or I can't help you."

He crossed his arms and tucked his chin into his chest. His mouth pouted sullenly. "I don't want your goddamn help."

"Little fucker says he doesn't want your help," Flagg said heartily. "Why don't you let him go join his friends over there?"

"Don't tempt me." I grabbed Alex by the front of his shirt and stuck my face in his. "You're just another punk to me. I don't like dope peddlers. I don't like the idea that I'm aiding and abetting a felon. So give with the money before I break every bone in your scrawny little body."

He hesitated. It was enough to push me over the edge.

I lifted him out of his seat and jammed his back hard against the steering wheel.

"Look, you little bastard, give me that money or I'll push you right through the windshield!"

"Okay, okay!" He reached in under his shirt and handed me a bundle of bills tied in an elastic. I let him go.

The parking lot was swarming with people who had spilled from the bar to check out the action. A drug bust? Gee, that's better than watching the Sox lose on fourteen TV screens.

"Lotsa confusion now," Flagg said. "Good time to break out of here."

"C'mon, Alex." I pulled him out of Flagg's car and stuffed him into my truck. "Let's be in touch," I told Flagg. "And thanks."

"No thanks needed. But remember what I said. Leave that ship business up to the big guys. You did the dive, you're out of it."

"Thanks anyway."

I took a shortcut across the Cape. Neither one of us

talked. Back at Little Taunton, I scouted the neighborhood, but apparently the cops didn't know where Alex's gang lived. At least not yet.

I parked in front of the darkened cottage. "You do any dealing from here?"

He shook his head. "Too risky," he mumbled. "We always did parking lot drops."

"Go get your stuff. You got any more dope inside?"

"No." Alex was a lousy liar.

"Don't bullshit me, Alex. Get your ass in there and get that stuff. All of it." I reached over and opened the door for him.

"What were you doing at the bar?"

"I followed you the other night. You and your smart buddies didn't know you'd been invited to a policemen's convention. They set you up like bowling pins. Now get me that shit. Pronto."

He got out of the truck and went into the cottage. A few minutes later he came out and handed me six baggies of white powder.

"Is that all of it?"

"Yeah."

I glared at him.

"That's *all* of it, for Chrissakes."

"It'd better be. Where'd this stuff come from?"

"T.J. was getting it from a dealer in Jamaica Plain. We'd cut it and planned to sell it for a big markup. We made some contacts in the restaurants with the kitchen cleaning business. The guy said he was the biggest distributor on the Cape. We figured he was a good connection."

"You figured wrong. He was a narc. Where does Steve Olney fit in?"

"He was the money. He bankrolled the cleaning business and laundered the dough through his bank accounts."

"How come he wasn't in on the score tonight?"

"He didn't want to come. Says he's taking a big enough risk with the other stuff."

"Smart kid."

Alex looked pathetic. His narrow shoulders were hunched. His head was down. The wise-assedness had drained out of him. I felt sorry for him, sorry for his parents, who didn't need any more grief in their lives, and I felt sorry for me because I really liked the kid and things would never be the same again.

He shrugged and turned away. "I've got to get moving. See you."

He was looking for a reply from the old Uncle Soc, some hint that things were still right with the neat dude who thumbed his nose at the world and lived a happy-go-lucky life by the side of the sea, not knowing there never was such a person.

I did Alex one more favor. I didn't answer him. I started the truck and left him standing there alone.

Chapter 26

Warm rain powered by a fitful gust slanted through the bedroom screen, splattering my face and pillow. I groped over and slammed the window shut. Lightning slashed the sky. A thunderboomer rumbled across the bay and echoed off the islands. The clouds emptied out. The steady drumbeat on the roof lulled me back to sleep. It was daylight when I awakened. Falling raindrops wrinkled the bay like an old man's skin. I would have liked to sleep in, but I had to make another try at seeing Solange.

I crawled out from between my clammy sheets and dressed for a soggy Cape Cod day: cutoffs, T-shirt, Red Sox ball hat, and yellow slicker. I stopped at Elsie's for a large coffee and a glazed doughnut to go, then took Route 6 toward Provincetown.

I drove with the headlights on, splashing through great puddles caused by flash flooding. At Fort Hill the parking lot was deserted. I pulled up to the split rail fence, facing toward the ocean, and turned on the radio. A local station was playing Mozart. I sipped my coffee and gnawed at the doughnut. Sooty clouds scudded over the Atlantic.

At ten past nine, lights crept up the access road. A late-model black Lincoln Town Car parked next to the pickup. The window rolled down and Solange beckoned me over. I got out and dashed through the rain.

She greeted me with a worried smile. She was dressed in a white one-piece cotton jumpsuit that underlined the velvety texture of her skin. "I wasn't sure you'd be here. I'm sorry I didn't come yesterday. It was impossible to get away."

"You're here today, that's what counts." I offered her the doughnut. "Bite?"

She shook her head. "Why were you on the beach the other night?"

"I saw some strange lights."

She looked puzzled. Then she laughed. "Oh, the lights. That's nothing. They just had to do with the television filming."

I finished my coffee, then stuffed half the doughnut into the empty cup.

"We could waltz around this all day long, lady, but it would be a waste of your time and mine. You're not part of a television crew. I know the lights were laser position finders and that you were using them to look for the *Pandora*."

The smile vanished. Her doe eyes piníoned me in a level gaze. "Who are you?"

Solange was scared. She was frightened to death of Nigel and Jack. That came across the other night on the beach, and she was sending me the same message now. Fear was the only leverage I had with her and I wasn't too proud to use it. "Maybe I'm someone who can help you."

"Are you from the police?"

"Not exactly."

She shook her head, dazed. "Then you're with the government?"

"Let's say I have government connections. We can help you, but it's not a one-way deal. I want information."

"What sort of information?"

"For starters, what's Nigel got to do with the *Pandora*?"

She studied me for a moment. "If I tell you, then what?"

"I'll help you."

There was doubt in her eyes.

"I'm your best chance," I pressed.

"I don't know."

"Consider your alternatives before you answer." I was betting she had none.

She took a deep breath and let it out slowly. "I don't have any."

"Then we have a deal?"

She nodded. "Nigel was waiting in Boston," she said. "When the ship didn't arrive, he decided he'd been double-crossed, that the cargo had been diverted."

"What changed his mind?"

"He read about the first body coming ashore after the storm. The attacks at Quanset Beach gave him the idea. We would say we were filming the story for TV. We'd be just one more TV crew. It would be the perfect cover."

"Cover for what?"

"To search for the ship."

"Do you know what the *Pandora* was carrying?"

"No. Only that it's very dangerous."

I searched her face for a sign she was holding out, but all I saw was a very scared young woman.

"Has he found the ship?"

"Yes. The night I saw you on the beach. You're right, they *were* using lasers to pinpoint the wreck somehow. I don't really know how it works. Nigel wanted to dive yesterday, but he saw a fishing boat working over the ship."

"What does he plan to do next?"

"I don't know. Nigel doesn't tell me everything. I assume he'll dive as soon as he thinks it's safe to do so."

The wind caught a fistful of raindrops and flung them against the window. The glassy rattle startled Solange.

I wiped a peephole in the fogged windshield. "The storm is moving fast," I said. "The sun should be out in a little while."

She smiled tentatively.

"How did you get into this mess?"

She looked out at the black clouds racing over the ocean. "It's a long story. I was born in the Bahamas. My family moved to London when I was eight years old. My father was a civil servant—not a high position, but a responsible one, having to do with the ministry of banking. There was a scandal. A case of embezzlement. My father was accused and convicted. He was not sentenced to prison, but his job was gone, his reputation was in shambles." She paused. The memory was still difficult. "He killed himself. My mother was never the same after that. She went in and out of fits of depression, trying vainly to find someone in the government who would clear my father's name. Nobody would help; after all, he was just a colonial, and a black one at that. Eventually, quite by accident, the real embezzler was caught. But by then you see, it was too late."

"Is that where you met Nigel? In London?"

"I was doing graduate work at the University of London. I met Nigel at a cocktail party. He was from a wealthy old English family. He seemed the epitome of all their pompous and arrogant ways. I'd had a few drinks, and all my anger came out. To my surprise, he agreed with me. He said the upper class who ruled the country were a bunch of prigs who didn't care about anything beyond their inflated positions and fat salaries. We began to see each other."

"Did you know what he did for a living?"

"Not at first. He sounded me out. Apparently, I passed the test. He began to tell me of his business dealings. Selectively, of course. He said he was procuring arms for African rebels who were fighting the remnants of colonial power. It was exactly what I wanted to hear, of course, and Nigel knew that."

"You said Nigel was English."

"Yes, and the world was his for the asking, but he claimed he'd die before he'd put on a bowler and take a financial position in the City. He was in the army, some sort of elite commando group from what I can glean. They learned how to scale buildings and drop out of helicopters in frogman suits. Now he calls himself a military consultant."

"What made you change your mind about him?"

"I was so naive at first. Or maybe blinded by my hatred. It didn't take me long to discover this isn't a war of one army against another. It's the slaughter of the innocents. Angola. Somalia. The Sudan. South Africa. Yugoslavia. Northern Ireland. Arms and hatred breed war. I wanted no part of that. You know, people never think about the injured. They read about them and say, oh well, that person was fortunate only to be injured. If people could only see the victims . . ."

She was shaking with anger. We sat, listening to the rain pelting overhead.

After awhile, I said, "Why haven't you walked away from Nigel?"

"That's what I should have done. But I was in love. Later, when I came to my senses, I should have simply left him, but instead, I talked to him, told him I wanted out. He said I was in too deep. I know too much. He said he'd track me down, and if he couldn't find me, he'd kill my mother."

"What do you know about Jack Morgan?"

"Only that he's American army. In demolitions. Jack has an almost sexual attraction to explosives. He and Nigel met several months ago. I'm deathly afraid of him."

I put my hand on the warm smoothness of her arm. "There's a way out of this, Solange, but it won't be easy. Nigel's got to be caught and put away for a long time."

"But what can you do alone against the two of them?"

"I need some time to work on this. I'll have to talk to you again."

"It's impossible. If Nigel's not watching me, Jack is. I told them I was coming into town to shop today. I can't use that excuse all the time."

"Can I call you at the Dwight house?"

She shook her head. "Too dangerous."

I got out my wallet and gave her my business card. "Then you'll have to call me."

She looked at my card. "A private detective? You said you were a fisherman."

"I'll explain later. If I don't hear from you soon, I'll accept Nigel's invitation for cocktails."

She looked at her watch. "I must go," she said urgently. "I told them I had to buy clothes. If I don't come home with something they'll get suspicious."

"Keep in touch."

She stared at me a moment, then leaned over. Her lips brushed my cheek. Again, I smelled rose petals. Then she started the engine. I climbed out into the rain. The Lincoln pulled away. I watched the red taillights vanish around a bend and wondered if I should trust her.

The thunderclouds were moving offshore. I drove off the hill, glancing casually across the rolling downs. About two hundred yards away, a man dressed in a green army surplus poncho and rain hat stood near a grove of locust trees. He seemed to be peering through binoculars. Crazy bird-watchers. They'll go out in the crummiest weather.

Chapter 27

A silvery-blue comet blasted through the intersection. It was Rollins, hunched over his Kawasaki like the Lone Ranger in hot pursuit of rustlers. The Kawasaki disappeared down the rain-puddled road toward Quanset. The light turned green. I spun onto the beach road and mashed the accelerator. Rollins was outside the administration building, notebook in hand, talking to a cop. He saw me, broke off the interview, and came over.

"Unfriggingbelievable." He shook his head. "This is nuts. Crazy. There's another dead guy on the beach."

"So what? That's like saying there's seaweed on the sand. Bodies have been floating ashore all week."

"Don't count this one, unless the high tide left him in a dune shack."

Gary came out of the administration building. "I'm

taking the press for a beach ride, Soc. There's room for you in the Jeep."

Hell, it was getting so my day wasn't complete unless I'd seen a corpse. Gary stopped at the beach buggy shack. The red patrol truck lumbered off the beach. Waiting EMT's hoisted a body bag into their ambulance and drove off with roof lights flashing. Gary pointed the Jeep south onto the beach road.

"Fire started in one of the beach shacks early this morning," Gary said. "Somebody in a nearby shack got up to use the outhouse and smelled smoke. He called for help on his CB. Usually when a shack catches fire, it just goes. The wood is old and dry and it's impossible for the fire department to get a pump truck out here. Luckily, that hard rain we had smothered the fire before it got the beach grass going."

"Who was in that bag?" Rollins asked. "The cops didn't want to say until next of kin was notified."

"That's a laugh. Everybody in town will know before the day is out. Besides, Huggins didn't have any next of kin."

The name was drowned out by the snarl of low gear. "Did you say Huggins?" I said.

"Yeah. You must know him. He was sort of the town's unofficial historian. Always putting on slide shows."

"Holy shit," Rollins said. "He was the guy who fed my esteemed editor and publisher the crapola on the pirate curse."

Gary said, "Sure, I remember seeing his name in the *Gazette.*"

"Hell," Rollins said, "guess the curse got him, too."

"Uh-uh," said Gary. "No curse. Looks like a suicide."

"Huggins killed himself?" I said.

"All I know is the guy who found him said he saw a shotgun next to the body."

The smell of charred wood came to our nostrils on the southwest breeze. The Jeep turned right and followed a sand track for about fifty yards.

The Huggins camp was, or had been, about the size of a large garage. Like most of the beach shacks, it was built originally as a duck hunting camp, then fancied up. The hip roof was surmounted by an oversized cupola big enough for a man to stand in. A couple of ancient wooden rockers with lattice seats rested on the porch. The front of the building looked like the false front of a movie set. The backside looked as if it had been scorched with a giant blowtorch. All that was left was a pile of charcoaled shingles and studs and a brick chimney. Fingers of smoke rose from the still-smouldering wreckage. Someone had wisely dragged the propane tanks away from the shack.

Over the front door was a crude quarterboard. It was carved with the words HI STORY, a punnish gesture toward the camp's nascent second floor and Huggins's passion with the past.

A fire department pickup truck was parked nearby. A dozen kibbitzers strolled around inspecting the damage. I knew the fireman standing in front of the place.

"Mind if I go up on the porch and take a look?"

"Yeah, I guesso," he said. "Just don't go inside. The fire marshal's coming out to poke around for cause."

"Any idea what started it?"

"Coulda been anything. Kerosene lantern. Cigarette. My bet is lightning. Most of these shacks are firetraps when you come right down to it. Just lucky the gas tanks didn't explode."

I went up on the porch and peeked in the front door. The shack had basically been one small room. The kitchen area had survived. There were a couple of chairs, an old wooden table with a metal top, a gas refrigerator, some shelves with canned goods on them. Where the bunks must have been was a pile of soggy black wood.

On the floor near the table was a dark sticky-looking stain.

I stepped off the porch and noticed a sliver of paper between two warped floorboards. I picked it up, glanced at it, and put it in my wallet. Then I walked around back. Gary was talking to the fireman. Rollins finished interviewing some spectators and came over. "Well, what do you think?"

I scratched my head under the baseball cap. "It doesn't make sense."

"Suicide never does. Maybe the guy was sick or something."

"No, not that. The fire doesn't make sense. How did it start?"

"The fire guy thinks it was lightning."

"That's what he told me, but try this on for size. Lightning strikes, the place catches on fire, and while it goes up in flames around him, Huggins blows his brains out. That's a little dramatic, don't you think?"

"So Huggins kills himself, *then* the lightning strikes." Rollins looked at me for encouragement, found none. "See what you mean. You really would have to believe in a pirate curse to swallow that kind of coincidence. Maybe it wasn't lightning. Maybe the guy started the fire by accident before he shot himself."

"I don't buy it. Huggins would have forgotten all about killing himself. He'd have tried to put the fire out."

"So maybe he started the fire on purpose."

"Why would he do that? If you're going to kill yourself, why torch your place first? Just in case the bullet doesn't work?"

"Maybe it was like a Viking funeral. He was a historian. Maybe Huggins loved the shack, so he didn't want anyone else to use it after he was gone."

"Maybe clams fly at night."

Rollins loped after me like a hungry puppy. "What are you saying?"

"I saw that storm. The rain came through about the same time as the lightning. I don't think fire would have had the chance to do this much damage in the time between the lightning and rain. But there's the reason I think the lightning theory is bogus." I pointed to a thin vertical rod attached to the cupola.

"Lightning rod?" Rollins said.

I nodded.

"Could be the guy was cooking something and the stove got out of control?"

"Could be you're reaching."

"Aw, c'mon. Hey, waitaminute. Do you think it wasn't suicide?"

"I'm just saying it looks funny."

"This is incredible. I can't believe I've been trying to get a job with a city paper. The stuff I'm covering will last me the rest of my life. Are you and Gary through here? I want to go back and interview the fire chief."

"I'm done."

"I haven't forgotten our deal. You remember, about helping each other? You just helped me, so I'm going to help you. I started asking around about Huggins after we talked at the paper the other day. He had a skeleton in his closet. He used to be a Boy Scout leader in upstate New York years before he moved here. Old houses weren't the only things he liked to take pictures of. Cops brought him in for child molesting. He beat the charges, but he had to leave town."

"Who else knew that?"

"The local cops are aware of it, but they figured Huggins was too old to cause any trouble, just as long as he didn't volunteer to be a den mother."

It was time to go. I had seen enough, and I wanted to catch up with Sam.

You could tell Sam's place was a fisherman's house just by looking at it.

Sam and Mildred lived in a neat one-hundred-fifty-year-old Greek Revival house of gleaming white clapboard. Colorful lobster buoys hung on the weathered shed. There were Day-Glo spherical plastic floats in the backyard near a pile of rotting lobster pots. A skiff lay upside down on two sawhorses, ready to receive a new coat of paint. It had been there since I started fishing with Sam.

I expected Mildred to answer the bell, so was surprised when Sam came to the door. He gave me a horse grin, allowed how it was nice of me to come by, and invited me inside. The television was tuned to a black-and-white rerun of *The Honeymooners.*

"Always liked Jackie Gleason," Sam explained. "The new fellas you see on TV don't seem quite as real as they used to be."

He looked as if he had gained ten years and lost ten pounds. Maybe it was seeing him in a bathrobe and PJ's in the middle of the day. Old people seem to age fast when an ailment strikes. As if they've been reminded of how old they are, and their bodies can't take the news. Sam seemed a little more hunched over at the shoulders than usual, and under his pale blue eyes he had shadows you never saw when he was fishing.

"Millie at home?"

He switched off the TV and settled into an easy chair. His duck-visored tan cap was on the arm of the chair, ready to go. "She went into town to do some errands. Be back in a bit." He slapped his knee. "Darn, it's good to see you, Soc. This hospital thing has been a real pain."

"What's the latest?"

He scowled. "Doc just wants me to take it easy 'til the tests are in. How'd you do yesterday with that dive charter?"

"Just fine, Sam."

"That's good, Soc. I don't figure it'll be more than a day or so before I get back to work. Millie'll probably kick me out of the house before that. I just can't seem to help being underfoot. Heard about those bodies on Quanset Beach. They have anything to do with whatever it is bit people?"

"My brain says there's no connection between the two things. But my nose has been twitching like yours does when bad weather's afoot."

Sam chuckled, then grew serious. "You got any idea what chewed up that man at Quanset?"

"Not yet. How about you?"

"Nope. But I've been thinking how the ocean's pretty predictable most of the time."

"Lot of people might argue that it's *un*predictable."

"I know they would, but think of it. She's going to be either nice or naughty. Trick is to figure out which is going to be which. It wasn't until people came along that things started to go out of whack."

"How do you mean, Sam?"

He grabbed his pipe, then put it down. "Not supposed to smoke," he said in disgust. "What I mean is, the ocean likes to keep things in balance. We come in, with our ships and our oil drilling rigs, our garbage dumping, our overfishing, and it throws things off. The ocean doesn't take kindly to us messing around with her. She reminds us who's boss." He flashed a mischievous grin. "Sort of like me and Millie."

"Which one of you is boss?"

"Which do you think?"

I got out of my chair. "I'll steer clear of that one.

How about getting together for a couple of games of checkers?"

"I'd like that, finestkind."

I told him I'd give him a call in the morning. When he shook my hand, I was glad to see that his grip was as strong as ever.

I called Norma when I got back to the boathouse.

"Put a clothespin on your nose, Soc. Phew, this whole thing stinks."

I grabbed a pad and pencil. "Clothespin's in place, Norma. What do you have?"

"First there's your friend, Mr. Costello. You didn't tell me he was a naughty boy."

"Yeah, he got sent to bed without his supper. What else?"

"Well, to begin with, Costello is the major trustee of six trusts. Those trusts own other companies. Somebody paid a corporate lawyer a lot of money to make it hard to figure out who is behind the companies, but we electronic snoops just don't give up. Here's a list of the top officers."

She reeled off the boards of a dozen companies. Olney was imbedded in every one of them. A few other names were familiar, too. The chairman of selectmen, for one. A few local businessmen. I asked Norma about the names I didn't recognize.

"They're all pols, Soc. Politically-connected fat cats who were shoehorned into jobs years ago when Olney was in the State House. They're on the big authorities like MassPike, MDC, or MassPort, where nobody can touch them."

"Anything else?"

"Just a little thing. That last company I gave you doesn't have anything to do with Mr. Costello. It was set up by Olney for his son. The kid's name is Stephen. Word I get is that the old man has spoiled the kid rotten, and he's financed him in some kind of business."

"What kind of business?"

"No details. I can check it out."

"That's okay, I think I know what it is." I remembered what Alex had told me about Stephen bankrolling the dope deals. I asked how Norma's diet was going.

"Max ordered me off it. Says he loves plump women. Isn't he a doll?"

"Yeah, Norma. You are, too."

I told her to forward any further information, hung up, and started going over the names, looking for a pattern. An hour later, all I had to show for it was a pageful of doodles. I went to the fridge. Oops, I'd forgotten to get more beer; I'd have to go out. First, I called Gary at the beach and asked how I could get in touch with Diana Trumbull. He said the state marine biologist had hung her hat at the town shellfish lab on the cove.

The lab was in a former garage a couple of hundred feet from the cove. The town shellfish biologist raised seed clams there and transplanted them to fallow areas along the shore. The door was open and I went in without knocking. Most of the inside area was taken up by wooden trays, stacked with space between them. Water circulating in from the cove gurgled through the pipes. There was the scent of old wood and the ghosts of long-dead shellfish. In one corner against the windows was counter space. Using the counter for a desk was Diana Trumbull.

She turned when I greeted her. To my great surprise, she didn't show her fangs. Her hair was tousled as if she had been running her hands through it, her eyes were dazed the way they get when someone's been reading too long.

She said, "Oh, it's you," with neither hostility nor friendliness.

I nodded toward an old wooden chair. "Mind if I sit down?"

"Go ahead. I was just finishing up."

I handed her a container of cranberry juice I picked up on the way. "Thanks," she said. "It gets hot in here with no air-conditioning."

"I know I'm not supposed to ask, but I wondered how your investigation was going?"

Diana sighed. "I may try your Loch Ness monster theory after all."

I opened my juice and stuck the straw in. "Look, Ms. Trumbull, I make my living on the water and so do a lot of my friends. I really would like to hear what you have to say."

She tapped a manila folder that was about an inch thick. "I have talked to lifeguards, witnesses, town officials, and to the surviving victim. I've examined autopsy and medical reports. I've looked into the habits of every predator in the Gulf of Maine and Cape Cod waters. I've even taken samples of the water."

"Conclusion?"

"I just don't know. *Some*thing attacked those people. I have photographs of those terrible wounds, and there's no doubt in my mind that they were made by a living organism or organisms, not gravel or an outboard motor propeller, as some people have suggested."

"Any idea what kind of organism?"

"Something with teeth. I've ruled out sharks, simply because of the bite. And bluefish. Nobody has ever gotten more than a painful nip from one. My educated guess is that one or more exotic, possibly dangerous fish wandered up here from southern waters because the water is unusually warm this summer."

"Any idea on species?"

"Absolutely none. But I'm going to assume that it was a freak occurrence and it won't happen again."

"Do you really believe that?"

"No. But that's what is going to be in my report. I can't do anything else. I'll have to recommend that the beach be opened."

"You can't do that."

Her stubborn chin came up at an angle. "I certainly can."

I realized I had snapped at her. "I'm sorry. I'm not trying to tell you how to do your job, but I'm worried someone might get hurt."

"It's out of my hands. The business people have been putting pressure on the town officials. They've been pushing my bosses. My bosses have been leaning on me.

If I can't come up with definitive answers, they are going to assume that the beach is safe, and frankly, I have no way to refute that."

"Then let me add something to your investigation. I'm not sure you'll believe me. But I swear every word is true. Not another fish story."

"Go ahead. I promise to listen to what you have to say."

I went out to my truck and brought in my scratched air tank and chewed-up fin. Then I gave her an edited version of my dive. I told her something had attacked me. I fudged the truth and said I had hunkered down on the bottom until whatever hit me had gone away. I described the flicker and the eyes I was sure I'd seen in the undersea gloom. I didn't mention the *Pandora.*

She said: "I believe there *is* something out there, and it is dangerous. But I can't do a thing about it."

"I know you're in a tough spot, but is there anyone who has the power or guts to act?"

"Sure, my superiors. Power, yes. Guts, no. They're just bureaucrats. They serve at the whim of the politicians."

"Thanks for being up front with me, Ms. Trumbull. When will you file your report?"

"I'll fax it up to Boston today."

"I guess that's it, then."

She nodded sadly.

"Maybe Sam was right," I mused. I told her about Sam's theory about the consequences of messing around with the ocean.

"Your friend Sam sounds like the original wise old

man of the sea. Maybe the creatures are warning us that they're angry over what we're doing to their habitat. We looked into a case not long ago where radioactive waste was dumped into Massachusetts Bay. Whether it's ozone depletion or rain forest destruction, we're changing the earth and the oceans. We'll have to live with the consequences."

"Then that's not the end of this thing."

"No." She shook her head grimly. "Probably not."

"Ms. Trumbull, I'd like to ask a favor. You remember the fisherman I told you about on the beach, the guy who saw something in the water and had his fishlines snapped? I'd like you to see him before you hand in your final report. I think I can get him to talk to you."

She lightly traced a line under her lower lip with a fingertip. Then she nodded. "A few hours won't make a great deal of difference."

I told her I'd be in touch, and set off to find Mac. His boat was at the dock, so he wasn't fishing. I tried the charter fleet pier, but he wasn't there. I found him at the 'Hole, where I should have looked in the first place. He was a little cool to the idea of telling his story to Diana Trumbull, but after I told him the interview would be confidential, described Diana, and bought him a few beers, he agreed to talk to her. I said I'd set it up. Then I went home, stopping for a six of Bud. Kojak was waiting at the door, doing his best imitation of a Dickensonian waif. I gave him an extra helping of food because I'd been so neglectful of late. I was gathering up my notes. There was a knock at the front door. I went to open it.

Nigel gave me his big-toothed grin. "Hello, old sport," he said.

Chapter 2 8

I grinned back, but Nigel had me outgrinned by a mile; I guess my heart wasn't in it.

"Hello, Nigel. Hi, Jack. What a pleasant surprise."

It was hard not to stammer or yammer, given what I'd learned about these boys from Flagg and Solange.

What the hell are they doing here?

"Hope we haven't caught you at a bad time, old sport. Since you haven't accepted our invitation to come by our place for cocktails and to talk about the bloody Blood Triangle, we dropped by to see if you could give us a few minutes of a film interview."

"No problem." I gestured them inside. "Couldn't Solange make it?"

His grin grew wider and even more equine. "She had some filming schedules she wanted to tend to."

"That's too bad. Maybe another time. I was just

about to have a beer out on the deck. Would you like to join me?"

Nigel cocked his head disarmingly. "Well, that's very kind of you." He turned to Jack. "Be a good chap and bring in the equipment while I get Mr. Socarides set up. We don't want to waste too much of his time."

I led Nigel into the kitchen. Casually, I picked up the yellow pad.

"Oh, I'm sorry, we interrupted your work."

I put the pad on top of the refrigerator. "I was just making out a shopping list." I opened the refrigerator. It was almost empty except for the six-pack of Bud.

"Yes, I see what you mean," said Nigel, crinkling his brow sympathetically. I pulled three cold beers out and offered him one. Then we went outside. Beer in hand, Nigel strolled to the edge of the deck and surveyed the bay.

"It's quite beautiful," he said. "A man could spend the rest of his life here."

"I certainly hope to."

He popped his Bud and raised the foaming can. "Well, here's to fulfillment of that wish." It was a friendly toast, but the big-toothed grin didn't go with the hardness in the green eyes.

Jack came through the kitchen and out onto the deck a few minutes later. He was lugging a tripod and an aluminum suitcase. He opened the case. Inside, cushioned by sponge rubber, rested a video camera. He took it out and put it on the tripod, then spread the legs. Kojak came by to see what was going on, but left when he discovered no chow was involved.

"Over there would do nicely," Nigel said, pointing

to a corner. "I don't believe we'll need the floods. The afternoon light here is quite adequate, don't you think, and it has a lovely soft quality about it."

He asked me to sit in a folding chair, attached a minimike to my T-shirt, another to his safari jacket, then sat next to me, notebook in hand.

"This is a test," he said to the camera. "Testing, testing. One two three."

Jack looked up from the camera and nodded. Nigel turned to me. "Well, then, we are interviewing Mr. Aristotle Socarides. Am I pronouncing your last name correctly?"

"Like the philosopher."

He grinned. "Mr. Aristotle Socarides is a fisherman who lives on Cape Cod." The grin vanished and he lowered his voice to a Bela Lugosi timbre. "And he was an eyewitness to the mysterious attack by *some*thing which killed a Canadian swimmer on holiday during a swim at Quanset Beach. Mr. Socarides, could you tell us what you saw at the beach that day?"

Nigel led me through the events at Quanset, skillfully drawing out details with intelligent questions. Not bad for a guy who buys and sells death for a living. It was hard to tell who was the better phony, Nigel or me. Jack didn't do much beyond tend to the camera. I wondered if there was film in it.

Finally, Nigel said, "Thank you, Mr. Socarides, for giving us your personal account of that bloody day at Quanset Beach."

He turned and faced the camera.

"What lurks beneath the dark sea that washes

Quanset Beach? Is it some great sea creature stirred into life by the curse of a doomed English pirate? And having satisfied itself, will it move on to new feeding grounds? Or will it strike again to satisfy its savage hunger? Many of the inhabitants of this small resort and fishing community are asking themselves these very same and deeply disturbing questions. This is Nigel Eden on Cape Cod, Massachusetts. Thank you and good day."

He drew the edge of his hand across his throat.

"That was bloody good, Mr. Socarides. You have an eye for detail and a flare for the dramatic."

"Maybe we both should have been actors."

He chuckled deep in his throat, but the green eyes didn't light. "That should do it, Jack. Let's collect this equipment and get it in the Blazer."

Jack gathered up the camera and tripod. Nigel and I walked outside. He watched his assistant pull down the tailgate.

"Jack doesn't say much, as you probably noticed. It's a quality which makes him a splendid assistant. He's the strong silent type. He never even asks for a raise."

I smiled. "When and where might I see this interview?"

"I think we'll wrap up our work here in a few days. We'll get it back to New York soonest and see what we've got. *Hard Copy* and *Unsolved Mysteries* have both expressed an interest in the story. I don't know how much shelf life this piece has, so I would imagine they would schedule it fairly soon. If there are more attacks or someone actually catches this thing that goes about nibbling on people, of course, there would be a film crew down here as quick as a wink. I don't know if it will be us, however. We may be on assignment on the other side of the world, chasing down the Abominable Snowman. Thanks again for your time, and for your beer.

We shook hands. They got into the Blazer and drove away. My blood pressure ratcheted down a few points. Why this chummy little visit? Had Solange betrayed our little chat? I put myself in Nigel's shoes, knowing that I was privy to their scheme. What would I do? I didn't like the answer I gave myself. I would get rid of the dumb gumshoe who had stumbled on my plans. So why hadn't they done it? I was alone. The boathouse is isolated. They could have taken care of me and thrown me in the bay.

I went back in the house and stood in the living room. Something was wrong. I felt it in my bones.

I shrugged and cleaned up the beer cans, then took my notepad off of the refrigerator. I had some pieces to the puzzle, now all I had to do was put them together. I heard a car come into the drive. My pulse quickened. Maybe Nigel was coming back to do the job.

I ran over to the front door and looked through the screen. Sally was walking toward me in the graceful easy saunter I had come to know so well. She saw me and smiled.

Chapter 29

Sally's kiss was long and warm. We played a game of square inches with our bodies. After a moment, she broke away gently and picked up the wicker basket she'd brought.

"I'm glad you're home. I took a chance you'd be here and brought something for dinner."

"I'm glad I'm home, too." I held the screen door open and she went inside. She wore dark violet shorts and a pale lilac tank top. Her breasts moved behind the thin cotton fabric.

"You didn't have to bring food. I could have whipped up something incredible. Remember my *zucchini creole à la Webber grill*?"

"How could I forget it? I also remember the Hamburger Helper topped with potato buds and Velveeta and your tuna, pepperoni, and ziti sprinkled with a subtle blend of Romano and Parmesan cheese and walnuts."

She opened the basket, extracted a neatly folded red-and-white cloth, and spread it over the kitchen table. Next she took out some plastic containers and a bottle of Piesporter Michelsburg, which she handed to me.

"A light, sparkly German wine. Just the thing for a warm summer night."

While I rummaged in a drawer for my corkscrew, Sally pulled out a baguette, cut off a few thin slices, opened the containers, and placed their contents on my chipped willow pattern dishes.

"Voilà. Pasta salad with spinach pesto à la yuppie. Cold mussels with aioli sauce and thin sliced beef. And for dessert, Ben and Jerry's Cherry Garcia."

I put a Vivaldi tape on the stereo, lit a couple of bayberry candles, and turned the lights off. We sat down and dug into the food. Sally talked about her dolphins. I filled her in about Sam. She told me about her ailing sea lion. Without going into detail, I told her about Cousin Alex.

After dinner I washed the dishes and Sally dried. Kojak licked the mussel and pesto containers, burped, and strolled off discreetly to bed.

Sally and I settled into the overstuffed green sofa with the faded flower print. We talked, not so much to each other, as at each other. Again, we did a conversational dance, waiting to see what kind of music the band played. Slaves to our hormones, we kept discomforting thoughts at a distance, for now at least, and if it wasn't the adult or even the wise thing to do, it felt very, very right.

I leaned over and kissed her neck. Her skin smelled of herbal shampoo and body silk. Her teeth nipped my ear gently, teasingly. We both knew where this was headed.

We left a trail of clothes all the way to the bedroom. I kicked Kojak off the bed and we slipped under the sheets.

There is no better place to make love than near the sea. You can hear the lonely call of the night birds in the marshes, as the tide whispers against the shore. The ocean air tosses the white cotton curtains and cools overheated bodies. We made love, the way it should be between friends, slowly and surely and deliciously, savoring each moment until the final one.

Later, we made love again. Entwined in a tangle of arms and legs, we fell into a deep sleep.

The sound seemed part of the images drifting through my sleep like flotsom on the ocean of dreams. I awoke, sat up, and stared into the shadows, confused. The phone rang again. I fumbled in the blackness and grabbed the phone. I managed to get it to my ear and grunt hello.

"You must get out of your house!" It was a woman's voice, loud and panic-stricken.

"Wha—?"

"Get out of your house."

"Solange," I managed, "is that you?"

"Yes, yes. I've been trying to call you."

Sally sat up and rubbed her eyes.

"Solange, what's going on?"

Sally became fully awake. "Who's Solange?"

"They put something in your house," Solange insisted, hysterically.

"Who put what where?"

"Nigel and Jack. In your bedroom."

Sally tugged at my arm. "Soc, who are you talking to?"

I shushed her, flicked on the lamp, and looked around. I got up, did a quick check of the closet and dresser drawers, not sure what I was looking for. There were some dust bunnies next to the bed. I quickly moved the lamp down from the night stand onto the floor. Its light outlined a package about the size of a shoebox, wrapped in brown paper and sealed with wide mailing tape. I knew it didn't belong to me.

They put something in your house.

The fingers holding the lamp turned to ice. Jack was alone in the house for at least five minutes while Nigel and I talked on the deck. More than enough time to slip a present under the bed.

Jack has an almost sexual attraction to explosives.

I yelled into the phone. "Solange, are you still there?"

"Yes, yes, but I *can't* talk now. *Please* go. Please. There isn't much time."

"How *much* time?"

"Two o'clock. It's set to go off at two o'clock. That's all I know."

The hands on the nightstand clock said three minutes to two. I dropped the phone. Sally was curled up under the sheets again in a fetal position, her way of saying she didn't like women calling me up in the middle of the night. I didn't blame her, but in this case it was too freaking bad.

"Sally, get up!"

She curled herself into more of a ball.

I whipped the sheet off her naked body, grabbed her wrists and yanked her off the mattress.

"Soc," she protested, more in surprise than pain. "What are you doing? You're hurting me!"

I wrapped the top sheet around her. "Sorry. I can't explain now, but we've got to get out of here." I steered her toward the front door.

She went reluctantly, tripping over the sheet. "Okay, *okay*. Just stop shoving."

"Get out of the house. Get as far away from it as you can."

She dug her heels in. Sally is hard to anger, but when she pops, her combined genes from County Cork and Palermo take over. She gets mad and stubborn at the same time. Now she aimed her chin at me like a lethal weapon.

"You just hold on, Aristotle Socarides," she fumed. "I have no intention of running outside into the night like some fugitive from a fraternity toga party—"

I glanced at the kitchen clock, a thrift shop acquisition that never ran on time. Two minutes.

I gathered her clothes off the floor and stuck them into her arms.

"Okay, take these with you, but get dressed outside. *Please* do what I'm asking. I have not gone crazy. I promise to give you an explanation."

"It better be good."

Clutching her clothes, she wheeled and stalked off with me on her heels. Halfway out the front door, I stopped.

"You go ahead," I said. "I'll catch up."

I dashed back inside, snapped the light on in the living room, and checked the sofa. No damned cat. Not on the wing chair either. I sprinted into the kitchen. Maybe he was having a midnight snack. Not there either. Damn! Where was he? I checked the bathroom to make sure he wasn't sleeping in the tub. Quick, think like Kojak. Where would you be? Of course. I dashed into the bedroom. He had snuck back onto the bed and was asleep with his head on a pillow.

"Kojak!"

His head came off the pillow. He glared at me with yellow eyes as big as pie plates. From his point of view, I was a screaming creature who was coming straight for him, arms extended, nasty hands curled. He jumped off the bed and tried to squeeze underneath. I grabbed his haunches just before they disappeared under the spring-board.

His skin stretched, but he was like a half-filled bag of suet and didn't come with it. He had dug his claws into the rug. His body got longer and longer. I looked at the clock.

The minute hand was so close to the twelve it wasn't worth looking at.

I reached in, dislodged his paws, yanked hard, and dragged him out from under the bed. I stood with him clutched to my chest, his legs dangling loose, then bolted through the house and out the front door.

"Sally," I called into the night.

"Over here by the woodpile."

The sharp edges of the clamshell driveway cut my feet, but I made it to the woodpile, and told Sally to get down behind it. Cautiously, I raised my head. All was silent except for the buzz of the insects. The lights blazed in the boathouse and it looked comfortable and inviting.

Sally clutched my arm. "Soc," she whispered. "*Please* tell me what's going on."

Kojak was squirming. I tightened my grip and watched the gleaming new shingles on the bedroom wall. It must be past two o'clock by now. Solange was wrong. Nothing was going to happen.

I turned to Sally. She deserved an explanation. "That telephone call I just got was—"

Whump!

My head jerked toward the explosion. The wall of the boathouse had gone white-hot. The night-adjusted pupils of my eyes closed down in reflex, but not fast enough to stop my retina from absorbing the full impact of the nova that had replaced my bedroom wall.

Night turned into day.

Sally raised her head. I pushed it down and ducked behind the protection of the double-stacked cords of wood. Splinters of wall and ceiling and new shingles rained down on us. Kojak went stiff with fear in my arms.

The blast echoed and reechoed across the bay. Then there was silence.

I edged around the logs and cautiously approached the house, blinking the stars out of my eyes.

The wall and part of the bedroom roof had disintegrated. There was no fire. The force of the explosion must have blown away the oxygen needed to fuel combustion. I felt a touch on my arm. Sally had come up behind me.

I was still standing in the debris-strewn yard, naked and holding a terrified Kojak in my arms, when the police cruiser swept up the drive, gumdrop flashing. The summer rent-a-cop piled out of the car and looked at the missing wall, then at me.

"Holy shit," he murmured, then ran for his radio. Sally raced behind the woodpile, clutching the sheet.

A fire truck showed up, followed by the rescue squad. The fire truck sprayed water around the wreckage. Sally got back into her shorts and top and loaned me her sheet. The EMT's looked me over, then put gunk on my feet where the soles had been cut by the shells in the driveway.

Everyone figured it was a gas explosion. I didn't argue with them. They'd change their minds as soon as they noticed the propane tanks were still intact.

My bedroom was open to the stars. The bed had been reduced to its basic molecules, but the rest of the house was in its usual disreputable shape. I located jeans, a T-shirt and sweatshirt, and high-top basketball Keds in an undamaged closet. Then Sally, Kojak and I drove to Sally's apartment.

I felt bad about my shingles. I had put a lot of work into getting them attached to the house. My garden, next to the bedroom, looked as if it had been hit by napalm. I always try to look on the bright side, though. Sally and Kojak and I were still breathing. And that damned tomato worm was gone.

Chapter 30

The boathouse looked much worse in daylight. My bedroom wall and ceiling had vanished. The bed was toothpicks and cotton balls. A pickup truck drove into the yard and two bearded guys got out. Bob and Joe, the carpenters I called from Sally's house. They gaped at the damage and asked what happened. I said I didn't know; I wasn't in the house at the time. That seemed to satisfy their curiosity and they left to buy plywood to lay over the holes.

Kojak had lost his normal feline aloofness and practically walked in my shoes wherever I went. I didn't blame him. A bomb must be a hard thing for a cat to comprehend. It was tough for *me* to understand. Sally had promised she would spoil him with piles of food and even let him sleep on her bed. It was pretty nice of her, considering she had almost been blown to bits. She mentioned that she didn't know practicing safe sex meant looking under the bed for explosives. Crazy sense of humor. That was one of the reasons I liked her.

I prowled around the yard and kicked at scraps of wood. A dull anger welled in my chest. I was angry at myself for involving Sally in this mess and for not being bright enough to figure out what Nigel and Jack were up to. Two cops showed up with someone from the county. I told them I thought it was a bomb. It would have been hard to explain otherwise. I said I got an anonymous warning call in the night. I said I had no idea who placed the bomb. It's not that I like to lie. But I wanted Nigel and Jack for myself.

They took pictures and picked up samples of junk, then left me alone. I went into the boathouse. A dresser was on its side but still intact. I piled a stack of clothes to take to Sally's apartment. The phone in the kitchen rang. New England Telephone was too tough to kill.

"Thank God! You're still alive. Are you all right?"

It seemed like a century had gone by since I last heard Solange's voice.

"Just dandy, but my bedroom has a new skylight and my cat needs therapy. Thanks for the wake-up call. You took a big risk."

"I wanted to warn you earlier, but Nigel and Jack were always around. I had to wait until they left to go to the beach. I thought I would go mad watching that clock."

"They came by yesterday for an interview. That's when they dropped their housewarming gift off."

"It's *my* fault. They knew I talked to you. I tried to deny it, but they'd seen us together."

The figure standing in the rain. "Guess I was wrong about the bird-watcher."

"What?"

"Somebody in a green poncho was watching us at Fort Hill."

"They went through my pocketbook and found your card. I told them you didn't know anything, but Nigel has a way of getting things out of a person. I heard them talking later. They were going to come over to force you to talk. Nigel decided that with time so short, it would be better to kill you. A clean surgical cut, he called it."

I looked through my bedroom door at the missing wall and ceiling. "Good thing he wasn't doing an appendectomy. Why is time short?"

"Too many people know about the *Pandora*. They're going to salvage what they can of the cargo. They went out early this morning."

"What else did they say about their plans?"

"Only that if they salvaged anything they would try to move it tonight."

Tonight. They couldn't salvage the whole cargo, but even a few canisters of nerve gas were big trouble.

"Can you leave the house?"

"They've taken the keys to the car."

"Listen carefully. Get out of the house and walk to the main road. It isn't far. Hitchhike into town and rent a car at the Mobil station. Write this address down." I gave her the name of a rooming house run by friends.

"Tell them to give you a room or I'll never speak to them again. Stay there until you hear from me. I'll call tonight or tomorrow."

"But what about Nigel and Jack? They'll find me—"

"No, they won't, because they're going to be in jail."

I held my breath while she thought it over and came to the conclusion that her options were limited. "All right. I'll do as you say."

"Good. And Solange . . ."

"Yes?"

"Thanks again."

I hung up and glanced around my bedroom. Thank God my mother wasn't here to see *this* mess. I owed Nigel and Jack a payback for their unsolicited remodeling job. But first I had to find them. I had a good idea where they might be. I called up Tillie Talbot and asked if someone could check from the bluff and tell me if a boat were anchored just offshore. She said she'd do it herself and call me back.

Ten minutes later, the phone rang. Tillie said a white boat appeared to be fishing a short distance from the beach. I asked her to call me if there was any change. I said I'd come by the camp later that day. I called Sam to let him know I was all right. Bob and Joe would undoubtedly stop off at Elsie's for coffee and I didn't want Sam to hear about the explosion through the Cape's coconut telegraph.

If I was right, there was no need to hurry. I raked the debris out of the house and kept out items that hadn't been damaged. The power was off, so I used up some mayonnaise and lettuce that was going bad in a tuna salad. Then I drove to the Quanset Beach Sailing Camp. Tillie was in her office dealing with a mound of paperwork. I told her I needed to tromp around her property.

"Does this have anything to do with the case?"

"I don't know. Maybe."

"Fine, be my guest while I catch up on this stuff. Stop by the office before you leave. And don't get run over by campers."

A minute later I was on the ocean bluff peering through binoculars. I had the lenses focused on a big Mako anchored over the *Pandora*. Nigel would have had a similarly good look at Flagg and me on the *Millie D.* A man with ginger hair leaned over the gunwale, looking down into the ocean. Nigel. As I watched, a Day-Glo head popped out of the sea. Nigel reached down to help the diver aboard. He stripped off what appeared to be a transparent outer suit. Then he got out of his drysuit. It was Morgan, double-layered for protection against K-22.

Jack had probably done a recon dive. Now he was talking it over with Nigel. I could guess what Morgan was saying. Salvaging the canisters would be tough, but not impossible. I went back to the lodge. Tillie hadn't made a dent in the mountain of bills. She pushed them aside and raised her eyebrows.

"I don't know if what I was looking at has anything to do with the camp," I told her. "Probably not. But I have information that does."

I sat down and told her what I had learned from

Norma. How Costello and Olney were partners, their ties to state and town officials. When I was through, she leaned back in her chair and looked out the window. Afternoon sunlight slanted through the pitch pine boughs.

"My husband and I worked like beavers to make a go of this camp. And these little men are trying to take it away from us. Why?"

"I think they expect to make some money. I don't know how yet, but I'm going to try to find out."

She reached over and took my hand. "Thank you very much for what you've done so far, Soc. You've already helped a great deal."

"There's still a lot to do. We've found out who our opposition is. Now we've got to figure out how to fight them."

"It's not your fight, Soc."

"I think it is. Like I said before, Cape Cod's been good to me. I came here with my brains scrambled, and the salt air has done more to clear my head than a hundred shrinks. I owe this place something."

"As you wish, Soc." She squeezed my hand and let go. "Well, it's back to the paperwork."

I stayed on the bluff until the sun went down and the shadows lengthened. At dinnertime a couple of campers came by with ham and cheese sandwiches, potato chips, soda, and cookies. I left my post only for bathroom runs, to get a can of Off! bug repellent spray, and to find a sweatshirt, for it was getting cooler and buggier.

Late in the afternoon, a double-engined plane circled overhead a couple of times. It looked like the plane that had buzzed Fort Hill on my walk with Flagg.

Sea and sky merged into a sheet of gray. Just before the light faded, the men in the boat began to winch something out of the ocean. A light went on where the boat was. My rear end was getting numb, my vision was starting to swim, and the mosquitoes were getting high on bug spray. Thoughts of the package Nigel and Jack left under my bed kept me glued to my seat.

Shortly after nine o'clock the light began to move north.

I went into the lodge and called Flagg. His answering service took my message and said he would get back to me immediately. Just have Mr. Flagg stand by for an important announcement, I told the service. Then I headed toward Quanset cut.

Chapter 3 1

Two miles from the camp, I spun the truck onto a rutted dirt road, drove a couple of hundred yards, and skidded to a stop at a white wooden barricade studded with red reflectors. I spilled from the truck and ran to the edge of a cliff. Quanset Heights is a prow-shaped headland that overlooks harbor and ocean. Moving across the great black sea like a space satellite was Nigel's boat. It was veering onto a westerly course that would take it straight to the cut.

Once inside the cut, Nigel could lose himself at a dozen hidden landings. I projected a mental map of Quanset harbor in my head. Nickerson Cove. The landing was isolated, hard to get to, and little used because the parking lot was smaller than a handkerchief and the water ankle-deep at low tide.

Minutes later, I was popping a quarter into a pay phone outside a convenience store. Flagg's patient answering service reported he was in the area, and that they could patch me through in a minute. I said there wasn't time. Just tell Flagg a load of trouble was coming in at Nickerson Cove and to meet me there pronto. I repeated the message to make sure it was understood, slammed the phone back in its cradle, and dashed for the truck.

The Nickerson Cove road descended from a bluff past older summer houses, narrowing to one lane as it meandered through a forest of scrub pine and oak bordering the harbor. A few hundred yards before the road dead-ended, I turned onto a sandy fire lane and left the truck. A path led through the woods and crossed a spiky swath of low dune blanketed with compass grass. I was panting when I came out of the dunes to the beach. Only the chuckle of the incoming tide and the chorus of night insects broke the otherworldly silence.

I squinted toward the harbor but saw only darkness. Maybe I had goofed. Nigel wasn't coming here. He was smart; he'd avoid doing the expected. I struck out quickly along the beach toward the unlit landing about fifty yards to my left. Twenty-five feet from the boat ramp, the scent of cigarette smoke came my way on the light kelpy breeze. I dropped to one knee. Ahead in the darkness, a man coughed.

I climbed back onto the dunes. Crawling on all fours like a child, I eased closer to the ramp, navigating painfully between razor-sharp clumps of beach grass. The sand was damp and cool under my palms. I stopped to listen to the distant whine of an outboard motor. Some passing fisherman on his way home? The noise grew louder. The boat was coming my way. Moments later, a light, softly diffused in the night mists, appeared like a will-o'-the-wisp around the corner of a marshy island. Nigel, if it *was* Nigel, had crossed the harbor faster than I figured.

The light blinked out. The motor sputtered to an idle. Then came the splash of an anchor. It was too shallow to bring the boat in. They would have to wait for the incoming tide. Now what, Socarides? I gnawed on my lower lip. This was insanity. I was alone. I didn't carry a gun. And I was about to go up against a dilettante thug and an ex-army guy who could eat a Granola bar and bench-press me with one hand at the same time. Maybe I could fake them out, claim my hands were lethal weapons. If that didn't work, I could throw quahogs at them.

In the end, I decided the best thing was to wait for Flagg. Ten minutes passed. Then twenty. Still no activity from the anchored boat. Patience isn't my forte. I was getting itchy to do something. I decided to check out their landing party. Was there more than one guy? Not that it mattered. One plus two that I knew of in the boat were three. Long odds. I inched forward on my belly.

The outboard motor started, the light came on and moved forward a few feet, then stopped. Still not enough water. The tide was coming in fast, and it wouldn't be long. I squirmed forward like a snake. There was a rustle in the grass off to my left. A rabbit? Then the soft scrunch of beach grass stalks crunched underfoot. I tried to get my legs under me. Too late. Out of the corner of my eye, I saw a fast-moving shadow. A hard knee jammed into the small of my back and pinned me down. A hand clamped against my mouth, jerking my head back.

I struggled like a beached flounder, expecting cold steel to slash me from ear to ear.

A finger drew lightly across my Adam's apple. A voice whispered, "Bang. You're dead."

Then came a soft chuckle. The hand dropped away from my mouth, and the knee withdrew from my back.

"*Damn*it Flagg!"

"Good thing I wasn't a VC. You'd be grinning out of your throat by now."

I was mad and embarrassed at being caught. "Where did *you* come from?"

"Here. Just where you told me to be. I was in the neighborhood, got your message, and found your truck down that dirt road. I figured you'd be working your way toward the landing, so I cut across the dunes and staked out a position near those goldenrod bushes. Glad I don't have hay fever. Next thing I know, you go slinking by like a big worm."

"You scared the hell out of me."

"My deepest apologies. You going to tell me what's doing?"

I scanned the darkness. "Nigel and Jack did a salvage job. I think they got some stuff off the *Pandora*."

"No shit. I had them in my sights all afternoon."

The circling Cessna. "Was that you in the plane?"

"Yeah, but how'd *you* know this thing was going down? Thought I told you to stay away from these guys."

"You didn't tell me to stay away from the girl."

"Huh. Shoulda known you'd get around it somehow. Guess you're in up to your neck."

"Guess I am. Got any ideas what we do now?"

"I scouted the landing. There's only one guy with the truck. We get in as close as we can and nail the driver. When the boat comes in, we hit the other two guys."

"How about calling the cops or coast guard?"

"No way. This has got to be quiet."

"What if there's some shooting?"

"What if there is? They're the ones that are going to get hurt."

"I don't like it, Flagg. A wild shot could hit one of those barrels of nerve gas. There are houses all along the bluff, people just sitting out on their decks or with their windows wide open. Lots of them have families with young kids. You said yourself nobody knows what the long-term effects of the gas are."

"I'm open to suggestion."

I lifted my head. All was still. "The tide's rising fast. They'll move soon. Stick with your plan to take out the driver. That's one less we'll have to worry about. I take his place. When they're out of the boat, away from the stuff, then you can come in and wave your cannon around."

"Whoo-ee, that's some ballsy scam. I like it." He thought for a moment. "Okay, give me five minutes to get around behind that truck driver. Then make some noise so he doesn't shoot you. Tell him one of your jokes. Maybe he'll just keel over with yuks. I'll do the rest." He crawled off into the darkness. Flagg was a big guy, probably two-fifty pounds, but he moved as silently as a thought.

I must have checked my watch a dozen times. Five minutes later, I scrambled off the dunes onto the beach and walked toward the landing, whistling Yankee Doodle with *fortissimo.*

Twenty feet away, a flashlight came on. The beam hit me square in the face.

"What's up, pal?" said a gruffly wary voice.

I raised my hand to shade my eyes. I tried not to think of the gun barrel that was probably pointing in my direction. Maybe this wasn't such a hot idea. "Fishing down the beach and got my matches wet. Thought I'd borrow a light if it's no bother."

There was a pause. The flash flicked down to my toes then back to my face again. "If you're fishing, where the fuck is your rod and reel?"

I advanced a few steps. "Biggest bass I've ever seen in my life grabbed the rod right out of my hand."

"Move over here, real slow, pal."

"Sure, no problem." Where was Flagg?

"What the hell—?"

There was a gurgle. The light dropped onto the sand. The driver collapsed as if his knees were wet noodles. I trotted over and picked up the flashlight. The driver was sprawled on the sand. Flagg was behind him. "For God's sakes don't kill him."

"Don't worry. I used the Vulcan death grip to make him sleepy. Get something to tie him up."

I found some line in the truck and we trussed the

driver hand and foot, stuck a rag in his mouth, and dragged him behind the dunes. I took his windbreaker and ball cap.

"Damn, Flagg."

"What's wrong?"

"It's a New York Yankees cap. I *hate* the Yankees."

He plunked the ball cap on my head. "No one'll see you in the dark."

The outboard motor stuttered into life. Flagg swiftly climbed into the back of the truck, which had a cover on it, and pulled down the canvas. I got in the cab and moved the truck down the ramp so the backup lights would reassure the incoming boat all was okay. Then I got out, strolled around behind the truck, and waited. I wasn't as cocky as I seemed. Nigel and Jack would have to be dumb as hockey pucks to fall for this scam.

Seconds later the motor cut off. Fiberglass thumped on wood. The boat was at the end of the small pier that extended out around thirty feet. Someone whistled three notes. There was a wheelbarrow next to the truck. I pushed the wheelbarrow across the beach on a line of planks laid out on the sand.

A man stood at the end of the pier. "Any problems?" he said. I couldn't see his face, but the gorilla physique told me I had finally heard Jack Morgan's voice. The guy standing in the shadowed boat would have to be Nigel.

"Uh-uh," I grunted, keeping my head down, and my lips clamped around the cigarette I had stolen from the driver.

314

"Good." He pulled the butt from my mouth and tossed it in the water. "Smoke later. Help me with this barrel. We've got five more after this."

We each grabbed an end of the canister. I curled my fingers under the lid and we hoisted it into the wheelbarrow. It weighed at least a hundred pounds, but Jack carried his end as if it were made of air. He followed as I pushed the loaded wheelbarrow off the pier and onto the beach. We put the canister in the sand. With Jack leading the way, I took the wheelbarrow back to the boat for another load.

My gut tightened. Hunching over, silently praying nobody would turn on a flashlight, I helped hoist another can onto the wheelbarrow.

"Need any help?" Nigel said.

"Naw," Morgan answered. "We can do it."

We hauled in three more barrels. My mind stumbled over the possibilities. Flagg could jump Jack and that would leave only Nigel. Jack could be persuaded by a gun in the neck to call his partner in. But Nigel took the matter out of our hands. Something about me didn't click. Maybe the driver was a talkative guy. Maybe my silence bothered him. We were halfway down the pier when Nigel called out.

"Wait!" he said.

I turned in reflex. A light went on. The blinding bull's-eye hit me smack between the eyes.

"You!" Nigel yelled.

I spun on my heel, blasted a right uppercut to Morgan's heart, then sent a short hook to his midsection. His washboard muscles were relaxed. He bent over in pain. I grabbed his head and kneed him in the face. I heard his nose crack under my knee. It wasn't nice, but planting a bomb under my bed wasn't nice either.

I vaulted over his sagging body and ran toward the truck.

Flagg must have heard the ruckus by now. I could picture him squinting over the sights of his gun looking for a target. Nigel was probably doing the same. A crossfire was no place to be. The second my sneaker touched the beach, I did a sharp right-hand turn, hit the sand in a tumbler's roll that knocked the wind out of me, then planted my face in the mud and tried to imitate a burrowing clam.

Cuh-rack!

A gunshot, close by. Two more shots answered. Followed by an outboard starting and throttled hard.

Flagg was out of the truck and running toward me. He sank to a kneeling position, his arms extended, his gun clutched in both hands, aimed toward the fleeing boat.

"Flagg," I yelled desperately, spitting wet sand out of my mouth. "Don't shoot! They've got a barrel on board!"

Slowly, he lowered his gun.

"You okay?"

"I'm fine. I like eating sand," I said, brushing off my knees. "Nigel noticed I wasn't the driver. I had to make a run for it."

"He tried to nail you, but I got off a shot first. Don't think I hit him, but it spoiled his aim. Guy on the dock jumped into the boat. Well, at least we got five barrels."

316

I walked over and tapped one of the canisters sitting in the sand. "Unfortunately, they've still got one can. They can still have a party with that, can't they?"

"Nothing you'd want an invite to," Flagg said grimly. "I'll call the Coast Guard from my car phone and get somebody to come in and take this crap away. Meantime, I wouldn't stand too close to that barrel. Maybe it was one of those that was leaking."

I edged away, quickly. "You still don't want to bring the cops in?"

"This place will be swarming with cops after that shoot-out. But this has got to stay at the federal level. I can enlarge the jurisdiction, bring in the FBI. Even the frigging Marines. But no local involvement. Them's my orders."

"Okay, Flagg, but there are a lot of inlets and coves those guys could put into."

"Don't worry. We'll get them." He headed back to his car.

The cops came by to investigate a noise complaint. Then some hard-eyed guys Flagg knew arrived to pacify the local gendarmes. I went by the Dwight house with Flagg and a couple of his friends. There was some good booze in the refrigerator. But no Nigel or Jack. And no Solange.

Chapter 32

Something was wrong. I could tell by the way Flagg evaded my eyes and the tight set to his mouth. He showed up at the boathouse the morning after the Nickerson Shores shoot-out. I gave him a tour of the bomb damage.

"They sure wanted your ass bad," he said.

"They almost got it, along with a few other parts I'd prefer to keep."

I poured us mugs of coffee and we went out on the deck. He got to it in his usual roundabout way. "How are the Red Sox doing?"

"They're still in third place and sinking fast. The pitching has never been better, but the batters can't find the ball, the runners have lead in their pants, the infielders are catching grounders with their noses, and all the outfielders have sun in their eyes." I slurped my coffee.

"You don't give a rat's ass about baseball, Flagg, so what are you trying to tell me?"

"The salvage ship has arrived and they'll start cleanup operations tomorrow."

"And the bad news?"

"Eden and Morgan are still on the loose."

"With the nerve gas?"

He nodded.

"Not good, Flagg. Did you squeeze the truck driver?"

"Til he's dry, but he's just a mule and doesn't know anything. Don't worry," Flagg added, "they'll pop up before long."

"They'd better. Nigel and Jack owe me some re-modeling costs."

Flagg took a check out of his wallet. "This should cover the charter of your fishing boat, and your new wall. We're keeping an eye out for the girl, Solange. You heard anything?"

I folded the check and put it in my pocket. "I've got a favor to ask. I've got Solange stashed away. But she needs some friends with connections who can help her keep a low profile until her former playmates are taken out of circulation."

He raised an eyebrow. "I figured you did something like that. Sure, we can take care of her. Give us a chance to see what she knows."

"I wasn't figuring a third degree in the deal, Flagg. She'll talk to you if I ask her, but it's got to be done one-on-one or she'll clam up or cut and run."

"No problem. Give her my number and tell her I'll be expecting a call." Kojak came onto the deck and headed toward Flagg. "Uh-oh. Here's that hungry cat. Better get moving before he chews my leg off for breakfast." Flagg stood up to go. Kojak rubbed against his calf. I walked Flagg to his car. He asked how Cousin Alex was doing. I told him I hadn't checked.

Before he left, I asked Flagg if he could arrange a little experiment I'd been thinking about. He gave me a funny look and said he would see what he could do.

The carpenters passed him on the way in. While they stripped off plywood and got busy on the new wall, I went inside and called Solange. I gave her the bad news about Nigel and Jack right away. Before she had a chance to go into a panic, I said:

"Here's the deal. I have a friend who can help you. He'll do whatever you want. Take you to a safe house or an airport."

"What does your 'friend' want in return?" Solange was no dummy.

"Information. Anything you know that might give him a lead on Nigel and Jack. He's promised not to lean on you. It's not a bad deal, Solange."

She didn't think so either. It only took her a moment to decide. I gave her Flagg's number and told her to call me if things didn't work out. If I needed a reminder that I still owed her, all I had to do was listen to nails being pounded into my shattered house.

With the posse after the bad guys, Solange taken care of, and the *Pandora* about to be relieved of its deadly cargo, I had more immediate concerns. Tillie Talbot, for one. Her camp was still on the firing line, and I had been hired to do something about it. I pulled out my yellow pad and examined it again.

Tillie was clearly the object of a three-pronged attack. Olney was pulling strings at the state level. Costello was doing his thing locally. And through his newspapers Thacher was keeping the pressure on. I circled their names. I didn't have the clout to go head to head against the three of them, but individually there might be a chance.

Next to Olney's name I wrote *Steve & Co.* Next to Costello's, I wrote, *dope.* Small d. I reached into my wallet, pulled out the sliver of paper I had found at Huggins's burnt camp, and placed it over Thacher's name. There was waxy stuff on the back of the paper and on the front black type that said PORK SPECIAL. I folded the sliver inside the paper, and stuffed it into the pocket of my jeans. I picked up the Federal Express package from Norma I'd been going through when Flagg showed up. It had been waiting for me the night before. Inside were the breakdowns of each of the corporate entities Fast Freddie and Olney were involved in. Nothing terribly incriminating, I was sorry to admit. But maybe enough to cause some trouble. Hell, it was worth a try.

Jack Olney's gambrel-roofed mansion was surrounded by a big lawn that looked as if it had been painted on. Each bay of the four-car garage was bigger than my boathouse. The garage had His and Hers Cadillacs, a GMC four-by-four, and a red Corvette. The whole setup overlooked a pretty salt pond.

I tucked the Fed Ex envelope under my arm and strolled up the front walk. A middle-aged woman who had Steve Olney's complexion and hair going to gray answered the door. I gave her my name and asked to see the lieutenant governor. She smiled pleasantly and led me around behind the house. Olney was on the back lawn standing near a gentle knoll.

"My husband's practicing his pitching and putting," she said with the resigned indulgence of a veteran golf widow. "He's got a game later today and he doesn't want to go in cold."

I thanked her and walked outside. A one-hole golf fairway had been set up on the lawn, complete with green, flag, and Scottish bunker.

Olney was bent over his putter trying to sink a fifteen-footer. He tapped the ball and it shot across the smooth greensward. I thought the angle was too far to the right, but the ball curved off a small rise and plopped neatly into the cup.

I clapped my hands. "Smooth shot."

Olney looked up and grinned. The putter was like a kid's golf club in his big hand. "Beginner's luck." He offered me the club. "Care to try one?"

I took the putter. About a dozen balls were lying on the green. I moved one a few inches away from the others, then lined up the shot.

Golf isn't my game. I've tried it a few times. It's hard not to on Cape Cod where there are so many golf courses you can practically hit a ball off one and have it land on another. I like the idea of the game. Walking across pretty rolling hills in useless pursuit of a little ball has always appealed to my innate spirit of slothfulness. But I've never been able to adapt my body comfortably to the unnatural positions you need to hit the ball properly. So I don't play golf much. I have enough frustrations in my life without adding another I can't afford anyhow.

I stroked the ball and tried to send it to the right as Olney had done. For the first time in my life the ball went straight. It sailed toward the cup and rolled off to the left about two feet.

"Not bad," Olney said generously.

"Not good either." I handed the putter back. "Nice club."

"I had it custom-made." He moved another ball away from the pile and sank it with an easy swing. "Hope I can keep my edge for the real thing later." He extended his hand and said, "Jack Olney," as if I didn't know who he was. His handshake was long and firm, a legacy of his politicking days.

I gave him my name and he mulled it over. "That's Greek, isn't it?" I could see the wheels turning in his head, pigeonholing me politically, lumping me into an ethnic group, doing a quick mental poll out of old habit, trying to figure out if I was a possible vote, whether I had any money to give him, whether I could help deliver a ward.

"That's right."

"Lots of Greeks up around Lowell."

"I was born there."

"You don't say? I've always admired Greek-Americans. Hard workers, and honest, too. In the old days when I was out in the hustings some of my top campaign contributors were Greeks. Have a seat."

He indicated a small circular patio table and two

chairs next to the putting green. On the table was a silver carafe. Olney poured a pale drink into a tall glass. The strong aroma of juniper berries mingled with the fragrance of newly cut lawn.

He offered the glass. "Care for a sip?"

It was late morning, but still too early for gin, even for me. "No, thanks. I never drink before the sun's over the yardarm."

"Neither do I, normally, but I just want to loosen up for my match."

Olney looked pretty loose to me. He was wearing baggy white pants, a turquoise golf shirt, and a white cotton cap. The foppish outfit looked all wrong on his railroad builder's physique, with its thick thighs and powerful shoulders. His angular face was built out of slabs of red-veined marble and he had the cruel hard mouth of a whorehouse bouncer.

He sipped his drink and set it down. "Have we met before?"

"Yes. At Fred Costello's party a few days ago."

"Oh?" He raised his eyebrows. "I must apologize. I didn't recognize you."

"I wouldn't expect you to. There were a lot of people there. We shook hands briefly. You were pretty busy, as I recall."

"Well, it's nice to see you again." His eyes flicked over the Federal Express package I'd rested on the table. "Now, what can I do for you, Mr. Socarides?"

Olney was a political anachronism, a "Last Hurrah" type ward heeler at heart who was not surprised to have perfect strangers arriving on his doorstep hat in hand looking for a favor. I slid a manila file out of the envelope

324

and gave it to him. Olney took a pair of reading glasses out of his pocket and went over each paper. After several minutes he looked up. The grin was still there. But now it had an unpleasant rawness to it.

"I don't like to beat around the bush, Mr. Socarides. What the hell is this all about?"

"It's about power and money and influence as I see it, Governor."

His blue eyes became glacier cold. "Who the hell *are* you, anyway?"

"I'm a friend of Tillie Talbot's who doesn't like the way some people have tried to push her around."

"Ah, *now* we're getting somewhere." He removed his glasses. "So tell me about these papers. What are they supposed to mean?"

"They mean that you and Fred Costello, and a few other characters, have been engaged in a conspiracy to drive Tillie off her camp so you can buy it."

He shook his head with disbelief that I could be so crassly stupid. "All these papers show is that a group of businessmen have gotten together under the laws of this great Commonwealth to do business."

"You're missing the point, Mr. Olney. I think they indicate that a former politician who still has powerful connections at the State House is playing footsie with a convicted felon."

He flung the papers at me. "You think you can cause trouble with this bullshit? Half the people in this town do business with Costello. They may hold their nose when they're around him, but there's one thing they don't mind, and that's the smell of money. Costello attracts it and they know it."

I watched the papers blow away in the breeze. "Don't worry about them. I have copies."

He bunched his fist into a ham and waved it in my face. "Let me give you a little lesson before I throw you bodily off my property. If you mess with somebody bigger than you, you'd better be carrying a club."

I reached into the envelope again. "Here's my club." I thought he was going to throw the papers I handed him at me again, but he put his glasses back on and read. His expression changed.

"You're getting into family business now, and that's not smart." He spoke with dangerous calmness.

"It wasn't smart for you to set up a company for your son and give him seed money. Young Steve's quite the entrepreneur. He's used the money you gave him for the restaurant-cleaning operation to go into the drug business."

It's not the brightest thing in the world to tell a guy who is nearly seven feet tall that the apple of his eye is a dope dealer. Olney's hand shot out, grabbed my shirt, and lifted me out of my chair.

"I'm going to rip your face off," he promised. His breath was heavy with the smell of gin.

It is hard to talk with your collar up around your ears, but I managed to croak out two sentences, and that's all I needed. "Ask your son if it's true. Ask him about the drug score that didn't go through the other night."

He glared at me for a couple of seconds, then dropped me back into the chair. "Don't move," he snarled. He stalked across the broad lawn and banged into the house. I contemplated getting into a safer line of work. Something like making faces at enraged grizzly bears.

About ten minutes later he returned. Steve straggled behind him like a schoolboy on his way to the woodshed.

"Do you know this man?" Olney demanded of his son.

Steve squinted with sullen eyes. There was a slight glint of recognition in them from our encounters at Costello's party and Alex's cottage. He said nothing.

"Well, he knows you," Olney rasped. "This gentleman here says you've been using the company I set up for you as a front to peddle drugs. Now what do you say to that?"

Steve's lips curled. I cut in before he could speak. "I know all about the beach house in Little Taunton. I know about Alex, T.J., Chili, and Tanya. And I know about you."

The kid's head jerked back as if I'd just squirted him with Mace. "You a cop?"

"I might be."

He nodded and turned away. "Take it up with Pop's lawyer. I got a date."

But before he had taken a step, Olney's long arm grabbed him by the collar and spun him around. His other hand smashed the kid's cheek. The blow sent him sprawling. He looked at his father, half in terror, half in defiance, and got to his feet. The side of his face was as red as raw hamburger.

"Fuck you!" he screamed. "FUCK YOU!" Holding his cheek with his hand, he ran back to the house.

Olney watched him go, his face flushed. Then he

327

crumpled into his chair, leaned forward, rubbed his forehead as if it ached. Hatred burned in his eyes.

"How much money do you want?"

I shook my head. "Blackmail's against the law, Governor. What I want is information. Why are you and your friends so interested in Tillie Talbot's camp?"

He gave me his best glower, which wasn't bad. "There's a plan to make it into a state park. It's surrounded by conservation land. The camp would link all that together. Like Olmsted's emerald necklace around Boston."

I let the information sink in. "I'd guess you heard about the project from your political connections. You figured to buy the camp real cheap. You could probably do it without even opening your wallet. It's all done on paper, with you as middleman. Just come up with a down payment, transfer the land to the state, then sit back and count the money. What kind of dough we talking about?"

"Maybe a couple of million clear split among the investors."

"Not a bad day's pay. Trouble is, Tillie wasn't about to sell, so you and your buddies decided to force her. You'd take care of bullying her around at the state level, and the chairman of selectman did his job at Town Hall. How'd you get Thacher into the deal? He was supposedly incorruptible."

He showed me where his son had picked up the contemptuous sneer. "You think *any* man is incorruptible if the price is right? Thacher's been in financial shit ever since he expanded his paper. I helped him out." He stuck his face in mine. The patina of class he affected had worn off and the bully boy was showing through. "So what's the payoff? You want in on the deal?"

"No deal. I want you to keep your hands off Mrs. Talbot and her camp."

"That's it?" He was having a problem dealing with someone who didn't have a hand out for baksheesh.

"For now. What are you going to do about Steve?"

"I'm going to call my lawyer and have that corporation dissolved, for a starter."

"While you're on the phone, I'd suggest you call a doctor and get your son into a serious detox center."

His skin color got more apoplectic. "You have kids, Mr. Socarides?"

I shook my head.

"Too bad. Maybe you can understand anyway. Steve has always been tough to raise. We spoiled him. Always gave him what he wanted. You've seen that Corvette in the garage. It's his third. He cracked up the other two. Lucky he wasn't killed. We sent him to the right prep school to meet some good kids. He ends up hanging around with a bunch of hoods from Jamaica Plain. It's just the kind of environment we were trying to keep him out of. The kind of neighborhood I grew up in. So when Steve asked me to advance him some money and set up a corporation for his summer cleaning business, I was ecstatic." He ran his hands through his silvery hair and sighed. "I guess there's too much of me in him and not enough of his mother."

In a way I felt sorry for Olney. But not that sorry. He had broken too many bones in his career to be an object of pity. He was the one who taught the kid that dishonesty bought you Corvettes and big houses on the water. Even now, smarting from the revelation that his only son was an ungrateful little bastard, he was as dangerous as a wounded bull.

I didn't say good-bye and neither did Olney. I walked across the sweeping lawn and looked back once. Olney was on the putting green. He tried an easy shot and missed. He was probably vowing to himself that he wasn't through with me.

I wasn't through with him, either.

Chapter 33

I stopped off at Quanset Beach to chat with the gate man. Ten minutes later I walked into the *Gazette*'s lobby and asked for Rollins. The receptionist waved me into the newsroom. Rollins was slouched in his chair, arms crossed. He was staring at a word processor as if he hoped it might sprout feet and walk away.

"Hot scoop?"

He looked up with glazed eyes. "Yeah, hot enough to cook cherrystones. Thacher's pulled me off the beach stuff. I'm trying to give a Hemingwayesque twist to an advance about the clambake to benefit the Board of Trade. I'm calling it 'the Clams of Kilimanjaro.' "

"I'll wait for the movie. Anything new on Huggins?"

He cocked his head, brightening. "Yeah. You did

good, Mr. Private Dick. The cops are making noises that it wasn't suicide." He frowned. "Thacher's taken me off that story, too. Says the town's getting a bad image and I'm too hungry. Can you imagine any editor telling a reporter he's *too* hungry? What the hell is going on?"

"Don't dismay. I may have something." I crossed the newsroom to Thacher's office and knocked on the doorjamb to be polite. Thacher sat erectly at an old Underwood typewriter, pipe in his mouth. "Can't talk to you now," he said through clenched teeth. "Got to finish this editorial. I'm on deadline."

"This will only take a minute. I've got a terrific story for you." I stepped in and sat down. Thacher's snowy eyebrows did a slow rise toward his hairline. He took his pipe out of his mouth. "Guess you're determined to stay, son." He slid a pocket watch that was lying faceup on the desk in front of him and grinned genially. "A good newsman never ignores a tip. I'll give you three minutes, Mr. Socarides. Then you'll have to excuse me while I get back to this important editorial on the bandstand some folks want to erect on the town green. Now, what's your tip?"

"This one's a real tearjerker. It's about a bunch of bullies ganging up on an aging widow who's trying to keep a kids' camp going in memory of her dead husband. How's it play so far?"

The grin twitched at the corners, but managed to hold. He stared at me, then got real busy knocking the glowing embers from his pipe bowl into a metal ashtray. The pipe sounded like a sledge hammer pounding a railroad spike.

"You should have been a newspaperman, son. I teach my reporters any story can be summed up in a single sentence."

"I cheated. There's more. One of the bad guys is a country editor who smokes a pipe. I don't know what kind of tobacco he uses."

"Can't be too bad a fellow then." Thacher's grin contracted into a tight, mirthless smile. He reached into his drawer, pulled out a can of tobacco, dipped his pipe into it, and lit up. "I use a special blend they make at Erlich's. I pick it up in Boston when I go to the Harvard Club." He took a puff and his grin disappeared behind a wreath of blue-gray smoke. "What's on your mind, son?"

"I talked to Olney a little while ago. He told me the state wants to buy Tillie Talbot's camp for a park. He said he and some investors hoped to make a big score if they could get Tillie to sell it to them before she learned of the state's plans. He mentioned you were one of the investors."

Thacher shook his head. "The lieutenant governor has never been at a loss for words, has he?" He ran his eyes over my face as if he were seeing me for the first time. "Doesn't look too good, does it, country editor like me who's fought hard against development, crossing over to the enemy?"

"A little like Benedict Arnold selling out to the British."

He gazed over at the wall which was covered with award-winning plaques. "If there's one thing I've learned in all the years I've spent in this business, it is the importance of black ink, especially on the accounting books. You can't pay good reporters or buy top equipment if you're operating in the red. And you can't operate in the best interests of your community. I'll admit it looks like a conflict of interest, but on balance it's not a bad deal. The state gets a park, the town gets open space, Tillie gets that white elephant off her back, and this newspaper gets the money that will enable it to defend this town in the really big fights against developers."

"I think they call that sophistry, Mr. Thacher. You don't have to run with the James Brothers gang because the banks have too much money."

His forehead wrinkled. "Maybe my business partners aren't as lily-white pure as you or I would like them. But this is America, son. The *Gazette* may be an institution, but newspapers are pure capitalism. There's no law against making a good deal."

"There's no law against using your newspaper to soften Tillie up so she'd sell out. Every time she sneezed she made headlines. She got more ink than Chappaquiddick."

"That's a pretty farfetched accusation."

"No more farfetched than your pirate curse story."

Thacher puffed on his pipe. "We were just having fun. Nobody believed that story."

"Nobody believed it, but you said it yourself: the *Gazette* is an institution. You knew the TV stations in Boston and New York would grab that garbage and run with it, that it would go national."

"I think you're overestimating my influence, Mr. Socarides. Readers are more sophisticated these days.

People love that kind of stuff but they don't take it seriously."

"Maybe not, but they take murder seriously."

His face paled. "What are you talking about?"

"Huggins."

Thacher stared at me and pursed his lips. He'd forgotten all about his pipe. He got up, closed the office door, and came back to his chair.

"You've got a lot on your mind, son," he said quietly. "Maybe you should get to the point."

"It all goes back to the Talbot camp. Tillie was tougher than you and your friends thought. She didn't buckle under to legal pressure. All the bad publicity didn't work. When the two swimmers were attacked at Quanset Beach, and bodies started floating ashore, you saw a golden opportunity. You made sure everybody who read your paper knew the camp was next to the beach. Then you got playful. You figured TV likes to pick up an oddball story, so you concocted that fairy tale about the pirate curse. You needed a credible source, so you went to Huggins. I'd guess you knew about his problems with the cops in upstate New York. You used that as a persuader. Huggins went along, but got nervous when people like me started asking questions. He wanted out."

"He was killed over the pirate curse story? That's quite a leap in logic." He picked up the pocket watch, rubbed the crystal on his sleeve, and put it back on his desk.

"Just call me Baryshnikov. Huggins could open a nasty can of worms if he recanted on the pirate story. People might wonder why he fibbed in the first place.

The trail would lead straight back to you. Then to the other investors. It might spoil your chance to get the camp. The money on the land sale to the state wouldn't come through. You could lose your paper."

"I think I see where you're heading, son, and I'm not sure I like it."

"Yeah, it stinks, doesn't it? I'd guess Huggins arranged to meet you at his shack. You were on the beach that night. You had time to think about it, to get angry. He arrived, you blasted him. It was a sloppy job. That makes me believe it wasn't thought out and you were probably just going to try to scare him. Afterward, you tried to make it look like a suicide and a fire."

"I'm going to have to take back what I said before. You're too easy with the facts to make a good reporter."

"How's this for a fact?" I reached into my shirt pocket. "I found this on the porch of the beach camp the day Huggins was murdered. It looks like an ad headline from your pasteup department. There's wax on the back of these things. I picked a couple off my sneaker the day you gave me the tour."

Thacher studied the paper for a moment. An experienced criminal would have coolly handed it back to me and said I could have picked it up anywhere. But Thacher was an amateur. Before I could make a move, he ripped the paper to shreds, crumpled the pieces and tossed them into his wastebasket. He looked pleased with himself, like a tough kid who's just thrown your hat in a puddle.

I reached into my pocket, pulled out a handful of

paper pieces, and dropped them on his desk. "I've got plenty more. I picked them up on the way in. The real one is in my truck."

"I covered court for years and know the system inside and out. You can't go around making accusations like that on the strength of a piece of ad copy."

"You're right. That's why I checked the beach buggy log the night Huggins died. There's a record of you going down a half hour before he did."

"I often go down the beach at night to go surf fishing. Lots of people do."

"But lots of people don't have the future of their newspaper riding on the purchase of a piece of land. Once the cops start digging, I promise you they'll find something. All a grand jury needs is probable cause."

Thacher deflated like a leaky balloon. His shoulders sagged. He slunk down in his chair. His pipe had gone out but he didn't relight it. I rose from my chair. "I guess my three minutes is up."

"Wait," he said. I waited.

He got up and looked through the glass at the newsroom, still holding his dead pipe in his hand. "Y'know, this was just a sleepy little newspaper when I bought it twenty-five years ago. Now it goes to subscribers in every state in the Union. Ends up on the coffee tables in offices of dozens of top corporate officers and congressmen. They like the combination of folksiness and street-smart wisdom." He looked at the plaques lining the wall. "I've got more prizes for editorials, picture and news coverage than any other paper this size in the country. Presidents have written to praise my editorials. This paper has done more to preserve Cape Cod than anyone." His voice was almost a whisper. "I thought the end justified the means. That was my big mistake."

"No, it wasn't."

He looked at me, a question in his pale blue eyes.

"Your big mistake was killing someone," I told him.

I went out into the newsroom and stopped at Rollins's desk. "Come by the cop station in about an hour and ask them if they've got anything new on the Huggins death. If your boss doesn't want to run the story, *The Boston Globe* has a guy down here. You can talk to him."

"I don't understand . . ." Rollins began.

"You will."

I walked out of the newspaper office and took a deep breath of clean air. I got into the truck. The face in my rearview mirror seemed to be somebody else's. Somebody with the same cynical hardness around the eyes and mouth I'd seen on cops who were on the job too long and cons who had done hard time. I'd seen it on my face before I quit the force and moved to where I thought all would be peaceful and quiet. It wasn't my fault that Thacher lost his moral compass bearings. He would deserve whatever he got. But I had trashed an American icon, and I felt sick about it.

Tillie Talbot was on the sailing dock surrounded by a gaggle of noisy campers. She looked tired.

"How nice to see you, Soc. I was just organizing the children's sailing classes."

"It looks as if you're going to be sailing for some time to come, Mrs. Talbot."

Her beautiful face lit up. "Do you have some news for me?"

"I've talked to some of the principals in the group that wants to buy your camp. They admit to being over-zealous. I said you didn't like it. They've agreed to stop bothering you."

"Then it *wasn't* my imagination," she said triumphantly. "People *were* out to harrass me into selling this camp." Now anger blazed in her eyes. "Is there *anything* I can do to hold them to accounts?"

"Probably not the way you'd like to. There *is* something that will make them very, very unhappy, and there may be some consolation in that." I told her about the state's interest in buying her land.

"I'm stunned, simply stunned," she said. "Even so, I'd never think of selling. They'd have to take this camp by eminent domain. I'll run it until my last breath."

"It may not have to be so drastic. I've been think-ing about this whole thing and I have a suggestion." I laid out my idea.

After I finished, she smiled her lovely smile. "Why Soc, that's a wonderful idea." She looked fondly at the kids, who were getting into their sailboats. "You know, I've been so busy with paperwork that I haven't been sailing since Hector was a pup. It's a shame, since Bill always said I do my best thinking at the helm of a boat. I believe I'll go out with this class and consider your proposal. I can't think of any more appropriate place to make an important decision about the camp than on one of Bill's boats. If you'll excuse me, I'll let you know what I decide. We can settle up after that."

"No big hurry," I told her.

The carpenters were still at work on the boathouse. The electricity was on and the refrigerator worked. I had a beer. It tasted pretty good, so I had another and went out on the deck. I should check in with Sally, but for the time being I was content to sit and watch the light change on the waters of the bay. I sat there, drinking beer, pondering Tillie's question. Could the bad guys be held accountable? And my answer. Probably not. I was being realistic. But it didn't make me any happier. I felt guilty about being a lousy role model for Cousin Alex. I should have been more worried about the *good* role model the bad guys are. They show the next generation of up-coming punks that you *can* get away with it.

Big Jack Olney could bitch about his son all he wanted to, but he was the one who showed the kid you could beat the system. Fast Freddy had done the same. Everyone who was ever tempted to cheat on his income tax or skim a few bucks off a deal could look at Freddie or Big Jack and say that even if you're caught, nothing happens to you. The attitude pervades the whole system. Nobody's responsible anymore, from the nutcase who blows away his wife and kids with a hunting rifle to the lawyer who embezzles a couple of hundred grand from an elderly client. God, I was starting to think like a Puritan.

Flagg called. He gave me an address in Boston and told me to come up the next day.

I dozed off. When I woke up, the carpenters had gone and it was dark. I went into the house, fished a flashlight out of a kitchen drawer, and went down to the beach. I reached under the cuddy of the skiff on shore and pulled a rusted old Maxwell House coffee can out from the pile of line that covered it. I opened the can and counted the plastic bags of dope I'd taken from Alex. Some Colombian farmer probably worked real hard to raise the coca plant the stuff came from. Maybe good could come of his labors.

I put on a pair of garden gloves and poured the contents of the bags into a larger plastic bag that didn't carry my fingerprints. Then I put the drug money in an envelope addressed to the state police. I dropped it in a mailbox on the way across town, enjoying the buzz from the beer I'd swilled down on an empty stomach, and the way the alcohol wore off the sharp edges of my judgment. The back road I was on changed into a dirt lane that ended in a tiny town landing. I parked and got a tool kit out of the truck, then walked down the boat ramp and along the quiet beach for about a quarter of a mile until I came to a steep set of stairs leading up the side of a sloping embankment.

I climbed to the top of the stairs. The lights were on in the big house. Nobody moved against the windows. Staying in the shadows cast by a row of red cedar trees, I headed to the garage, grateful Fast Freddy didn't have a dog. The doors were locked. I went around to the side and quietly cut a hole in a pane big enough to get my hand through to the lock. I slid the window open and pulled myself inside. The Mercedes was unlocked. Removing the door panel would be too complicated. Instead, I levered up the cushions of the back seat and tucked the bag neatly in a corner. Moments later, I was trotting back across the lawn to the stairway.

On the way home I stopped at a pay phone and called the state police. I told the cops the drug task force might be interested in checking under the backseat of a Mercedes owned by one Freddie Costello. I gave his address and his car registration number just to be helpful. Then I hung up.

The way I figured it, Freddy should have gone to the slammer a few years back. It was only through the efforts of a sharp lawyer, and the timidity of the cops who wanted to sweep the case under the rug because one of their own was involved, that kept him out of jail. I didn't like the things he had done to Tillie Talbot, either, and there should be some accounting for that. Justice served late is still justice in my view.

I navigated the truck back to the boathouse, breaking a few laws myself, and flopped onto the bed. Maybe it was not having Kojak around to hog the sheets, but I slept sounder than I had in days.

C h a p t e r   3 4

Flagg was waiting for me in the lobby of the JFK Building, where the Environmental Protection Agency has its
offices. He pinned an ID badge on my chest and led the
way into an elevator that took us to an office maze on the
umpteenth floor. I followed him through an unmarked
door into a darkened room. Taking up one wall was a
glass window that looked into a chamber about twice as
large as the one we were in.

Two people in protective white suits with air tanks
on their backs stood next to a metal lab table. On the
table was a fish tank about six feet long and four feet
high and wide. Swimming around in the tank were two
bluefish.

Flagg picked up the phone. "We're ready."

One of the lab techs waved at the window. He went

to a refrigerator and used a set of tongs to extract a vial less than two inches tall from a rack. Carefully, he opened the vial and poured its contents into the tank. Then he capped the container and placed it in a metal box on the table.

The bluefish skittered nervously at the intrusion.

The other lab tech went to the refrigerator and took out a steak cod that probably weighed twenty pounds. He hooked its mouth onto a line attached to a metal bar. He and his colleague straddled the bar across the top of the tank so the fish hung into the water. He set a timer next to the tank.

The blues swam away from the cod at first. Then they bumped it with their noses.

For a few minutes, there was no change in behavior. Then the bluefish began to swim around the tank in spastic, jerky motions, banging their pointed snouts against the glass. Slowly at first, then faster. Sharp teeth glinted. Their large muscular jaws snapped at nothing. Then at the codfish. Their canine teeth voraciously tore off big pieces of white flesh. Within minutes, the cod was reduced to floating scales and shreds.

The target of their attacks demolished, the blues turned on each other. One fish raked its companion. The injured fish slashed back. The silent, deadly battle raged until both fish were dead and their body parts mingled with those of the cod. Blood clouded the water. The tech pointed to the timer. Four minutes had gone by.

"Holy shit," Flagg muttered under his breath. "This is the second time I've seen this, and I *still* can't believe it. How the hell did you know this would happen?"

I shook my head. "I wasn't sure, but I'd been thinking about bluefish for a long time. There are big schools up and down the New England coast all summer long. Some get to be a couple of acres in size."

Flagg said, "I've seen them chase pogies right up onto the shore back on the Vineyard, but the most I'd ever heard is them taking a nip out of somebody's leg. That's a long jump to chewing someone to death."

"That's what I thought, too. Blues are aggressive as hell. They'll plunge into a school of baitfish slashing left and right, but they don't usually go after something bigger than they are. Then someone said something about the fish getting back at us for all the toxic waste we've dumped on their heads."

Flagg grinned bleakly, his eyes dark. "So you figured they'd chew on a few swimmers to show they were pissed off at us."

"Not exactly. I kept thinking about K-Twenty-two and what it did to me. Instant paranoia. A fish's nervous system is a lot less complicated than a human's, but what if the stuff leaking from those drums jammed their circuits somehow, confused them so they went after anything that got in their way, no matter what it was? Maybe the fish just went beserk and made a mistake."

Flagg pointed to the lab room. The techs were cleaning up. "Those guys tried the same experiment yesterday. They used just a little bit of the stuff from those barrels Nigel pulled up. Same thing we just saw happened. They figure maybe the fish absorbed some of the leaking gas. Some chemical in it hiked up the level of aggressiveness. It wouldn't take much. Whole schools of blues must have gone beserk, snapped at anything that moved. Probably what hit you on the *Pandora* dive."

"That's my guess. Now answer one for me. What about that blob my friend Mac saw?"

"Could have been bioluminescence. Could have been the light hitting the scales on one of those big schools of fish. Could have been something entirely unrelated to this. Sea's a mysterious place. We don't know all the answers."

I looked at the bloody tank. "Maybe we don't know any of them."

On the way home from Boston, I stopped at Sam's house. Millie gave me a wide smile.

"Soc, how lovely to see you. Sam was hoping you'd drop by. He tried to call you this morning."

"I had a few errands, Millie. How's the old guy doing?"

She rolled her eyes. "See for yourself."

I expected Sam to be in his bathrobe and slippers lounging in front of the TV the way I'd seen him on my last visit, but instead Millie led me through the kitchen to the back door. Sam was in the yard stacking fish boxes. He wore tan work pants and shirt, and the matching cap with the duck-billed visor.

"Should he be doing that?"

Millie shrugged and smiled. "The hospital gave him a clean bill of health. All the tests proved negative, thank goodness. It was just a simple case of exhaustion. The doctor said Sam's heart had a lot of miles on it, but not to tell Sam because he'd get cocky and use them up in one day. He just warned Sam not to work so darned hard when the sun is hot. Think you can keep him from doing that?"

I put my arm around her and squeezed gently. "I'll try, Millie."

"I know he can be stubborn," she said fondly, her eyes on him, "but I'm awfully glad he's not ready to retire. It has just been an absolute trial, having him around the house all week. When he retires I'll probably murder him. Please take him fishing again as soon as you can so I can get something done around here."

"You bet I will, Millie, but first I'd better give him a hand with those boxes."

When he spotted me, Sam waved and gave me a big grin. He looked like his old self. I stayed at the house a couple of hours. We did very little work actually. Most of the time was spent listening to Sam expound on the deficiencies in the American medical system. We agreed to try fishing in a day or two. Sam said he'd sniff out the weather.

"That reminds me, Sam. I was worried for a while that you'd go to the grave without telling me how you do that."

"Heck, it's easy, Soc. It's just knowing where to point your nose."

"Okay, so where do I point it?"

"Same place I do." Sam's grin was sly. "Turn on the NOAA forecast and point it at the radio."

. . .

From Sam's house, I went home and called my mother.

"Cousin Alex is home, Aristotle. His mother and father are very glad. You did a good job. Uncle Alexander and Aunt Demeter say to thank you and come up for dinner some time."

"I'm glad to hear Alex is doing okay," I said, heaving a sigh of relief. "I wish I could have done more."

"Nono*no*," she scolded. "You did all you could. Alex is not a little boy."

"I know that. I just feel Alex wouldn't have gotten into trouble in the first place if he didn't look up to me."

"Poof, Aristotle, you make me very angry when you talk like that. You have a good heart, anyone can see that. If they don't, it's their own fault. You can't make Alex civilized. Nobody can. He has to do it himself."

"Thanks, Ma. It makes me feel good to hear you say that."

"*Kala,* Aristotle. But there is one thing you *must* do something about."

"What's that, Ma?"

"Your *house,* Aristotle, your house . . ."

I looked through the gaping hole at the scorched tomato patch.

"I'm working on it, Ma," I said truthfully.

Chapter 35

The selectmen reopened Quanset Beach the next morning. Busy fishing with Sam, I missed the opening. A few days later I sat in my pickup listening to the engine go *pockety-pock,* thinking that I really should get it to Hoppie's garage before I heard a death rattle. Traffic was creeping along on the beach road. I slipped into a space at the far end of the parking lot.

People were lined up at the snack bar. The boardwalk looked like Broadway on New Year's Eve. Hardly a square inch of sand was visible between the blankets and chairs spread out from the edge of the dunes to the waterline.

Gary and Mo were on their tower watching the mob of bathers splashing about in the surf. Gary climbed down to shake my hand.

"Busy day," I commented.

"Yeah, *too* busy." He kept his eyes on the water.

"Problems?"

He frowned. "Just the usual. Lost kids and cut feet." He scanned the beach. "I just hope it doesn't happen again."

"I've got a feeling, Gary. I think that marine biologist Diana Trumbull was right. This was just a fluke. A freak accident."

He turned to me, searching for reassurance. "You think so, Soc?"

"Trust me."

Gary couldn't be blamed for worrying. I would be jittery too, if Flagg hadn't told me the *Pandora* had been cleaned out. The curious were told the salvage ship was working on a NOAA survey of ocean currents. The *Pandora*'s lethal cargo was loaded in nets during the day and hoisted aboard at night. It was a slick job. Maybe in time, sport divers would discover the wreck. They'd wonder where it had come from, but for now, the sea hid the *Pandora*'s dark secrets from all but the fish.

Diana Trumbull was closer than she knew when she said it was a wonder all the creatures in the sea don't attack us in revenge for ruining their home. With the nerve gas containers gone, the marauding bluefish should return to their normal habits of chasing pogies, and leave people alone.

I looked toward the bluff that marked Tillie Talbot's camp. Tillie had followed my suggestion. The deal was still in the works, but the prospects looked good. Tillie simply made the state an offer it couldn't refuse.

She would sell the property for a token payment of one dollar. There were a few conditions attached, of course. The state park would have to include a sailing camp. She'd run the camp as long as she could, then it would be operated by a trust, with the bucks the state would have paid her for the property as seed money. The campers would come from the inner city and other places that aren't healthy for kids. The new camp would be named after her husband.

Temperatures had dropped to more comfortable levels so I no longer had to worry about Sam keeling over. Alex was in a detox center. He'd be out in a few weeks, and from what I heard from my mother, he was planning to go back to school. Flagg had disappeared once more, but he'd surface again. Mac McConnell was fishing full-time, and he'd found something to occupy his off-hours. I'd seen Mac and Diana Trumbull playing kneesies at the 'Hole.

Fast Freddy Costello has hired a lawyer to try to persuade a jury the cocaine in his Mercedes was a plant. Wes Thacher might be spending a few dollars on legal help, too, after the grand jury meets. Big Jack Olney may squirm a little when his connections to Costello get around, but he's survived worse. I guess I could have told somebody how he financed his son's drug operation, but maybe having to deal with a kid like Stephen is punishment enough. All the breaking news has my pal Rollins typing his fingers off. He's still building up his portfolio, but sometimes he wonders if he could get some money to buy the *Gazette,* now that it's likely to be on the market.

Kojak is back home. Sally claimed he was taking

over her apartment and eating all her food. He and I are still sleeping on the couch, but the carpenters swear they will have the bedroom finished in a couple of days. I haven't seen them around lately, but they did leave an old hammer and a stepladder. I expect they'll be back in three or four years.

Solange left the safe house and disappeared without a trace. I hope she calls sometime. I'd like to tell her she doesn't have anything to fear from her former boyfriend. A plain envelope was tacked onto my door the night before. I guess Flagg delivered it. Inside was a clipping from *The Boston Globe.* The article said the bodies of two men had been found in a drifting boat several miles off the coast of Cape Cod. Both had been shot to death. The police said it looked as if they killed each other. The men were identified as Nigel Eden and Jack Morgan. In the boat was an empty barrel marked chemical fertilizer. Maybe one of Flagg's wild shots hit a mark after all.

"Still interested in that outboard?" I asked Gary.

"Yeah, but I can't leave the beach to look at it until this afternoon."

"Give me a call tomorrow. I'm going to be busy today."

Sally had the day off. Tillie Talbot had offered the use of a sailboat, so we were going to sail over for a picnic on the outer beach. I said good-bye to Gary and walked up to the boardwalk. Wham! A beach ball bounced off my cranium. The kid who owned the ball was standing there with a guilty look on his face, but he grinned when I threw it back to him. I paused at the boardwalk and took a long look around. Yep. Just another quiet day at Quanset Beach.